THE JOURNAL:

raging tide

DEBORAH D. MOORE

A PERMUTED PRESS BOOK

ISBN (trade paperback): 978-1-61868-622-0
ISBN (eBook): 978-1-61868-623-7

RAGING TIDE
The Journal Book 4
© 2015 by Deborah D. Moore
All Rights Reserved

Cover art by Matt Mosley

PERMUTED
PRESS

Permuted Press
109 International Drive, Suite 300
Franklin, TN 37067
http://permutedpress.com

Also in *The Journal* series:

Cracked Earth (Book One)
Ash Fall (Book Two)
Crimson Skies (Book Three)

Look for the fifth installment of *The Journal* series, coming soon!

Also by Deborah D. Moore

A Prepper's Cookbook: Twenty Years of Cooking in the Woods,
coming in Summer 2016!

ACKNOWLEDGEMENTS

I'd like to thank my family and friends who have encouraged and supported me during the process of writing this series.

This would not be complete if I didn't thank Boyne Soozie for giving me the leather journal that started all of this.

Special thanks to personal friends who allowed me to include their names in the stories: Bob C. & Kathy O., Guy & Dawn M., Pastor Carolyn, Dee Streiner, Ken Krause, Harold Wolfe, Marie, and especially my sister Pam and my two sons, Eric and Jason. My apologies if I've forgotten anyone.

Another thank you to all the ladies on my woman's group – you're the greatest and I couldn't have done it without you.

And to Michael Wilson at Permuted Press for taking a chance on this unknown, unpublished author – thank you for your trust in me.

Felicia Sullivan, my editor and now my friend, who has patiently sorted out my manuscripts and made them readable. Thank you SO much. I hope you know how much and how valuable you are to so many of us.

BEING SINGLE IS GREAT

I have so much freedom!
I have the freedom to paint any room any color
I have the freedom to spend money I earned the way I want to
I have the freedom to spend my birthday working and come
home to an empty house, but it's MY house, all mine, and no
one can take it away from me, not even the bank
I have the freedom to get up and read or write at 2am if I
have yet another sleepless night
I have the freedom to have soup for breakfast and oatmeal
for dinner without someone telling me it's wrong
I have the freedom to make a mistake without someone
telling me I'm stupid
I have the freedom to leave the dinner dishes until morning
I have the freedom to leave the outdoor Christmas lights up
all year and turn them on in May or August just because they
make me smile
I have the freedom to avoid petty arguments that stem from
jealousy or fear because we are both scared and uncertain
I have the freedom to reach over and feel the cold sheets on
the other side of the bed

I have the freedom to be the only one worrying that the cat
hasn't come home in two days
I have the freedom to spend Christmas morning alone, with
no tree and no presents
I have the freedom to always be the odd-one out at every
New Year's Eve party
I have the freedom to ache for a sincere hug
I have the freedom to cry myself to sleep at night because
I'm so lonely for someone to love
Yeah, being single is great…

D. Moore

To everyone who has ever needed a second chance.

"Life always offers a second chance,
It's called Tomorrow."
—Author unknown

The world is shaking apart and the North American continent is at the heart of it. A seemingly minor tremor escalated into ripping the country in half at the New Madrid fault line. Shipping ceased and sent the country into a tailspin, with small towns like Moose Creek, Michigan suffering the most. Recovery came slow as the country pulled itself together, until another more terrifying quake hit, awakening the sleeping caldera beneath Yellowstone. The deadly ash thrown into the atmosphere decimated those who were unprepared or unwilling to accept it could affect them. The ash that now circled the world disrupted weather patterns everywhere, blotting out the sun and stirring up massive storms.

Moose Creek survived – barely. Life goes on in the small town in the Upper Peninsula of Michigan. An infusion of residents came on the heels of the devastating fire in a nearby city, and with the repopulation came more problems, including a killer virus that claimed the life of Allexa Smeth's husband. An unprecedented earthquake during the funeral of Dr. Mark Robbins divided the Upper Peninsula in half, sending billions of gallons of Lake Superior surging into Lake Michigan, resulting in the destruction of many coastal communities.

CHAPTER 1

April 1

"What do you mean you're going on a road trip?" Jason demanded, placing his fists on his hips as his brother Eric scowled at me.

My two boys, men now, were so much alike yet they were so different. Jason, with his green eyes and dark hair, was outgoing and quick to laugh. Eric, with clear blue eyes and sandy hair like his father, was quiet and reserved, mostly from years spent in the military where he learned to keep his own counsel.

"Just what I said," I shot right back. "And don't you two dare try to tell me what I can and cannot do!" I was tempted to shake my finger at my two adult sons. "Look," I pleaded with them, "I need to do this. I need to do *something*. I can't just sit around all day, every day. Mark is dead, I'm not."

My voice hitched saying his name. The flu that swept through Moose Creek late last fall claimed over two hundred lives, including the life of my husband. We had only four months together, four months of love and happiness and I will cherish that time forever.

"When is this supposed to happen, Mom?" Eric asked, his mouth pulled into a straight line.

"We haven't decided yet," I answered truthfully. "The colonel is antsy to get going, however, I've convinced him we need to wait for several reasons. The first and foremost will be the weather. Regardless of how temperate it's been here, I'm not willing to risk being snow-bound in a tent in the middle of nowhere from a late season storm. Plus, I want to pack carefully and make sure we don't forget something vital."

"I'm just not sure about you running off with Colonel Jim, Mom. I like him and all, but isn't it… a bit soon?" Jason frowned.

"A bit soon for what? Jim is my friend, nothing more, and I resent what you're implying." I turned away from them and poured myself another cup of tea, trying to control my temper.

"I'm sorry, Mom," Jason said, hugging me from behind. "We worry about you, that's all."

"I know you do, and I appreciate that," I replied, softening some. "This is something that I don't need to do, I *want* to do it! I want to do something new to get my life back. Please understand that."

"What can we do to help?" Eric asked, capitulating.

*

"Are you sure you want to be doing this, Allex?" Tom White asked.

"Oh, not you too." I shook my head and sat down across from the town's new mayor. "Tom, you've been my friend for years. When have I ever done something that I haven't thought long and hard about?"

"You married Mark on rather short notice," he said matter-of-factly, leaning back in his big leather chair.

"That doesn't mean I didn't think it out first."

"Is he giving you a hard time, too, Allex?" Colonel Jim Andrews said from the doorway. "Ever since I mentioned this road trip to him, Tom has been trying to talk me out of it." He came into the room, grabbed the nearest chair and turned it around, straddling it.

"That's not true, Jim, I just want you to take someone else. I need Allex here," Tom said.

"No you don't, Tom. I haven't done anything worthwhile or helpful since… well, in months," I answered, standing so I could pace. "It's hard to explain. I want to do something new, something… exciting, before I'm too old to have an adventure."

*

"So, Allex, if I know you at all, you've been making lists," Tom said, while the three of us sat around the kitchen table at the house on the lake later that afternoon.

I had made dinner at home and brought it over so we could have a planning meeting without my sons interfering. Homemade pasta and a large kettle of spiced venison sat in the center on a folded towel to protect the polished wood from the heat of the pot. The delicate aroma of the cinnamon wafted around the room on the gentle breeze coming off Lake Meade. I set a basket of fresh baked rolls between the two men.

I took a moment to look at these two men who had become so important in my life. Tom, with his chocolate brown eyes and dark honey colored hair that was inching away from his forehead at an alarming rate, had been my friend for many years. Since he was only in his late forties, it must be the stress, and God knows we'd had enough of that this past year. When we first met during emergency management training, we felt a slight attraction that ended quickly when he met the woman he was to marry. We left our relationship as good friends, never to be anything else.

And Colonel James Anderson, was fiftyish and married to the military. His steel gray eyes fit his gray buzz-cut hair. Jim's six foot two frame towered Tom by a good four inches. We met only a year ago when Eric and Emilee arrived unexpectedly at Sawyer Air Force Base after the first of the earthquakes. With Jim's weekly visits these last few months, on the pretense of playing cribbage, we've gotten to know each other well, almost better than I knew Tom. Our relationship, though, is the same: just good friends, never to be anything else. I've loved - and lost - two men this past year, my heart won't allow for anything closer than just friends.

"Earth to Allex, are you joining us?" Tom laughed and I sat.

"So what have you come up with for us to take?" Jim tore open a warm yeasty roll and dipped it into the brown gravy that oozed around the venison.

"It's only a preliminary list so far, much will depend on how long we'll be gone. Any idea on that, Jim?" I questioned.

"I'd say anywhere from two weeks to two months. It shouldn't take any longer than that to find out what we need to know," he said around the bite of bread.

"*T-two months*??" Tom stammered. "Why so long?"

Jim gazed at his friend and house mate, and smiled. "Jealous?" he asked with a smirk.

Tom glanced at him, and then at me. "Yeah, in a way," he confessed. "I envy the adventure. It gets boring pushing paper around my desk all day."

"Tell you what, Tom, if you help us get ready for this, next time you can come with us," I offered with a chuckle.

*

The step-van filled with a store full of liquor that Jim had sent us six months ago when Marquette was evacuated, was steadily depleting. Mark had tagged it The Christmas Truck and we had agreed to keep the contents to ourselves. I know that was a selfish thing to do, but the few of us with access to it truly enjoyed the normalcy it provided, like now, as we sat on the deck overlooking Lake Meade, having an after dinner drink. Besides, had we shared it with the town, it would have been gone in a week and could have caused a multitude of problems.

"What's on your list, Allex?" Jim asked, handing me a small glass with lots of ice and a shot of my favorite spiced rum.

"Well, on the gear and supply list, I have a tent, sleeping bags, air mattress, pillows, two extra blankets, a tarp, kerosene lamp, camp stove, cast iron Dutch oven and fry pan, a cook-kit, tin coffee cups, French press and percolator, Berkey, bucket, flashlights, batteries and matches/lighters… and a can opener."

"You do know the Humvee has limited storage space, right?" Jim snickered.

"Yes. I also know you can remove those two seats in the back. They're only held in place with turn lock pins," I replied with a grin.

"Eric?" he asked.

"Eric," I confirmed. Eric has been a wealth of knowledge when it comes to military vehicles. "Besides, all of that will take very little space since it packs into itself."

"What about personally? You still need clothes and food," Tom said.

"So far on that list I have my medic bag, towel, washcloth, soap, comb, toothbrush and paste, two pair of jeans, sweatpants, hooded sweat shirt, two long sleeve and two short sleeve t-shirts, socks, underwear, shoes and boots, jacket, gloves, rain gear and a hat. All of which fit in my backpack, with the exception of the medic bag, and I'll be wearing one set of the clothes at any given time." When my list was met with silence I looked up. "What?"

"That's a pretty concise list, Allex, I would have expected more," Tom said.

"I grew up camping. We were taught how little you really need. And I'm sure we will be coming across streams and rivers where we can wash what we need to."

"I've no doubt you've already thought about food, right?" Jim asked, the corner of his mouth twitching to hide a smile.

"Of course. The only thing fresh we'll take are eggs, and maybe a day or two of meat. Other than that, I think it's best to take only dried or canned items that don't need refrigeration, like oatmeal, beans, Spam, tuna, all in disposable containers. Plus, coffee, flour, sugar, yeast, lard, and salt. We should be able to find some food along the way, too. Before we leave I'll make regular bread and a batch of Ezekiel bread."

"What's that?" Jim asked.

"It's a high protein, high fiber batter bread," I said. "It's been said that it contains all the nutrients the body needs to survive, and that this was the only food that Ezekiel ate during his journey, *Ezekiel 4:9*. It's also rather tasty and because of the lack of certain ingredients, like eggs and milk, it stays fresh a long time."

"Sounds like you've thought of everything," Tom murmured quietly.

"I'm sure there are things I've forgotten, Tom, that's why we three are going over these lists, to fill in the gaps." I was getting the feeling that Tom was feeling very much left out of our plans. "Anything else you would suggest?"

"What about fuel?" he asked. I turned to look at Jim. I was *not* going to be making all the decisions here!

"The Hummer is a diesel, however it gets lousy mileage, maybe ten miles per gallon. It does have a twenty-five gallon gas tank, though, and with the extra weight of the seats gone," he glanced at me, "it could be more. That's two hundred and fifty miles, which covers a lot of ground. We can also strap four or even eight jerry cans to the sides and back, and that would give us an extra twenty to forty gallons."

"One of those fuel cans needs to be kerosene for the lantern and camp stove," I said, writing that down on my list. "What else should I know about the Hummer?"

"It has four wheel drive of course, and run-flat tires. That's how I made it back after driving through the fire. There is a second tire within the visual tire and why they're extra wide. Plus high clearance wheel wells for tactical maneuverability. The body itself is extra wide, a good six feet across. One can sleep widthwise in a pinch."

Tom sat a bit straighter in his chair. I think he was starting to get into the planning with us. "Have you considered the possibility of running into other communities or other individuals? What about trade-goods?"

"What would you suggest?" I asked, facing him so he couldn't see that was already on my notepad.

"Nothing we can't replace, of course, but something useful," he took a sip from his glass of bourbon and the ice cubes tinkled around the golden liquid.

"I've got enough toothbrushes to last twenty years. I could spare a few," I said, and wrote that down.

"I know it's only been eighteen months since the first earthquake, however, most people weren't half as prepared as you, Allex. What about something that could now be considered a luxury, like scented soap or razors?" Tom suggested.

"Yeah," I said, "and pins and needles, fishhooks and line, nail files or a comb."

"Matches!" Jim joined in.

"I've got an extra five gallon bucket we can set up just for trade items," I offered. "I'll ask the nuns to make up small sewing and fishing kits. Maybe two fishhooks stuck into a piece of cardboard with ten yards of line wrapped around it. One pack of fishhooks and one spool of line could make two dozen kits, we can spare that; same with sewing needles and thread."

We finally decided on a five gallon bucket filled with fishing kits, sewing kits, toothbrushes, combs, a bag of a dozen matches tied with a rubber band, several baggies with a half cup of salt, a bar of soap cut in quarters, generic aspirins, cable ties, emery boards, and baggies with one cup of rice. It was a good thing the food warehouse truck had a case of sandwich baggies.

JOURNAL ENTRY: April 2

I spent several hours last night going over my lists and separating them into work-oriented projects, ones that I can enlist others to help with.

I took my newly revised barter list and let myself into the store front that was once the Downriggers Bait Shop. The nuns, Sisters Agnes, Margaret and Lynn have done wonders to the shop that now holds all the supplies that were removed from the Walstroms store in Marquette before the city burned to the ground.

The main floor has a children's play area with all kinds of colorful toys and a well-padded floor to prevent injuries to the little ones. It is a warm and cheery place now. The main floor also houses the rooms that have been converted into displays of children's and adult clothing. Upstairs, and logically away from the curiosity of little fingers, are the rooms filled with bath and cleaning products, lotions and hygiene care, as well as bolts of colorful cloth and rows of soft yarns.

~~~

"Good morning, Allexa! What can I help you with today?" Sister Agnes beamed.

"I'm hoping I can enlist your help with a few things I need for our trip."

"Darn! I was hoping it was to help talk you out of going," she lamented.

"Not you too," I pouted. If it weren't rude, I'd turn around and leave. "I really am tired of hearing what a bad idea this is."

I was only half joking. The entire town was abuzz with the pending road trip, not all of it good.

Sister Agnes looked chagrined. "Oh, no, please. I was teasing. I know many people feel this trip is going to be too dangerous, though I don't. Actually, I think it might be fun and just what you need. What can I do to help?" The sadness in her eyes flickered for only for a moment.

"I plan on taking a bucket full of different items to trade with others we may find along the way. Useful things, like thread and needles. I have a list, though if there are any other simple items you can think of, please feel free to add to it." I handed the piece of paper over to the nun.

The three nuns had taken to dressing very casually and only wearing a short white coif head cap to express their station in the church. Father Constantine quickly got used to wearing whatever he felt like, with the addition of his clerical collar. There were times it looked very odd with a bright plaid shirt and jeans.

"That's a generous and noble act, Allexa. My apologies for my comment earlier," Sister Agnes. She started reading the list. "Ah, teach a man to fish... These are very practical items for the most part. Do you have a preference how these are set up?"

"I was thinking two, maybe three fishhooks, poked into a half of a three by five card, then wrapped with maybe ten or fifteen yards of fish line around the card. If we use one package of hooks and only one spool of line that will give us many to give away without shorting the people here. I'd like the needles done the same way. Maybe two sewing needles, six pins, a safety pin, and a selection of different colored threads. What do you think?"

"Yes, those would be practical and desired. I'll get our staff working on these right away," Sister Agnes said.

"Staff?"

"Sort of," she chuckled. "The younger children can cut the cards in half, while the older ones can handle the pins and hooks. I think the mothers that help out here would be best at winding the threads neatly. Most of the adults are looking for something to do, and so are the children."

"It's good to see everyone working so well together."

"Well," she hesitated, "not everyone gets along, but we've managed to rearrange the schedules to accommodate the difference in personalities."

"Good. Oh, here is a box of a hundred sandwich baggies to put things in. I don't think we should have too much to give away.

Everything needs to fit into one bucket and we don't want anyone to think we have unlimited resources."

"One of the boxes we found in the trailer was filled with travel sized items. Would you like some of those for your bucket?" Agnes asked.

"About the only thing I think would be handy would be aspirin, Ibuprofen, or allergy meds. Anything else I would prefer to stay here," I replied. "Oh, and I need a haircut. Has anyone shown a talent in that area?" I absentmindedly ran my fingers through my now shoulder-length hair.

"Sister Doris always did ours," Agnes answered softly. "When Doris died from the flu last November, so much was lost with her. We do have a retired barber that has been helping out once a week. He will be here in an hour if you care to wait."

"Please have him save me a slot. I'll be back shortly." I made my way across the street to see Marsha Maki about some food supplies for the bucket. I didn't mind in the least using my own storage and supplies for our trip, but not to barter away; some of that could come from the town. I'd given enough.

*

I found Marsha in the back room that she and her husband Arnie had designated for home-food supplies. It was her suggestion that people needed to fix some of their own meals and until they could grow gardens, that food came from the warehouse trailer, with Marsha keeping a close eye on it.

"What is that?" I asked as I watched her filling in a grid on a chalkboard.

"It's the pool we've started, trying to guess how long you and the colonel will be gone," she stated. "Many of the people are really excited about this trip and what you will find out. This is their way of sharing in the mystery of it."

"I see," I said. "What's the prize?"

"There isn't any, it's only bragging rights," Marsha said. "Now, what can I do for you?" she asked, dusting the chalk off her hands.

"I'd like some staples as barter items," I requested. "Like a half cup of salt in a baggie; one cup of rice; a quarter cup of yeast, things like that, I'll let you decide. Not too much, I don't want to put a strain on our town supplies. Ten baggies of each should be more than enough."

"When do you need it by?"

"We plan on leaving in a couple of days. Is there a pool on that too?" I asked.

"Not that I know of. Your departure is going to be common knowledge. I'll get your trade items ready by tomorrow."

With that taken care of, I went back to get my hair cut.

CHAPTER 2

April 4

"I see you waited for me to put the tent up," Jim joked as he helped me stretch out the dull green four man nylon tent.

"One person can do this easily, and I think we both should be able to do it without the other person," I said to him.

We pounded the stakes in and attached the lines to the corner loops. The poles were next, and with a bit of tightening on the lines, the tent was up. I unzipped the outer door, then the screen.

"Do we really need that much room, Allex?" Jim asked. "This is a four man tent and it's just us."

"The roominess is deceptive. Once we get the air mattresses and sleeping bags in, there will only be a small aisle down the center. Four people can fit, sure, elbow to elbow! Plus we should also keep our duffels, weapons and ammo cans with us at all times, don't you think? There may be times we will be forced to cook inside the tent. It's going to feel cramped if that happens."

"Now that you've brought up weapons, what are you planning on taking?" Jim asked.

"I'm used to my 9mm Kel Tec, and thought I'd bring the M14 too. Plus I've got that knife. You remember, the one that Virginia soldier stabbed me with?"

"I'd rather forget that whole debacle. I should have seen through Marlow sooner than I did. I'm sorry, Allex," Jim said, sounding truly saddened. "Anyway, I have no problem with your Kel Tec, though I do think we should upgrade you to an M4 Carbine. It's lighter, has a collapsible stock, and is usually a more reliable magazine feed than the M14. Don't worry, I've got extra."

*

We spent the better part of the afternoon packing and rearranging the gear in the back of the Humvee. We agreed on only one cooler since once the ice melted it would only be a storage chest. Using an empty cooler allowed us to get a good feel for how everything would fit.

"I have to be honest, Allex, I didn't think we would get everything in. Hummers aren't noted for their storage capacity."

"Most everything can be nested, as you can see. That makes a big difference. The only thing I see I want to change is to add another bucket. The buckets are functional, though while we're traveling they're protection for the more delicate necessities."

"Like what? I thought nothing was glass."

"I know it seems redundant to have two coffee pots, the French press, *and* the small percolator. The percolator will mainly be for boiling water, and we can't heat water if it's full of coffee. Then there's the Berkey; it has three fragile ceramic filters we need to protect. This will be our source of potable drinking water. The Berkey and the press can sit together in one bucket, and the kerosene lantern with its glass globe will stay in one by itself. That one we shouldn't use for water anyway since there might be some fuel leakage."

"Makes sense." He looked into the back again. "I see there's still room for the duffels and sleeping bags. Are you sure we need the air mattresses?"

"They take up next to no room. You can leave yours behind if you want, but I don't want to sleep on the cold ground. I really think that cheap piece of plastic is going to make a world of difference in our comfort."

"We can always sleep in the Hummer," Jim suggested. I looked in the back again and raised my eyebrows. "You win," he laughed. "Okay, it looks like we're ready."

"Yeah, it does." I took a deep breath. "How about we leave in two days? I need to bake tomorrow."

April 5

"Mom, you *have* to go with us to the Inn tonight," Eric pleaded.

"Why?" I asked. I know my sons all too well, and I'm sure they have something planned.

"I didn't want to ruin the surprise, but there's a 'going away' party for you and the colonel. Everyone wants to say goodbye and wish you a safe journey."

"That sounds like we're not coming back! It will only be for a couple of weeks, two months at the longest and we *will* be back," I assured him. The look in his eyes said I hit a sore spot. My son was worried. "Okay, I'll be there."

"Good! We'll pick you up at five."

"Before you go, there's something I need you to do for me," I said hesitantly. "Even if it's only for two weeks, I'd like you to move in here. You're the best one to tend the green house and start the garden if we're delayed getting back. And to watch over Tufts. Plus it will give you and Rayn some privacy."

Eric looked relieved.

"That will give us a good break," he said. "I love my brother, and I really like Amanda. She and Rayn get along well, but…" he paused, "there's such a thing as too much closeness!"

"So you'll do it?"

"Of course, Mom, we'd be happy to."

*

"It looks like most of the town turned out for this farewell party!" Tom said, handing me a cup of punch. It was a fruity drink, and too much sweetness for my taste. It would be a good drink to nurse all evening.

"I hope this shindig doesn't last very long," I said. "There are still things to do and since we plan on an early start, I need some sleep."

"Suck it up, princess. Your fans want to see you before you leave," Tom joked.

"Ah, there you are," Colonel Jim said. "Ready for the big day tomorrow?" He rubbed his hands together in obvious glee.

"Oh, yes," I said. "What time do you want to get going?"

"Best time is always daybreak."

CHAPTER 3

JOURNAL ENTRY: APRIL 6

I didn't sleep well last night; I think it was the anxiety of today's events. We've been planning this trip for a month and now it's finally here.

~~~

"Did you remember the ice, Jim? I forgot to ask you about that last night," I said when the colonel arrived shortly after six o'clock in the morning. With the city-sized power plant running the town for ten hours every day, it was much easier for him to freeze a gallon jug of water than me.

"Yes, ma'am, it's right here," he replied, setting the old plastic milk bottle next to the cooler. "I also had Earl Tyler go over the Hummer front to back with a tune up and oil change. He's been an unbelievable help. Auto mechanic, diesel mechanic, and when he said he could make anything he wasn't kidding. Wait until you see the racks he made and attached to the sides for carrying the jerry cans! Oh, and he's assured me he will keep the generators in top working order while we're gone."

"Do you have a car kit for the Hummer?"

"Like what?"

"Basic tools, air compressor, towing straps, things like that."

"Standard issue, all in the built-in panels," Jim replied. "Stop worrying, Allex. We've got it covered."

I sighed, knowing that I *do* tend to worry too much. "Then let's get packing!"

I looked around the kitchen at the piles of stuff to pack, wondering if it was too much or not enough, and then decided we would make do, no matter what.

While we were loading the back of the vehicle, Jim noticed the second cooler I had set by the parking spot.

"I thought we were only taking one cooler?"

"We were, then I realized I only had a cardboard box for all the canned and dried foods. Cardboard is rather flimsy. Not only will the cooler be more stable, in the event we need it, it's also water tight," I explained.

I loaded the fresh foods into the cooler with the ice: eggs, bread, butter, cheese, a couple of potatoes, tomatoes and lettuce from the greenhouse, and more water. The second cooler with canned meats, jars of bouillon, pasta, flour, sugar, salt, yeast, oatmeal, peanut butter, and jam was heavy so went in first. The heavy ammo cans were next. The rifles were right behind the seats and accessible, our personal weapons already on us.

"Last in, first out," Jim said as our duffels, sleeping bags, and the tent went on top of everything else. The chainsaw was the very last item to go in since it might be the first thing needed.

I slipped back into the house to find Tufts. With all the activity making him nervous, I found him under the bed. I pulled him out and cuddled him for a few minutes, stroking his silky black fur, knowing it would be weeks before I saw him again.

I looked around the kitchen one last time, not finding anything we might have forgotten. While Jim waited outside, I noticed him open each door and spray the hinges. Must be a bit of auto maintenance he does.

My family came across the yard, one by one giving me a hug and shaking the colonel's hand. There were a few tears, though I do think we all felt this was a good and joyous occasion.

Emilee, now almost as tall as I and approaching thirteen years old, gave Jim a brief hug, very sternly saying, "You better take good care of my Nahna!"

"Yes, ma'am!" Jim said jovially. "I will do that!"

*

"I hate goodbyes," I sighed as we sped north on 695 to the 150 road and turned west.

"So do I," Jim concurred. "That's a wonderful family you have there, Allex. There's so much love and warmth." He coughed, embarrassed, and we were quiet until the next turnoff.

"Make a right turn here," I instructed. "This is the new road leading to the mine and we shouldn't have any obstructions for the next fifteen miles."

"You sound pretty confident about that," Jim commented as he maneuvered the big vehicle north again. He gazed over the panorama of the wide asphalt road with wider shoulders. The forest landscaping was free of trees for a hundred yards on either side. "Oh, I see what you mean."

We drove another half hour in companionable silence, until the next turn.

"Now we make a left onto that dirt road," I said, pointing to a break in the trees and we were heading south again.

"You seem to know your way around way out here," he remarked.

"This is where Kathy and I would come blueberry picking and mushroom hunting," I replied, gazing out the window, remembering all the good times we had. "And yes, I miss her."

Another turn had us going west and then south.

"Let's stop here," I said when we came to a clearing that was more like a wide spot in the road. "I want to go over the map with you again, now that we're here."

The light morning breeze ruffled the edges of the map I spread out over the hood of the vehicle so we could both look at it. I traced our route with my finger.

"From this point on, I'm not sure what we will find. The mine started building a new road they could haul the ore over without disturbing the population of Moose Creek. I've heard they had finished clearing the trees away before being forced to halt construction. It seems they ran into a wetland area and the government made them stop." I looked around and pointed. "Over there should be the beginning of that road. If it's as good as I think, it should take us all the way to US-41 west of Marquette."

"Sounds good to me," Jim said enthusiastically. "I'm anxious to see how the Shopmore store survived the earthquakes. We should be able to pick up a few more supplies before we head to Sawyer."

"Sawyer?"

"I want to refuel, and get some intel on what we might find ahead."

"Makes sense. Are you concerned at all they may ask you to stay, or even detain us?"

"No, Allex, I'm not. I wouldn't put either of us in that kind of danger. I'm still a colonel in the United States Army. Only a brigadier or major general outrank me and last time I checked, there was only a major there," Jim replied.

"Okay. Let's try this road then and see what kind of time we can make," I said, anxious to be on the move.

*

The road turned out to be better than I had expected. It was cleared of trees and smoothed out, even packed down, and we made steady progress heading south. It was noon when we came across the first house.

"I doubt it's worth checking out. What do you think, Jim?" I asked, looking at the scorched beams of what was once a large log cabin set far back from the road.

"Looks to be an old fire. We could take a closer look if you're curious," he answered.

I pulled my binoculars from a side pocket and searched the area.

"No movement at all. Let's keep going," I said, putting the eyepiece away.

"I didn't know you brought those. That was a good idea."

"I'm not real anxious to get too close to something I'm not sure of. I'd rather check things out from a distance. I've got a longer range scope in my pack if we need it."

An hour later we came upon the first wetland area and it wasn't much, only a bit swampy to the east.

Jim snorted. "They stopped the road because of that?"

"Maybe it's bigger and wetter at different times of the year. I don't know. Stop a minute, Jim, I want to check something." I got out of the Hummer and walked to the edge of the new road. "Look here, there's some serious erosion. I bet this section does flood at some point." I opened the map up, guessed where we were, and drew blue lines through the road.

We passed a few more houses, none of which looked occupied. The closer the houses were, the rougher the road became, and then there was pavement. A mile later we came to US 41.

"Hot damn!" Jim said, slapping the steering wheel gleefully. "We made it!"

"Marquette is about twenty miles northeast," I said. "Let's break for something to eat. It's already two o'clock and I'm getting hungry."

"Me too," Jim said. "I was so excited to finally being on the road again, I skipped breakfast."

He found an abandoned and locked wayside rest area and pulled the Hummer to a stop.

"Egg salad or tuna?" I asked, digging around in the top cooler. I handed out the sandwiches and retrieved two bottles of water for us. We sat on an old wooden picnic table that had seen better days and ate the sandwiches I made up this morning.

US-41 was relatively free of vehicles, though we did come across a couple of accidents that were off to the side of the road.

"Jim, look over in that parking lot. Isn't that semi-trailer like the one in Moose Creek?"

"It sure is," he said, cutting across the four lanes and into the near empty parking lot. Upon further inspection, we agreed it had once held supplies from Walstroms.

"Colonel Andrews?" a voice said from deep within the trailer. We both drew our side arms and a young man emerged.

"Do I know you?" Jim asked.

"Probably not, but I know you," he replied. "I was at the sports arena and was one of the evacuees going to Escanaba. I was driving this truck when we were hijacked."

"What happened, son?" Jim asked, holstering his weapon. I kept mine drawn.

"We were in the convoy, buses in the front leading the way, followed by the medical van, then the food truck and this supply truck, with the tankers bringing up the rear, just like you told us to do. The buses and medical truck passed an intersection a half mile east of here, and then a garbage truck pulled out of a side street and blocked the road.

"We were surrounded by a group of people, although a mob is probably more accurate. They pulled the drivers from the cabs and gave us a choice: join them or get shot. Not much of a choice. We drove the trucks and tankers into a small town south of here, Rosemont, where this mob was living. As soon as we parked where they told us to, they swarmed the trailers like ants, taking everything."

"What happened to the buses?" I asked.

"They slowed down at first, then they must have realized what was going down and they sped up and got out of here. These folks didn't want more people anyway, they only wanted the food and supplies. After the trailers were empty, they had us drivers move them out of the way."

"How far is this town… I'm sorry, son, what's your name?" Jim said.

"Mickey, sir. The town starts a few blocks in from 41. It's mostly rundown trailer parks and a few bars."

"How many people are there, Mickey? And are we going to have a problem?" Jim asked, his voice steely.

"There won't be any problems, Colonel. They didn't ration themselves, not at all, and the food was gone in a month. That's when they turned on each other. Darn near killed each other off, too. The few that survived took off into the woods.

"During that month, I hooked up with a nice gal. She was terrified of the rest of them, even the women were violent. When the fighting broke out, she and I took off."

"How have you been managing, Mickey?" I asked.

"We've been doing fine by scavenging. There are some nice subdivisions along here and a surprising amount of food left in the pantries. We aren't struggling, though it is challenging. Funny thing is, I've never felt more alive than I do now. It's not the kind of life I imagined having, but I'm not unhappy." He smiled broadly.

This startled me and put into perspective something that had been hovering on the edges of my thoughts. These past eighteen months had been a challenge, but not really a struggle for my family since I was prepared. I hadn't been challenged lately; maybe that was why this road trip meant so much to me.

"What happened to the tankers?" Jim asked.

Mickey frowned. "During the free-for-all fighting, someone got stupid and set the gas tanker on fire. It started a chain reaction since they were all parked together and the explosion is what killed a lot of those people. Dumb asses."

Jim extended his hand to Mickey. "I appreciate the information and wish you well, young man. We need to get back on the road."

Down the road a bit, I asked Jim, "Do you believe him?"

"Yes, I do, about what happened anyway. Do I trust him? No. I kept getting the creepy feeling of being watched," Jim answered. "I think as long as we were out in the open, and not making any move to take things ourselves, we were okay. At some point though, we would have been in danger."

I shivered. "I'm glad to be out of there too."

*

The pavement rolled a bit and there were some major cracks we assumed were the result of the earthquake last December. Jim easily maneuvered around the worst of it, and those twenty miles still took us over an hour to travel.

"That wasn't so bad," I said as the silent traffic light in front of Walstroms came into sight. It hung like a silent reminder of a past era. Jim spotted the entrance to the Shopmore center and turned, following the broken pavement.

"Damn!" he exclaimed, screeching to a halt.

In front of us lay Shopmore. The north and west walls had completely collapsed, leaving the rest of the structure listing precariously. Jim parked the vehicle as close as he could without running over blocks of busted concrete and scattered red bricks. We both got out of the Hummer.

"I'm going to see if there is still a way inside," he said.

"Are you kidding? That building could collapse any minute," I said, taking a step backward.

Jim smiled wickedly. "Where's your sense of adventure, Allex?"

"It's parked right next to my sense of claustrophobia!" I shot back.

"Really? I'm sorry, I didn't know," he apologized. "Walk with me, Allex, that's all."

We spent the next hour checking the crumpled building from all angles.

"I can't seem to find a reasonable way inside," Jim said crossing his arms and leaning against the Hummer.

"Well, that's a relief," I said, glaring at him. "Look, if you were to crawl inside and get crushed, I'd have to turn around and go home. I don't want to do that. Don't get yourself killed, Colonel Andrews!" I stomped around to the other side of the vehicle and yanked the door open. I could hear him snickering behind me.

"It's almost six o'clock. We should find someplace safe to spend the night," Jim said with a touch of sudden sullenness.

"Mickey's comment has been hanging in the back of my mind. There's a very nice subdivision up behind Walstroms. Five acre lots, big houses. My guess is those people were the first to head out of here, so we should have our pick. We might even find some supplies."

*

The higher the road went, the worse it got. There was broken pavement and broken trees. Everywhere I looked, it was a mess. We drove around the majority of it and stopped only when we would have needed to cut our way through with the chainsaw. A large spruce tree lay partly across a paved driveway that wound up and out of sight.

"This looks as good as any to try," Jim said, swerving up the steep incline.

The house was a massive three-story Tudor, complete with dark stained contrasting board and bat accents on the cream stucco and brown bricked arches.

"Wow," I said. "I've always wanted to see inside one of these houses." I let my thoughts trail out silently as I took in the majestic home.

Jim walked up to the front door and rang the bell. I laughed at his gesture. Then he twisted the ornate doorknob and walked in. I was right behind him.

The foyer was black slate with matching benches and led into the cathedral ceilinged living room. A massive fireplace, done in Michigan Fieldstone, graced half of one wall and complimented the dark ivory walls. For such a large room, it had a cozy feeling to it.

"Weapons drawn, Allex. Let's check and clear the rooms on the main floor first."

Jim was all business and I knew he was right to be so cautious. One by one we checked the various rooms to find nothing except a layer of dust and soot and eerie quiet.

We silently ascended the sweeping staircase, our footfalls muffled by the thick dark rose carpeting. In the second bedroom we found her. It was difficult to pin an age on the body; it was dehydrated, yet still in the early stages of decomposition, possibly preserved because of the cold winter temperatures. Her auburn hair fanned out across the pillow and looked to be a natural color, so I guessed her to be in her late thirties.

"Looks like she's been dead several months," I said, circling the large bed. "She's in a nightgown and there's a box of tissues next to the pillow. I see a pile of crumpled tissues on the floor and the shades are drawn. She was sick." Because of the dim light I missed the other two smaller figures lying on the floor near the closet, wrapped in blankets.

"I didn't look real close, but there doesn't appear to be any injuries on the children. Likely it was the same sickness that took their mother," Jim said after checking under the blankets.

We backed out of the room and closed the heavy door behind us. The rest of the rooms were as empty as the ones downstairs. The third floor was a large vacant attic.

"Let's check out the kitchen," Jim said as we descended to the main level.

We opened cupboards and pulled out cans and bottles, setting everything on the long center island. Jim reached for the refrigerator.

"I wouldn't do that!" I said. When he gave me a quizzical look, I continued. "The power has been out since at least October. The seal on the door has been keeping all rotten smells trapped inside. Do you really want to let them out?" He dropped his hand.

"I know there's a couple of corpses upstairs, Allex, but this looks like a good, safe place to stay the night. What do you think? Can you sleep with bodies in the house?" Jim asked, and then realized what he had said, remembering that's exactly what I did when Mark died in December.

"We're okay, Jim, really." I turned to the six burner stove done in black enamel. I turned a knob and could smell gas. "We can have a hot meal tonight!"

"I'm going to check the garage, make sure I can park inside and out of sight," Jim said, opening one of the doors on the furthest wall of the large kitchen and closed it. "Basement." He opened another. "Powder room". On the third try he walked into the three car garage, leaving me to continue checking the kitchen out.

The work island now held an array of smoked oysters, sardines, gourmet olives, a one pound canned ham, canned asparagus spears, olive oil, pricey vinegars, different sauces, and fruit cocktail. I opened a lower door, and to my delight I found a full twelve bottle wine rack, all bottles resting easy on their sides. I pulled one out, a Napa Valley red blend.

I heard the garage door lift and went to see what Jim was doing.

"You might not want to come in here, Allex!" Jim warned me too late. The first thing I saw was the body hanging from its neck, the rope tied to one of the beams. I stopped in my tracks.

Jim came over to me and looked up at the rafters. "I would venture to say the father couldn't deal with it." He paused for the longest time. "This is a big garage. I'd rather have the Humvee in this slot, closest to the house, so I'm going to move the body." Jim turned me by the shoulders. "Are you okay with this?"

I nodded. "I've seen my share of bodies, Jim, including those of children. It never gets easier. If we do this together, it will get done that much faster."

I got a sheet from the closet and we went back for the father. Wrapped in the sheet, it was easy for us to each take an end, and make the long walk up the stairs again. The four family members now rested eternally together, the children on the bed between their parents.

*

The interior doors that connected the three garages opened easily on well-oiled hinges. In the furthest port was a deep blue Mercedes. In the center port was a soft pink Cadillac: his and her status symbols.

By the time Jim backed the Hummer into the garage and retrieved our duffels, I had the wine opened and two ornate crystal glasses filled. We drank the first bottle in silence, sitting on the floor in front of a roaring fire, munching on smoked oysters and stale crackers.

"We probably shouldn't have built a fire. It's a breach of security and might alert someone to our presence," Jim said. "However, what's done is done, and I'm rather enjoying it."

I drenched the heated asparagus in the jar of warmed Béarnaise sauce, fried slices of canned ham in olive oil, and dribbled the garlic flavored balsamic vinegar on the lettuce and tomatoes I had picked from my greenhouse before we left. I set two plates on the coffee table we had moved in front of the fire. Dinner was served.

"So much for roughing it," Jim chuckled as he poured another glass of wine.

"I doubt we will have many more meals like this, Jim. Enjoy it while you can," I raised my glass in a mock toast, and speared a salty, onion stuffed olive.

*

"I'd rather not sleep on the floor when there are beds available, and I'm also uncomfortable about separating," Jim confessed. Did I detect some embarrassment?

"Why don't we drag two mattresses in here and sleep by the fire?" I suggested. "We don't even need our bags, not with all the blankets available."

CHAPTER 4

April 7

I woke to the sun streaming in through the dusty plate glass doors. The fire had gone out and it was cool in the room. Jim was gone from the mattress on the other side of the room.

"Are you ready for some coffee?" he said from the kitchen.

I sat up with a start and winced at the pain in my head. There's nothing worse than a wine hangover, except maybe finding four bodies in a really nice, posh house.

"I will be as soon as I find some aspirin," I moaned, and made my way to the door in the kitchen where Jim had found the powder room. I opened the medicine cabinet over the sink and found that the lady of the house was the perfect hostess. There were two toothbrushes still in wrappers, travel sized toothpaste and floss, plus a variety of painkillers: ibuprofen, aspirin, acetaminophen, in generic and name brand. I set the ibuprofen on the sink and checked the tank of the toilet. It was more than half full, enough for a full flush. I was tempted.

As I closed the mirrored cabinet, I noticed a second mirror, also on hinges. I opened what turned out to be the circuit breaker box with everything neatly labeled. At the very bottom of the first row, was one that said "generator", set in the off position. I took my ibuprofen in search of some drinking water.

"Headache?" Jim snickered.

"A bottle of wine does that to me." I washed down the pills, and then accepted the cup of brew he handed me.

"We should probably get on the road soon," Jim said. "I'd like to make it to Sawyer before dinner."

"We haven't completely explored this house yet."

"What's more to see, Allex?"

"The basement," I said. "Those olives last night were martini olives, yet I haven't seen any liquor."

"Okay, I'll get the lantern. It's going to be dark down there," he said, rising.

"I'm not sure that will be necessary, Jim. I found something very interesting in the bathroom. It's the house circuit box and one breaker is marked as the generator. I'm guessing this place is wired to run off of it. It would make sense to put the circuit box somewhere easy to locate, and I can't see these people, with their upscale lifestyle, using gasoline, so I'd say it's hooked to the propane."

Jim's eyes brightened. "Let's try it."

I pulled the main off out of habit, and flipped the other switch to on. At first there was nothing, then I heard a ticking. The clock in the bathroom had come to life.

"I think we should check the tank level before depending on it to keep the lights going while we're downstairs," Jim said.

I looked into extensive backyard from the glass doors. An elaborate oak stained wooden pergola dominated the poured cement patio and a matching structure further back looked like a child's playhouse. Right behind the garages, hidden from view to the street, sat the large green propane tank.

"It's behind the garage," I called out to Jim as I opened the sliding door.

The protective cap lifted with a little effort and exposed the meter gauge. We were in luck.

"Seventy percent? They must have just had it filled," Jim observed. "Why is this tank green when ours are all blue?"

"A different company, that's all."

*

Even with lights shining the way, we still descended the stairs cautiously. At the foot of the stairs was a row of light switches, each one a dimmer. I turned them on, one at a time. In front of us lay a parquet dance floor, at least thirty foot by thirty foot, highly polished. Off to the left was the long professional wet-bar in laminated cork and six bucket style stools in burgundy leather lined up neatly. I turned slowly in a circle.

"I bet it has a dynamite sound system too," I sighed while Jim explored the bar. Six small bistro tables were at the other end of the dance floor on plush forest green carpeting. Chairs that matched the barstools sat two each to a glass top table. These people really knew how to entertain.

"The bar is fully stocked, Allex." Jim frowned. "We wouldn't be able to take all of this with us."

"I think we should leave it here …"

"What?"

"… for now. I suggest we stop on our way back and take what we can." I paused, thinking. "In a way it feels like stealing though."

"We're not *looting*, Allex, that's stealing. We're *scavenging*. There's a difference. The world has fallen apart and we know the owners are dead. Whatever we find that isn't already claimed is fair game."

I looked at Jim and knew he was right. I nodded my head in agreement.

"I wonder if they have a wine cellar." I grinned. It didn't take long for us to find the hidden panel that popped open to applied pressure. How Jim knew to press the corners I didn't ask.

"Oh. My." I breathed. The room had cases and cases of wine stacked, all labeled with name, type, and year. "We would need the Christmas Truck to get all of this. Come on, let's close it up." I stepped back, taking one bottle from the nearest open case: A Cap d'Haute, 1996. It would deserve a special dinner.

"We need to keep looking. I wouldn't be surprised to find guns too."

"We really don't need any more guns, Allex."

"Perhaps not, but we can keep them out of the hands of others."

We started at the top of the house and worked our way down, finding only one gun cabinet with a half dozen rifles and two handguns.

"Not what I would have thought, though at least we found the few they had," I said, as Jim put them inside the wine cellar and closed the panel. I ran a towel over the mirrors, removing any smudges that would draw attention.

"I've been thinking about what that Mickey had said about the nice houses he'd found. Maybe we should scout around this neighborhood before we move on," Jim suggested.

I stood at the stove scrambling some eggs into the remaining ham. We had a late breakfast with the eggs made into sandwiches and we finished the coffee.

"I think that's a great idea. I'll get my notepad from the Hummer so I can write down addresses in case we find anything worthwhile."

Four hours later we had covered only half of the estates. That's what they were, really—estates. Some had bought two or three of the five acre lots and situated their house accordingly. We walked back to the Hummer pulling a red wagon we found in one of the backyards. The wagon was piled high with an assortment of exotic canned goods, liquor bottles and wine. And guns. We didn't take all that was there, except for the guns, and I had the addresses and a list of what was left.

"I say we stay until we've searched all the houses," Jim said.

"Agreed. It's not like they are expecting us at Sawyer, so we've got all the time we want to take."

"I hate to admit this, Allex, but I'm actually having fun going through someone else's house. Is that sick or what?"

"I think it satisfies a voyeuristic side that is part of human nature, Jim. Though I *am* glad we haven't found any more bodies!"

"Yet," he reminded me.

"Yet," I agreed.

"Did you leave the generator running?" he asked me.

"Yes, I wanted to heat the water in the tanks. I'm really looking forward to a hot soaking bath tonight. And a shower in the morning," I said wistfully, missing my hot tub. Without grid power I had to drain it right after the big quake, right after Mark died. We set boxes on the floor and bags on the counter in the kitchen. "We can go through these later and see what we want to take and what we can leave to pick up on our way home," I said. I turned and stared out the window.

"What's the matter?" Jim asked, approaching me from behind.

"I feel kind of odd. We're staying in this really nice house and we don't even know who these people were or what their names are."

"That's easily remedied," Jim said, going out into the garage. He returned a few minutes later with the car registrations. "Linda and Richard Iverson. I also found his briefcase." Jim opened the slim attaché. "He was an attorney from the looks of all the legal papers." He closed the case and set it aside. "Does that help?"

"Yes, thank you." I smiled with satisfaction. One less mystery on my mind. "How about some lunch before we start on the other houses? We have some smoked salmon, roasted red peppers, kippers, albacore tuna, chicken breast, and a couple cans of clam chowder."

"I'll take a chicken sandwich and some soup," he said. "Do you want me to do anything to help?"

"You could see if there's anything to drink downstairs."

I set two bowls of clam chowder on the island and two plates with chicken sandwiches. There was enough lettuce left to put two small leaves on each sandwich. The polished island had four swivel bucket barstools made of birds-eye maple and deep green leather, and I guessed that this was a common and casual place for the family to have quick meals.

Jim returned with a tray sporting two glasses filled with ice and two liquor bottles.

"Ice?" I exclaimed.

"The bar has an icemaker that's been churning away with the generator on. I know it's a bit early in the day, but we aren't driving anywhere so…"

After lunch, I rinsed the bowls and put everything in the dishwasher, something I was definitely looking forward to running after dinner later.

We took the empty wagon and set out in the opposite direction. The casual walking felt good. Jim and I had spent many hours talking about ourselves during our weekly cribbage games this past winter that the silence we now shared wasn't awkward in the least. There was a light cloud cover and the sun strained to be seen through the filmy gray.

The first house we came to held nothing for us. The second house had bodies.

"Looks like a murder/suicide," Jim remarked as he circled the table where the bodies slumped. "From the hole in the skull, I would say he shot her from behind, then sat down and put the barrel in his mouth."

I was looking around the room and trying not to focus on the two corpses. I spotted a piece of paper stapled to the side of a dark mahogany cupboard in the kitchen that was very much out of place. No one *staples* notes to expensive woodwork, not unless they want the note found.

"Jim, come look at this," I said quietly.

"Hmmm," he said, reading the note contemplatively, with his hands resting gently on my shoulders as he stood behind me. "Pretty much the way it went down, Allex. She was an invalid and he was sick with the flu. I say we look through the house quickly and leave these folks in peace." Jim picked the revolver up from the floor where it had fallen, and spun the chamber. "The gun is empty. I guess he knew he would need only two rounds." He set the gun on the island, below the note.

After the eight houses we had scoured today, we had a working rhythm. We started at the top and worked our way down. This house produced nothing we could use and we locked the door behind us, taking the empty gun.

"Only two houses to go and we can call it quits for the night," I said as we made our way up the street to the next McMansion. "I'm exhausted, and a little emotionally drained."

"I understand, Allex. If you would rather wait here, I can go through these next two on my own," Jim offered.

"No, as you said before, we shouldn't be separated. I'll be okay," I murmured, trudging along.

Thankfully, there were no more bodies for us to discover. To speed things along, after clearing the upstairs rooms, Jim and I each took a room looking for guns, then the same for downstairs. Our biggest finds were always in the kitchens or the finished basements, usually in the way of canned goods and liquor. The liquor we left behind, with me making a note what was in each house, the canned food we took with us. We were done and headed back to what we were referring to as *home*.

Jim had locked the garage door when we left, so we approached the front door to let ourselves in again and found the door ajar. Jim stopped, motioning me to stay back as he pulled his gun. I drew mine, too, and followed him anyway.

There was an elderly man standing in the living room, looking out into the backyard. His dirty clothes were too large for him and I could smell him from ten feet away. "Oh there you are, Linda! I was wondering where you were. Say, you cut your hair, I think I like it better long," he said, when he saw me.

Linda? That was the name of the lady of the house. He must be confusing me with her. "Hi," I said quietly. Jim and I cautiously stepped closer. The old man didn't appear to be threatening, just confused.

"Rich, when did you get so gray?" the old man said, cocking his head to the side. "I see you brought work home. That will send you to an early grave for sure!" he said, waving a shaky, liver-spotted hand toward the briefcase that was still on the floor. "Where are those grandkids of mine? I haven't seen them since you put me in that home." He frowned and seemed lost in thoughts again.

Ah ha! This must be Linda's father, and ill with dementia or Alzheimer's.

"Ah, the kids are… having a playdate with some school friends… Dad," I ventured, giving Jim a quick look. "What are you doing here? Won't the center be worried when they find you missing?"

"They ignore me all the time, Linda. I don't like it there. When I couldn't find anyone to get my dinner today I walked out! That will teach them," the old guy said angrily, looking away. When he turned back to us, he was all happy again. "Say, Rich, can you get me one of those fancy beers you keep downstairs? I'm thirsty and tired.." He lowered himself into one of the plush chairs facing the fireplace and closed his eyes.

"Sure thing, give me a hand, Linda," Jim said, taking me by the arm.

"What the hell is going on, Allex?" he asked once we were downstairs. "That old man thinks you're Linda and I'm Richard? Is he crazy?" Jim went behind the bar and opened the refrigerator. He selected one of the more exotic beers and opened it.

"I think he's got dementia and that's why he was put into a home, Jim. I'm not sure what we're going to do about this. I mean this *is* his daughter's house!"

"Maybe he'll get confused again and walk out," Jim sighed and we went back upstairs.

"Here's your beer… Dad," I said, extending the bottle to the old man. He didn't move. I touched his shoulder, thinking he'd fallen asleep. He still didn't move. I backed up. "Jim... I think he's dead. Would you get my medical bag from the Hummer?" I stood there, looking at how peaceful the old guy looked.

Jim handed me the brass studded black leather purse that I had converted to a medical bag a few years ago, the one Mark had used until he died. I removed the stethoscope and listened for a heartbeat. Nothing. I stepped back again and put the stethoscope away.

"At least he died content, thinking he was back with his family," I said.

"Let's move him upstairs so he really can be with his family," Jim said softly.

I got another sheet from the closet. We wrapped him in a blue floral shroud, then carried him up the stairs and laid him at the foot of the crowded bed.

We finished putting most of our finds away in the basement, with the exception of the canned foods and a few bottles of wine. It was now eight o'clock, and in spite of the shock of the old man waiting for us, and then dying, I was hungry. I took a jar of pasta sauce from the basement pantry and another can of flaked chicken.

Once again, we sat on the floor in front of a fire. Dinner was spaghetti and more wine. We finished off the first loaf of bread mopping up the sauce.

April 9

After breakfast I emptied the dishwasher and put everything back like it was. The few remaining canned goods went into our box of food along with an assorted case of wine from the upstairs cache and the basement. I left my notes of what was where in this ritzy neighborhood under the silverware tray so I wouldn't lose it.

It was time to get back on the road.

CHAPTER 5

Jim steered around yet another chunk of asphalt that was jutting up and in our way. "This road is a mess, Allex. We've made only five miles in the past hour and we need to put more distance behind us. Do you know another route or do we go off-road?"

"I say it's time for me to see your true driving skills," I teased. "There are a few places the shoulders dip away and deep for rain runoff, otherwise I don't think there is anyone around to complain about you driving over their lawns. Just don't break the wine bottles."

"Do you think there are many houses like the one we just left?" he asked, running down a plastic pink flamingo lawn ornament.

"Seriously? No, I don't. Tom said people were leaving every day, and I doubt they would leave behind that much food." We had found a second pantry in the basement, filled with canned goods and more gourmet foods. "That house was off the beaten path and well hidden even from within that subdivision. Anna had said there was so little food left before the evacuation that she only managed to get a few cans from all the houses surrounding where she was. So, no, that house we found was a rare treasure trove. Maybe the Iversons were planning on riding out the disasters by hunkering down and then got sick. I hope the house is still secure when we return."

"Any idea how much further to Sawyer?" Jim asked. "I'm not that familiar with this route and things look different to me."

"It's maybe another ten miles, if we don't run into any blockages."

*

We pulled up to the security gate at Sawyer Air Force Base and an armed guard stepped out of the new shack. Jim rolled down the window.

"ID, please," the young man said. Jim pulled his ID from the visor and handed it over.

The guard saluted, and said, "Welcome back to Sawyer, Colonel Andrews!" He looked into the Hummer at me. "I'm sorry, sir, orders are no more civilians are allowed on base."

Jim's gaze became very stony. "Lieutenant Smeth is not a civilian, Sergeant. What she is is out of uniform, and we're here in part to rectify that."

Me a lieutenant? I wish Jim had warned me, though I could play along if I had to.

The sergeant went silent for a moment. "My orders—"

"Do your orders include questioning a senior officer? Open this gate, Sergeant," Jim snapped testily.

"Yes sir!" The gate lifted.

Once Jim had parked the Humvee, he turned to me and said, "I'm sorry about that, Allex. I've been wondering if we were going to meet some resistance, now I know. As far as we are concerned, you're now a first lieutenant, under my command. I had to rank you over that guard, and over ninety percent of the soldiers here for your own protection. How familiar are you with ranks in the military?"

"Not very."

"Okay. Basically, a captain, a major, a general and a colonel outrank you. It sounds like a lot, however there aren't that many high ranking officers here. They have to salute me, so if I salute back, you salute them, okay? I'll try to mention their rank at this time. And if in doubt about what to call someone, Sir or Ma'am will suffice. First thing on the agenda is to get you some military duds," Jim said as he started to get out. "Oh, lose the shoulder holster, Allex. Military doesn't wear them. I have an extra Beretta that will fit on your belt."

I slipped off my jacket, and then removed the holster. "I'll have you know I feel half naked without this," I said as I wrapped the straps around the Kel-Tec and shoved it under the seat.

"You can put it back on when we clear everything military. Until then, you need to act like Army." He handed me a leather holster and I threaded it on my belt.

When we entered what used to be the airport terminal, I noticed how much it had changed, even from just a year ago when I came here to pick up Eric and Emilee. There was a great deal of activity everywhere. I was feeling a bit overwhelmed and hoped I could keep my cover.

"Colonel Andrews!" someone called out. Jim stopped and turned toward the deep male voice.

"Steve! How's my favorite major?" Jim returned the salute. I came to a moderate attention and saluted the major. He returned my salute with a question in his eyes directed at the Colonel. "Major Steven Kopley, I'd like you to meet First Lieutenant Allex Smeth. Allex has been my right hand these past few months. We're here to re-outfit her. She lost everything in the Marquette fires."

"Welcome to Sawyer, Lt. Smeth. Where did you transfer out of?" the Major asked with a genuine smile.

I smiled back, stalling for time.

"Selfridge, Sir," I replied, dredging up some distant memories.

"Selfridge is an Air Force Base," he said skeptically.

"So is Sawyer, Sir. The Army has presence everywhere these days." I was starting to feel interrogated.

He looked at me suspiciously. "I spent some time there a while back. There was a cider mill I was rather fond of, on one of the Mile Roads, 21 I think."

"If it's Spencer's you're remembering, Sir, it's on 26 Mile Road. Best cinnamon cake donuts this side of heaven," I replied smoothly.

Major Kopley grinned. "Those were indeed the best I've ever had."

"Things look a bit different from the last time I was here, Major. Where is the PX located now?" Jim asked, swiftly changing the subject.

"Building H will have everything you need."

"After we get the lieutenant back in uniform, can we meet you somewhere for a briefing on this crack left behind by the earthquake? Our information is very limited," Jim said.

The major looked at his watch. "Meet me in the officers' mess at eighteen hundred hours for dinner and I'll tell you everything I know. Colonel, Lieutenant," he saluted and left.

Jim stared at me for a moment. He looked confused.

"What?" I said.

"I'm speechless, and that's hard to do to me," he confessed. "He was testing you, you realize, and you passed with flying colors. I'm impressed."

"Robert Heinlein, one of my favorite authors, once said there were three ways to lie. I adapted those by adding enough truth to the lie to make it believable without digging myself in too deep." We walked out the doors looking for Building H. "I grew up on the eastside of Detroit, Jim. Selfridge was well known to everyone, and the cider mill was a favorite hangout for us teens in the fall, and they really did make great donuts! I hope he doesn't ask me too many more questions because I've never been to Selfridge, although I have an aunt that spent a great deal of time there."

"Before we run into anyone else, we need to give you an AOC, an Area of Concentration— a line of work. Everyone does something, and since you're in Emergency Management already I think Public Affairs would suit you."

"What does a military public affairs officer do?" I asked perplexed.

"Basically, you civilianize military information; make sure what is going out to the public doesn't have anything classified in it. It's the perfect cover AOC for traveling," Jim said, obviously pleased with himself.

We found Building H easily and no one dared stop or question the colonel. Signs were abundant enough that we didn't have to ask directions to the Clothing Sales shop in the Post Exchange.

"Well, hello, Smitty!" Jim looked at the young man behind the counter.

"Colonel Andrews!" he snapped a salute. "It's good to see you again, Sir!"

"Corporal Donald Smith, this is First Lieutenant Allex Smeth," Jim introduced us.

"Ma'am!" Cpl. Smith saluted me, which felt very odd. I returned the gesture.

"The lieutenant lost everything in a fire, Smitty, so I need you to completely re-outfit her. Can you do that?"

"Oh, yes Sir!" Smitty looked at me appraisingly. "Size 8, five foot five?" I nodded, impressed. "How much, Sir?"

"I think two or three sets of fatigues should do; t-shirts, pants, shirts, cap, jacket. Do you have any sweaters here? Good, one of those too. And her bars." Smitty was busy writing. "Do you still have that embroidery machine?"

"Yes, Sir!"

"Good," Jim handed me a pen and I carefully printed my name to get the spelling correct.

The corporal quickly brought me a short stack of clothes, camo pants and a khaki t-shirt. "If you will try these on, Ma'am, to make sure I have the sizes right. The dressing room is right over there." He pointed to a curtain.

"I need a favor, Smitty," I heard Jim say while I was changing clothes.

"Anything for you, Colonel!"

"I need one shirt with her name and rank before we leave. The rest we'll pick up later," Jim requested. "And she'll need a new laminated ID."

"I'll get right on it, Sir, and I can drop everything off to the women's barracks, if you like."

I could hear the hum and clatter of a machine from somewhere in the shop. Soon Smitty reappeared with a handful of tags that said "SMETH" and set them on the table. From a locked cabinet, he brought out a box of officer insignias. I tried on the shirt he handed me and we went for a half size larger for comfort. He disappeared again and returned with my name tag sewn on and my officer bars on the collar along with the shield for Public Affairs, my new AOC.

"I'll have the rest for you within the hour." Smitty smiled at us. "Ah, sir, what unit do I send the bill to?"

"No need, Corporal, I'll pay for them. After all, I lost them." I shrugged. He told me how much and I removed the bills from my wallet. Thankfully I had taken some of the remaining cash from my envelope before we left. I added an extra fifty to the pile of bills. "I do appreciate you sewing all this on for me. I hate sewing," I gave him one of my best smiles.

"If you'll step over here, Ma'am, I'll take a picture for your new ID card."

*

We were well away from the PX and out of earshot, when Jim casually said, "I thought you liked sewing."

"Oh, I do, but Smitty doesn't need to know that," I answered. "Everyone needs to feel appreciated, Jim, *everyone*. And if Smitty thinks he's doing me an extra favor, so much the better. Besides, I think I just made a new friend and possible ally."

Jim laughed. "You learn fast."

*

We were back in the main terminal a few minutes before six o'clock, though I had to remind myself that I needed to say eighteen hundred hours. The officers' mess was up a flight of stairs, connected to what was once the small restaurant when this was only an airport.

Major Kopley had already secured a table and was waiting for us, a cup of steaming dark coffee in his hands.

"Got everything squared away, Colonel?" he asked.

"Yes, it was good to see Smitty still in charge," Jim replied. A civilian came to our table, poured us some coffee, and set a sheet in front of Jim with the daily menu printed in large block letters. "Tell us about the quake, Steve. We felt it up in Moose Creek."

"Before we get into that, Jim, can I ask how you ended up in that little town?" Major Kopley asked. "We all thought you were going to the Soo, and then you disappeared from radar."

"Very simple, I got stranded on the wrong side of the fires when I cleared out the civilians. I had already assigned Sanders, Perkins, Jones, and Smeth to temporary duty in Moose Creek, so it seemed logical to join them there until I could figure out where we stood," Jim said, casually fielding the question. He picked up the menu then handed it to me. "With winter approaching, there wasn't much choice except to stay put, and once the quake hit, all comms were down."

"Well, I'd say you certainly lucked out with personnel to be stranded with," Kopley said while smiling at me. "Lieutenant, there's a nice quiet bar across the road. Would you care to join me for a drink after dinner?"

"I appreciate the offer, Major, and I'm flattered, but I must decline. I know the Colonel likes to get an early start and I'm looking forward to a good night sleep," I said graciously.

"Oh, I could help with that too, Lieutenant," he said with obvious intent.

"Major Kopley, stop hitting on my lieutenant," Jim said very quietly, just loud enough for us to hear the underlying threat.

"I don't see a wedding ring, so it doesn't hurt to ask," Kopley's smile faltered.

"Allex is a recent widow, Steve, so back off."

"It's only been four months, Major. My husband was buried the day the quake hit," I said.

"My apologies, Ma'am, and my condolences."

Just then the civilian waitress brought the plates of pasta we had ordered.

*

The dishes had been removed and our coffee cups refilled. Major Kopley unfolded a colored laminated map of the Upper Peninsula and laid it across the table. A blue magic marker line made its jagged way from the Lake Superior shore to Lake Michigan. More blue lines curled away.

"The quake, which has been determined a 10.9, centered here, around what was Chatham. The Divide now runs from Au Train Bay to Gladstone along the Whitefish River. Instead of being fifty feet wide and twenty feet deep though, it's now five hundred feet wide and the depth in areas is still undetermined."

"What are these extra blue markings, Major?" I asked, pointing to the ones near Gladstone.

"Those are the new shorelines. Here, here, and here are completely flooded. Any survivors were evacuated inland. With the quake hitting at the time it did, the causalities were high."

"We've had some limited ham transmissions from downstate that indicate there's been flooding elsewhere," Jim added.

"With that much water spilling into Lake Michigan, most of the coastlines have been breached, including Chicago. Which is why this has taken on a priority status," Kopley said.

"Is there any way to get across this divide?" Jim asked, examining the map closer.

"The Army Corp of Engineers has constructed three bridges to access the other side, and they're working at trying to plug the hole."

"Plug it?" I asked. "How?"

"I haven't seen the area since they started construction, though it seems to be a Hoover-size dam," Kopley was all business now. "The biggest problem we're having on the other side is with the gangs, so no matter what you decide, be careful." He refolded the map and handed it to Jim.

"What kind of gangs?" Jim asked, concern lacing his voice.

"When the quake hit, all power was lost for a time and the prisons went down. There are, or were, two maximum security facilities at Newberry and the Soo. Eighty percent of the inmates have been recovered in one way or another, which leaves twenty percent still on the loose and causing a great deal of trouble for the locals," Kopley told us. "Some of them actually turned themselves back in once they got a taste of the wilderness. Those city boys can't hack the wild conditions of the U.P.," he added with a laugh. "Please be careful. I'd also suggest you start at the construction site. They can advise you which crossings are safest at any given time."

*

I let myself into the female barracks and found my new uniforms piled neatly on one of the beds. I found a khaki nightshirt and a towel on top of the pile; Smitty had thought of everything. I sat on the bed tugging at the laces of my jungle boots, thinking about the gangs the major had told us about. A shiver ran up my spine when I remembered the Wheeler gang and how many lives they had taken. I pushed the thoughts away and headed for the showers.

CHAPTER 6

April 12

"Are you ready, Lieutenant?" Jim asked as I emerged from the barracks. I had slept well and was looking forward to the new day. The few women sharing the large room had been full of questions that morning and were still milling about, curious about the new "officer" and her high ranking traveling companion.

"Yes, Sir," I replied, a smile tugging gently at the corner of my mouth. I would be very happy to get past this charade and back to our casual names. I picked up my new duffle and followed Jim out the door.

"Let's grab some grub before hitting the road," he said.

"Should I put this in the Hummer first?" I asked, referring to the duffle.

"No, I want the others to know we're in a hurry and will be leaving soon."

*

We followed 94 to Highway 57, then north where it intersected with M-28 and headed east. The roads had been cleared of buckled asphalt and broken concrete, which now lay along the shoulders in large, unsightly piles. The new dirt and gravel road slowed our speed and it took over an hour to reach the construction site, a trip that in the past would have taken twenty minutes. There was no mistaking the zone when it came into sight.

"Wow, that is impressive!" I gasped, seeing the beginnings of the massive dam. A half mile before the actual activity, we were stopped by another guarded gate.

"ID, please," the young soldier requested. We handed over our laminated badges. He carefully examined them, checking that the photos were indeed us, wrote something on his clipboard, and handed them back. "Your purpose here, Colonel?"

"Information, Sergeant, and a means of getting across the Divide to my unit in the Soo," Jim replied smoothly.

"Yes, Sir! If you ask for Captain Argyle at that small building on the left, the one with the red metal roof, I'm sure he can answer any questions." With that, he gave us a quick salute and we were on our way.

*

"As you can see, Colonel, our progress has been a bit slow," Captain Argyle said, leading us through a maze of dusty bulldozers, cables, and scaffolding, "Though we *are* getting there."

"How long have you been at this now?" Jim asked, squinting into the muted sunlight.

"Just over three months, Sir. We arrived two weeks after the rift opened. Our first objective was to establish a safe route between the two sides here where the work was needed. Then we set about to secure a secondary bridge for the civilian's further south. *This* is a restricted area, of course." Captain Argyle led us over to a map board on the wall of another building. "Our crossing is a quarter mile from here," he pointed down the new river at a metal bridge in view. "The civilian crossing is thirty-eight miles south of here, and ten miles north of the new shoreline. That gives the best coverage for any that need to get across." He indicated on the map where the other bridge was.

"I was told there were three bridges, Captain," Jim said.

"That was our intention at first. It was deemed impractical, and therefore unnecessary."

"May I ask, Captain, what are you trying to accomplish here, besides the obvious of stopping the flow?" I asked. "And what problems are you running into that is impeding your progress?"

"The obvious is our only goal, Lieutenant. The continuing loss of water from Superior has greatly diminished the shipping lanes. The water level is now down seventy-five feet, and while that may not seem like a lot when the lake has an average depth of over four hundred feet, it is. The lake bottom isn't consistent and navigating has become difficult." He looked out to the lake before going on. "It isn't just *losing* water from Superior, though. Our equally important goal is to stop the flow *into* Lake Michigan. There are millions of people being affected on that other end. I've got the governors from not only Michigan and Wisconsin calling me daily, but from Illinois and Indiana too."

"What is your biggest obstacle, Captain?" Jim said, re-asking my question.

"We can't find the bottom of the rift, Sir."

*

We accepted the coffee Argyle offered us, and stood fifty feet from the edge of the rift. The gushing water was mesmerizing. Fifty yards from the original shoreline the water funneled and turned choppy, swirling in mini whirlpools. The closer to the rift, the muddier the water became. It rushed and gyrated and sent plumes of misty spray several feet into the air, shimmering with rainbows as it formed an unseen waterfall beneath the waves.

"How far down have you measured?" I asked the captain.

"The instruments we have registered two hundred feet before they quit, and the current created is much too strong to send a diver down yet," he replied. "We are expecting a deep water submersible any day now that should be able to determine what we're up against. Meanwhile, we are continuing with what we can, hoping to slow the water down at least. The first two hundred feet or so on both sides have a bottom of seventy to a hundred and fifty-five feet. At least there we've got something to work with. It's that center hundred feet that has us stymied." He took a sip from his cup. "The good news is the water is cold, icy cold."

"Why is that good news?" Jim asked.

"If the water was warming it would mean this crack was really deep, lava deep, and there would be no way to seal it."

*

We left the construction site and drove the quarter mile to cross over to the other side. Part of the new construction was forming new dirt and gravel tracts on either side of the rift for the ease of monitoring the traffic. As far as the eye could see, the trees and brush had been cleared back for a hundred feet or so and a dirt and rock berm ran alongside the newly widened river.

As we neared the bridge, I saw another guarded gate and a road leading due west, away from the river.

"Corporal, where does that road lead?" I asked.

"It takes any civilians back toward Trenary, Ma'am, away from the restricted areas," he answered. I had been wondering how that would be handled.

We crossed to the other side in silence, the turbulent water below us.

CHAPTER 7

"This is a lot slower going than I thought it would be," Jim grunted. "Only twenty miles in two hours."

"We knew it wasn't going to be easy, Jim. Do you want to take a break? Maybe have some coffee?" I asked, reaching for the thermos I had filled at breakfast as we passed a small dirt road.

Jim stopped the Hummer and we both got out. I handed him the thermos and walked back to the road.

"What's wrong, Allex?"

"Nothing, I think we should do some exploring, that's all. Let's see where that road leads."

Not too far in another, much narrower road veered to the north: someone's driveway. Jim slowed the Hummer as the house came into view.

It was a peaceful scene with chickens scratching in the yard and sheets hung on a clothesline. A young blonde girl stepped out of the house, shotgun in hand. We stopped the Hummer and stepped out.

"Hi!" I said. "We see you have chickens. Do you have any eggs for sale?"

"Money's no good anymore," she said warily.

"Maybe we can trade something." I took one step closer and stopped.

"What have you got?"

"What do you need?"

"A doctor...."

"What's the matter? Maybe I can help," I offered, concerned.

At that she perked up. "Are you a doctor or a nurse?"

"My husband was a doctor and I learned a lot from him, and I helped him as his nurse. My name is Allexa. What's yours?"

"Annie," she replied. "Glenn ate something and now he's sick."

"Can we come closer, Annie?" I asked.

"Sure, if you think you can help him," Annie replied.

"Jim, would you get that medical bag for me?" I said walking to within a few feet of the porch. I could see Annie was young, maybe sixteen. "Where are your parents, Annie?"

"Out back." There was that frown again.

"How old is Glenn? Do you know what he ate?" I asked tentatively.

"He's seventeen and I think he ate some peaches," Annie backed up as Jim came closer.

"I bet he's throwing up and has diarrhea, right?" I said. Her eyes widened. "Sounds like food poisoning. Can we come in?" When she didn't move I said, "Annie, we won't hurt you or Glenn. I just want to help." I used my softest mom-voice to quell her fears. She lowered the shotgun and opened the door for us.

The house smelled of sick. Annie leaned the shotgun in the corner and led me to a room off to the side. The smell was worse in there, even though a window was open. The young man on the bed, presumably Glenn, looked pale and gaunt. At the sound of us coming in he turned his head, and dry heaved into a bucket, which Annie picked up and took into the attached bathroom.

"How long ago did you eat that can of peaches, Glenn?" I asked, sitting down on the edge of the bed. I pulled the stethoscope out of my bag, and a thermometer.

"Two days ago. I only ate two pieces because it didn't taste right," he said, closing his eyes again. I stuck the thermometer in his mouth and listened to his breathing. The use of the stethoscope was to give them confidence in me and served little other purpose. His temperature was 102.1, high but not life threatening. My first thought was the best guess: food poisoning.

"Was the can damaged at all, or leaking?" I asked.

"It was a bit swollen, but peaches sounded so good to me. I guess I shouldn't have eaten them, huh?"

"You got that right." I put everything back in the bag, with the thermometer upside down as a reminder to me to sterilize it. "Have you eaten or drank anything since?"

"No, I can't keep it down," he said.

"Well, I doubt this food poisoning will kill you or it would have already, but the dehydration might. You need to start drinking fluids. I'm going to give you a shot of antibiotics and that should help combat the gut infection." I swabbed his arm down with an alcohol pad and injected the antibiotics like Mark had taught me. "I'll help Annie mix up some rehydration fluids that will bring your electrolytes back in line." I stood up and moved toward the door, motioning for Annie to follow me.

"He's sick, but he's not going to die, Annie. We need to stop the dehydration though, and soon. Do you have any kaopectate? And we'll need some baking soda for the electrolyte solution."

"I... I... don't know," she stammered.

"Let's go into the kitchen and see what we can find." Once in the other room, I turned her toward me. "Annie, where are your parents?" I could see Jim had followed us and was leaning against the door jamb listening.

"Out back," she repeated with her lip quivering. "We buried them in the backyard under the apple tree."

"What happened, Annie?"

"About a month or so after the big earthquake some men came around. They were very mean and they wanted all of our food. My dad had to shoot one that was trying to come in the house. That's when everyone starting shooting, even my mom. First she made me take the twins into the basement to hide. When everything was quiet for maybe a half hour, I came upstairs." Her mouth scrunched up and the tears slid down her cheeks. "They were lying on the floor, all bloody. The men were dead too, but dad made sure they never came in." She lifted her chin and swallowed.

"Did you bury them by yourself, Annie?" I asked softly. This poor girl had been through a great deal.

"No, Glenn heard all the gunfire and came over. His place is down the road a bit. He helped me move them out of the house so Jared and Jodi wouldn't see them. Then I mopped the floor before I would let them out of the basement." Annie looked up at me with pale, spiky wet lashes.

"You did real good," I said and gave her a hug, catching Jim's eye as I did so. "Now we need to make Glenn better. Where did your mother keep the medicines?"

"There's some in the bathroom cabinet, but there's not much," she said, leading me to a different bathroom than the one Glenn was using. I opened the mirrored door and found a bottle of aspirin, a box of Band-Aids, some Neosporin, and some toothpaste.

"Any place else she may have kept things, Annie?" I asked. She looked down at her feet. "Annie?" I repeated.

"Mom said we should never tell anyone about what she had saved for us. She said most everyone would try to take it from us."

"Let's go back to the kitchen for now and mix up something for Glenn to drink," I wasn't going to push her, not yet. "We need some baking soda, sugar, salt, some powdered juice drink and water."

"We ran out of bottled water a few days ago. I've been bringing some up from the creek, but it's dirty and the twins won't drink it unless it sits for a couple of days," she said.

"Jim, would you get that gallon of water from the cooler and bring in the Berkey Traveler, please?" I turned back to Annie. "Okay, so do you have the rest?"

"Oh, sure," she said, opening cupboard doors and setting things on the counter.

With the water Jim brought in, I mixed one pint with one teaspoon of salt, and one quarter teaspoon of baking soda, and stirred it. "Here, give this to Glenn and make sure he drinks all of it," I said, handing it to Jim, then I set the water filtration unit on the counter. "Where is the creek water?"

Annie's eyes widened. "What's this?"

"This makes any water drinkable by filtering it."

"We have one of those!" She reached for a door off the kitchen and stopped. "You're not going to take our stuff, are you?"

"No, Annie, we are not. We have our own and don't need yours," I reassured her, and she opened the pantry door. We both stepped in.

"Oh. My. Your parents were preppers, weren't they?" I said, glancing at all the supplies.

"That's what Mom said they were, and reminded me they were not hoarders!"

"No, preppers are not hoarders, Annie. They are people who want to take care of themselves and the ones they love and believe in being prepared for bad times. And that's very good. Now, show me where you saw the water filter." She opened another door and we stepped into a smaller room. I spotted the Berkey immediately, and lifted it off the shelf and handed it to her. I took the cover off the top to see the ceramic filters were missing. On the shelf beside the now empty slot was a stack of what I needed. I took three and we went back to the kitchen.

"Didn't you know what this was for, Annie?" I asked.

"No, my mom said I didn't need to know yet, that she would show me when it was time. Then she died."

"Do you know how to use any of those things?"

She shook her head. "I've been cooking a lot of macaroni and cheese, tuna fish, and soups. The twins haven't complained."

"Okay, then you need some lessons. Watch how I do this." I took one of the filters and fitted it into a hole in the top unit and attached it with a plastic wing nut from underneath. "The filters can break so you have to be careful. Try it." I had her do the next two. "This unit looks like it will do two gallons. The first water to go through can't be used for drinking, since it's washing out loose particles inside the filters. After that though, it will be good. You will only have to do this once for every new set of filters, and each set is good for ten thousand gallons. It will be a long time before you have to replace these unless they break." I poured the creek water into the top unit.

"Oh, thank you, Allexa, the twins will be so happy!" She turned and gave me a hug.

"Now, while that drips through, let's mix up another batch for Glenn to drink to rebalance his electrolytes. We need three-fourths a teaspoon of salt, one teaspoon of baking soda, four tablespoons of sugar, three-fourths quarts of water, and one cup of juice, or all water and a tablespoon of powdered juice mix." Annie measured while I stirred. "Where *are* the twins, Annie?" I asked casually, seeing Jim at the door again.

"Oh, I told them to stay upstairs in their room until I call them down. They play for hours by themselves."

"Can I see you for a minute Allex?" Jim said.

"Sure. Annie, why don't you take a glass of this into Glenn?"

Jim and I stepped outside. He leaned against the front fender of the Hummer, crossing his arms. "Does this mean we're sticking around here for a few days?"

"I think we should. Her mother left them stocked really well, and with many manual appliances that Annie doesn't even know what they're for much less how to use them. When it comes to protecting their children, preppers are no different than anyone else, Jim, but not showing Annie how to use what is in that room has jeopardized their lives. One or two days, Jim, that's all I need to show her most of what's there," I pleaded with him.

He sighed. "I suppose I can busy myself cutting them some firewood."

*

"That dripped through really fast!" Annie said when she saw the top unit almost empty of water.

"Fresh filters are like that. It will slow down some over time. You won't have any problem getting ten gallons of drinking water every day as long as you make it part of your routine," I told her. I had her lift the second bucket of creek water to pour in, and then stopped her. "This looks dirtier than the first bucket."

"Yeah, I just brought it up this morning and it hasn't settled yet."

I asked her to get me a pillow case, which I fitted over the top unit of the Berkey, and we poured the dirty water in.

"Wow, that caught a lot of the dirt, didn't it?" Annie exclaimed.

"Yes, so remember that. Depending on how dirty the water is it might need to be pre-filtered. These ceramic filters *will* filter that out, however it will clog them up quicker and they'll need cleaning more often. A little extra work now will save you a lot of work later." I turned to her and said, "And Annie, remember too, that no matter how clean the water looks, it *must* be run through this filter before drinking, understand?"

"Yes, we learned about microbes, germs and such in school."

While Annie went down to the creek for two more buckets of water, I wandered through the pantry and selected a couple of appliances to show her their function. I also spotted a shelf with various over the counter medications and thankfully found some kaopectate which I gave to Glenn to help stop the diarrhea.

"I've been wondering what those are for," Annie said, setting the buckets of water on the floor.

"This one is a grain grinder, this is a pasta press, and this is a pasta drying rack," I explained, setting up a tinker-toy like device. "I know it's only four o'clock, however I think it's time we start working on dinner." I could hear Jim outside with the chainsaw and knew he would be hungry soon. Glenn would soon be ready too for some solid food.

I showed her how to mix up fresh pasta, and while it rested, we selected a couple of jars of home canned meat and veggies. We then ran the pasta through the press, cutting it into ribbons, which Annie carefully draped on the drying rack.

"I wish I could make us some pizza," she lamented, putting the last of the pasta in place.

"You need cheese for that," I said.

"There are more things down in the cold cellar. You want to see? I'm sure there's some cheese too. Can you make us a pizza?" she asked in awe, sounding much younger than her sixteen years.

We took a battery lantern and descended the wooded stairs into darkness. In a glass closet, obviously meant to keep the humidity regulated, were a couple of wheels of cheese coated in wax and several blocks of creamy white mozzarella still in air-tight wrappers. I handed one of the blocks to Annie, and then checked out the second glass cabinet to find ropes of smoked meat.

"I'm impressed, Annie! Where did your folks get all of this?"

"They made it. Dad did a lot of hunting last fall. He and mom made lots of sausage and she canned a bunch of it too," she replied, pride lacing her words. I cut one of the narrower links off and we went back upstairs.

I decided the pasta dish could wait until tomorrow. These children needed something to give them more confidence in us.

*

"Can we come out now, Annie?" a little voice called from behind a closed door sometime later.

Annie walked over to the door and opened it. "Yes, you can. We have company, so both of you behave!" she instructed the two redheads peeking out. "Allexa, this is Jared and Jodi, my brother and sister. They're seven years old."

"Well, hello!" I said, smiling at the two youngsters. Obviously not identical twins, they still looked a great deal like each other.

"It sure smells good in here!" Jim said as he walked in. The two kids scampered behind Annie.

"Allexa showed me how to make a pizza on the woodstove!" Annie exclaimed, and the twins jumped up and down in excitement, obviously forgetting their wariness of Jim. Jared was the first to pause.

"You two are soldiers!" he said in awe.

"Yes we are," Jim replied. "I'm Colonel James Andrews, and this is Lieutenant Allexa Smeth." He walked up to the little boy and held out his hand. Jared tilted his head back and stared. Jim's six foot two frame towered over the little boy. To his credit, Jared stuck his hand out too, which made Jim smile.

The military fatigues were so comfortable to wear I had forgotten I was wearing them. No wonder Annie was a bit submissive: we intimidated her. Just then, Glenn staggered from the other room.

"Your color is better, Glenn, how are you feeling?" I asked.

"You stink!" Jared interrupted, wrinkling his little nose.

"Perhaps you can get some water for Glenn so he can wash up," I said sternly. Annie took the twins by the hands and helped them fill buckets of creek water. As they walked out the door I heard her chastise Jared for being rude.

"Yes, ma'am, I'm feeling much better. I don't know what you made me drink, but it sure did the trick," Glenn finally answered.

"Good, because I think you're very much needed here and those three can't afford to lose you!"

*

It was a very shallow bath for Glenn with two buckets of cold creek water and one of hot I had heating on the stove for washing dishes. He definitely smelled better when he was done though. Later, when there was more time, I would see what else was in the pantry that could be used to make a bucket shower for these kids.

The six of us sat at the big kitchen table and ate the pizza covered with jarred spaghetti sauce, mozzarella cheese, and what turned out to be summer sausage, not the pepperoni I thought it looked like. The little ones guzzled the clean water and ignored the tomato sauce on their chins. Glenn had more of the electrolyte mix and Annie sipped her water. Jim retrieved a bottle of wine from the Hummer and the two of us enjoyed the relaxing meal. It almost felt…normal.

"Glenn, where are your parents, if I may ask?" Jim said casually.

"Well, sir, a couple of days before the men attacked here, they attacked our place. I had been out hunting and my dad was there alone. He didn't stand a chance; those guys in the orange jumpsuits overwhelmed him. When I got home that evening, the men were sitting on the porch drinking my dad's hooch, smoking his cigars, and wearing his jackets. I saw they had just tossed my dad in the yard, so when they were inside and it was really dark, I snuck in and took his body to bury it. I'm sure they thought a coyote had dragged it off." Glenn paused to sip his drink. "I have another hunting blind that's not too far from the house, and I took the deer I had back there and hung it high in a tree to cure. I stayed in the blind for three days, cooking only at night after those guys drank themselves to sleep. I would watch them from a thicket of brambles during the day. Then one morning they left, taking all the rifles my dad had and the rest of the food. Several hours later I heard all the shooting over here." He took a deep breath and looked up at the ceiling. "I've been sweet on Annie since we were kids," he looked at her and she blushed, "and the thought of those men hurting her made me mad! By the time I got here though, everyone was dead. I dragged their bodies into the woods for the wolves."

"You've been through a lot, son. I'm sorry about your dad. What about your mother?" Jim gently pushed the boy to continue.

"Oh, she died years ago. It's only been me and dad for over five years now." Glenn hungrily cut another slice of pizza.

I noticed the sun was gone and shadows were creeping into the house. "Are there any evening chores we can help with?" I asked.

"I need to change Glenn's sheets again. The clean ones are on the line and the chickens need to be cooped up for the night," Annie sighed, standing up.

"Why don't you tend to the bedding, I'll take care of the chickens, while Jim and Glenn light the lanterns," I offered.

"Are you staying the night then?" Annie asked, sounding hopeful.

"I think we can hang around another day. You still need a few more lessons on how to use all the great stuff your mother left for you and Glenn is still too weak to do chores. So, yes, we'll stay the night," I replied. These kids were hungry for adult companionship and guidance.

"Great! You two can have my parents' bedroom!" Annie grinned. Sleeping arrangements hadn't occurred to me.

"Allex can have the bed, Annie. I'm going to pitch our tent in the yard. Someone should stand guard tonight, just in case," Jim was quick to make the change and I breathed a sigh of relief. Sleeping in the same tent in separate sleeping bags was one thing; sleeping in the same bed wasn't something I had considered.

*

"All four of the kids are sound asleep," I said, settling into the rocker on the porch. Jim had retrieved our two liquor bottles from the Hummer and poured us each an evening drink.

"How much longer do you think we need to stay here, Allex?" he asked casually.

"I think we can get on the road again tomorrow afternoon. If that's okay with you."

"That's fine. I don't want them getting dependent on us, that's all."

"Good point. I'll show her a few more things and leave her lots of notes. I feel good about helping them, Jim."

"I know you do, Allex. I do too, but too much help can hurt." Jim said.

"How much firewood do they have now?" I asked.

"After I do some splitting tomorrow, I'd say about a month. That should give Glenn enough time to get his strength back," he said. The darkness settled around us, and we finished our drinks in silence.

CHAPTER 8

April 15

I woke to the sun streaming in through dingy lace curtains and a little redhead sitting on the bed next to me staring in my face.

"Good morning, Jodi," I said, and she jumped down off the bed and ran out the door, making me laugh.

*

"The colonel made some coffee for you, Allexa," Annie said, handing me a cup.

"I'll have to thank him," I said sipping the hot brew.

"Can I ask you a personal question?" Annie said, looking embarrassed.

"Sure. You can ask me anything you want, however I reserve the right to not answer," I replied, giving my standard reply to personal questions.

"Oh," she looked like she was rethinking what she wanted to know. "Are you and the colonel married?"

I was startled at her abruptness. "No, we're not. Jim and I are only friends. I can see where that might be misconstrued though, considering we're traveling alone together." I took a sip from my cup before continuing. "My husband, Mark, died four months ago from the flu. Needless to say, I took it very hard. I think Jim knew long before I did that I needed a reason to keep going, and this road trip is part of that healing process." I don't know why I shared so much personal information with this young girl, maybe I needed her to see me as just another survivor, like her.

"He seems like a good man," Annie said with wisdom beyond her years.

"He is, and I'm lucky to have him as my friend. By the way, do you know where he is?"

"He and Glenn are walking the edge of the woods looking for deadfall to cut. Glenn is doing so much better already. Have I thanked you for saving him?" Annie's lip quivered.

"If he had gotten enough fluids he would have healed on his own, eventually." I looked out the window at a movement, and saw the two dragging a small tree. "What would you like to fix for breakfast?" I asked changing the subject.

"We usually have eggs and biscuits," she answered. "Biscuits are something I've gotten good at making."

"I remember seeing a home canned jar of sausage on the shelf so how about sausage gravy for those biscuits?" I offered.

"I never learned to make gravy," Annie confessed.

"Have you thought of anything else you would like me to show you before we leave?"

"There's a ton of stuff I need to know, Allexa, and no one to teach me. I don't even know how to thread the treadle sewing machine. Are you sure you can't stay longer?" Annie pleaded.

"We need to keep moving, Annie, sorry. I tell you what, though, if we're anywhere close on our way back, we'll stop in. How's that?"

*

"That was really good," Glenn said, pushing his plate aside.

"Biscuits with sausage gravy plus fried and scrambled eggs. That's the way to win any man!" Jim agreed with a loud burp. "I'm almost too full to keep working!"

"Well, Annie and I have a couple more hours of going over some of these supplies. Why don't you repack the Hummer before doing any more physical work?"

Annie cleared the table and I sat with some fresh coffee and a stack of 3x5 cards, jotting down notes. Many of the small appliances in the second pantry room still had the instruction booklets so I didn't concern myself with them. She was a bright girl and would figure them out. She did need instruction with the grain grinder, the meat grinder and sausage stuffer, the juicer, and the dehydrator. Although the dehydrator wouldn't work without power, I could show her how to use it with solar and I still needed to see about a bucket shower for them.

"Remember, with the grain grinder it's easier on your arm and shoulder if you grind in stages. First grind is to crack the grain, especially corn. The second time through is for meal, and the third time for flour. Each time you need to tighten down the wheels," I demonstrated.

We discussed each piece that was on those shelves, making notes or taking notes. All the while, Jim and Glenn cut and split firewood while the twins played in the yard.

I found a solar camp shower in the back behind some other camping gear. "Is there an empty five gallon bucket, Annie? I want to make a shower for you."

I used a hand brace to drill a hole in the bucket right at the base, just big enough for the hose from the solar shower and used some tub caulk to seal it. From Annie's father's workshop, I found a heavy duty hook which I screwed into the ceiling in the shower and hung the bucket up. The sprinkler head hung down too low so I trimmed it back a few inches.

"Why couldn't we just hang the solar bag?" Annie asked.

"We could have. I find the bucket is much easier to fill and adjust the water temperature. It's a bit heavy when it's full, though I doubt Glenn will have problem lifting it. Until you get used to it, you might want to try lifting a less than full bucket." I took the empty bucket down and filled it with cold water to demonstrate how to use it. "The water is gravity fed, and even though it's slow, that slowness has an advantage: you can stand under it longer. It's like standing in the rain." I opened the valve and the water sprayed out the nozzle.

"Wow…" was all Annie had to say.

*

We continued with her lessons, making bread in the Dutch oven on top of the wood stove much like she made biscuits, and then we did flatbread on the griddle. Doing it this way made me ever grateful to have my wood cook stove with an oven.

"Now, where is the sewing machine?" I asked. She led me to it and I sat down on the chair. I flipped the top open and pulled the sewing head out. "The belt needs to be put on the wheel each time, and the machine won't collapse again until you disengage it."

"I've used it before but I don't remember how to thread it or wind the bobbin," Annie said.

"This looks very much like mine. Watch what I do." I put a spool of thread on the spindle, pulled out a foot, and threaded the machine from memory.

"You make it look so easy. I'll never remember all that."

"In time you will do it automatically too. My mom taught me a real easy way to remember. In fact, she used this method as she got older and her memory wasn't so good." I took some scissors from the little cabinet and snipped the thread off at the spool. "Just leave it like that, already threaded. It will always be a reminder of how it's supposed to go." That suggestion earned me a big smile. Next I showed her how to wind the bobbin and how to fit it in.

Soon it was four o'clock in the afternoon.

"It's sixteen hundred hours, Allex," Jim announced. "We need to get a move on to get some distance before finding a campsite."

"You could stay another—" Annie started.

"No, Annie, we can't, we have to go," I said, giving her a hug. "You will be fine now. Just remember to pre-filter the water and make clean water every day." I turned to Glenn.

"I know, I know. No more peaches!" he said, embarrassed.

"Allexa, here are those eggs you asked me for," Annie said. "With all you've taught me I wish I had six dozen to give you." I knew better than to refuse her gift, as that would offend her.

"One quick question, Glenn. Does this road go all the way through?" Jim asked.

"No, it curves north about a half mile from my place and then dead ends. There's another bigger road about five miles south of here. You'll know because it has a sign that says you're entering the Hiawatha National Forest Preserve. That road runs all the way to I-75."

*

After cutting away fallen trees twice, we finally made it to the turnoff almost two hours later, just as it started to rain.

"How about we make camp right here next to the river?" Jim suggested.

"Sounds good to me, it's been a long day."

We pitched the tent under the wide arms of an old and stately oak tree, in hopes that it would shelter us somewhat if the rain got heavier. The sleeping bags were unrolled to get the air mattresses out and blown up. They were thin and cheap plastic and I knew they would keep us off the damp ground. Even though it was still two hours until the sun set, the dark clouds, filled with cold rain, cast a gloom to the day and it felt much later than it really was.

I lit the kerosene lantern and hung it from a hook in the center of the tent, hoping it would keep out the dampness, plus it offered the necessary light as we moved around inside.

"This is a nice tent, Allex. I've been meaning to tell you it was a good choice. I can even stand up in it," Jim said. At six foot two, there were only a few inches between the top of his head and the center of the tent. Not having to stoop over all the time made a big difference to the comfort.

"Do you think we should run a tarp between the tent and the Hummer, Jim? If it rains much harder we'll get soaked the minute we step outside. Plus it will let me cook outside."

We set two ten by twelve tarps over a rope strung from the center tent pole to the Hummer, one for the rain and one to block the wind that was increasing. It made for a cozy and functional little room. I extended the legs on the camp stove and got to making fried Spam sandwiches for our dinner. Jim cast a questioning look at the meal.

"When I was a kid it seemed we always pitched camp in the rain. The girls' tent was the biggest and the first to go up so Mom would have someplace dry to cook while the rest of us unloaded all the gear and set up the other tent for my folks. My brother had a floorless pup tent over the trailer and slept with all the food," I said. "Fried Spam sandwiches were the easiest and quickest for her to fix. When you're cold, wet, and hungry, that hot sandwich was the best meal!"

"Sounds like you had a good childhood," Jim said. "Would you like Bordeaux with your Spam sandwich or a Merlot?" he asked with a straight face.

"I think the Merlot," I said, cracking a smile. We sat on the wide tailgate of the Hummer and ate our dinner, drinking fine wine out of tin cups. The rain was definitely coming down harder and I could hear a rumble of thunder in the distance. The air was collecting a distinctive chill so we took the rest of the bottle inside the tent and finished it over a game of cribbage.

*

April 16

The morning air was misty and humid as the sun struggled to break through the clouds. I shrugged on my jacket and stepped from under the tarp, my booted feet squishing in the water-logged grass.

"Good morning, Allex!" Jim said, coming from the front of the Hummer.

"You're mighty chipper this morning."

"I feel it's going to be a good day to travel," he replied, taking a deep breath of fresh air. "I'm going to start taking the tarps down so the dew can run off before I fold them back up."

"I think I'll get a bucket of water from the river to wash up the few dishes from last night, and then I'll help you break camp," I said, walking toward the river and swinging the bucket.

With the steady downpour from last night, the river was running even faster than before. It looked almost peaceful in its turbulence. I knelt near the edge and dipped the bucket into the water, leaning forward awkwardly since the water level was at least a foot below the edge. I didn't want the bucket to fill too quickly or it might get pulled from my hand. All of a sudden the soggy shore crumbled beneath my knees and the dirt gave way, propelling me forward even more, causing the bucket to dip deep and the fast current pulled hard at it, and pulled *me* headlong into the roaring river! I surfaced sputtering the dirty water, my clothes instantly soaked with the icy water. I was swept away before I could call for help.

I'd always been a good swimmer so I didn't panic. My mom made me take swimming lessons when I was seven, to learn how to swim on *top* of the water because I was always *under* it. It's funny what runs through the mind at a time like this. Only moments passed when I realized this was a very bad situation. My clothes were weighing me down, preventing me from doing much more than keeping my head above the waves, and a dark chill was already starting to seep into my bones.

I straightened out my body as best I could. The current tugged at my legs and arms and hidden branches caught on my clothes, dragging me lower. I thought if I tried to move *with* the water instead of fighting it, I might be able to get back near the shore. Might. My hip bounced off a rock below the surface and I think I cried out. I was getting tired quickly just fighting to keep my head up and my skin was already numb from the cold water. How long had I been in the river? Five minutes? It seemed much longer.

As I struggled toward the shore, I saw a bend in the river where a small tree had fallen in. If I could grab a branch as I went by, I could pull myself back. Who was I kidding? I was already exhausted! I felt something large beside me pushing my body. It was a submerged log perhaps, with a very strange feel to it: solid yet not. The tree loomed ahead and I raised my arms as best as I could. The tree slammed into my chest and I clung with the little strength I had left. I closed my eyes to rest as the water rushed by, pulling at me, and that log drifted away with the current.

I heard a voice calling me: "Let go, Allex. Let go." Was that Mark calling me to him? I felt the current dragging at the back of my wet jacket and I resisted, clinging tighter to the log. "Let go, Allex!" I was so tired of fighting. I let go.

*

I felt the hard ground on my back and pressure on my mouth. I turned my head and coughed out a mouth full of muddy river water.

"Allex, please wake up!" I could hear Jim yelling at me. I forced my eyes open and immediately started shivering. Jim made me stand and picked me up over his shoulder, fireman style.

"You have to get out of those wet clothes before hypothermia sets in," he was saying as I leaned against the door of the Hummer. Jim was tugging at my jacket, my zipper, my boots, and all I could do was shake. I was so cold it was hard to think straight. He pulled my wet shirt off over my head and wrapped a blanket around my shoulders, and then he pulled my pants and socks off. He took the blanket from me and wrapped my whole body with it and then picked me up to sit me in the front seat of the vehicle where the heater was blasting wonderful hot air at me. Still, I shook uncontrollably.

I felt the vehicle move then stop. I didn't care, the vents were still pouring the luscious heat at me and I closed my eyes.

When I opened my eyes again, I was in the tent, wearing my sweats and wrapped in my sleeping bag, the lantern blazing away, warming the air. Jim was toweling my hair.

"Well, there you are," Jim said softly. "You gave me quite a scare!"

"How did I get out of the river?"

"I pulled you out. You didn't want to let go of that damn log though! And then you didn't want to breathe," he said. The pressure I had felt; was he giving me mouth-to-mouth?

"How did you get to me? The river swept me away so fast." I shivered again.

"I saw you fall in, and suddenly you were gone. I jumped in the Hummer, following the river, and once I spotted you, I got ahead, thinking I could grab you as you went by. By then you had already hit the tree."

"How did I get in my sweats? I don't remember anything," I said, looking down at my dry clothes.

"You were shivering so bad, Allex, I had to get the wet clothes off of you," he said, embarrassed. "Hypothermia is a real danger and still is. That water is barely forty degrees and lowered your body temp fast. We need to bring it up. I've got some soup warming." Jim stood and went outside. I leaned forward toward the lantern. The heat it was radiating felt wonderful. A great deal of body heat is lost from the head and with wet, cold hair I was staying chilled. I fluffed my hair with shaky fingers, trying to dry it faster.

Jim set a bowl of steaming chicken noodle soup in my hands. The heat from the bowl on my cold hands caused me to give a quick shiver, sloshing the soup. He clamped his big, warm hands over mine to steady the bowl.

"Are you going to be able to handle that yourself, or do I have to feed you too?" he said gruffly.

"I'll manage." I spooned the hot soup into my mouth. The heat trickled all the way down, easing my aching chest. I winced.

"What's wrong?"

"My chest hurts," I said.

"That doesn't surprise me. You've got one hell of a bruise across your ribs and another doozy on your hip. How did that one happen?"

"I remember bouncing off a boulder, and I think the ribs were from hitting the log." I stared at my soup. He had seen those bruises? *Well, sure dummy, he stripped your wet clothes off so you wouldn't die,* I chastised myself. "You saved my life, Jim."

"Remind me sometime to ask you about those camouflage undies," he grinned.

"That's easy. They were a gift from Smitty."

*

"Shouldn't we be getting on the road soon?"

"You need heat and rest, Allex. We can stay put for an extra day. Besides, the tent is too wet to pack up anyway," he said. "Being hurt and almost drowned is not going to get you out of a rematch cribbage game though!"

*

During the night I felt warm and secure. I was zipped snugly in my sleeping bag and when I tried to turn over, I realized Jim was next to me on his mattress with his open sleeping bag over both of us, and his arm held me against him for extra warmth. I fell back to sleep listening to the wind.

CHAPTER 9

April 18

The day broke with a brilliant sun and a warm breeze. I was feeling rested and much better, although my bruises still hurt.

"We should be able to break camp today," Jim said, "unless you need another day to recuperate?"

"No, I'm doing fine, Jim, really, and I slept well. My hip still hurts, but it's not as if we're walking," I told him. "I'm going to scramble up some of these eggs to go on the last of our bread. Um, would you get me some water?" I asked. "I'm just not up to using the bigger bucket. I feel bad I lost the smaller one." He cocked an eyebrow at me and took the bucket without saying a word.

*

I finished washing the frying pan and the soup bowls from last night, then refilled the Berkey to filter as we traveled. The day was turning wonderfully warm. The road was little traveled, however, we did see the sign saying we were entering the Hiawatha National Forest, so we knew we were on the right track. A mile in we were stopped by a downed tree.

"I'm sure glad we brought this chainsaw along. It's getting a lot of use," Jim said, revving it up. "I hope we don't run out of gas for it." He bolted the long twelve-inch thick tree into sixteen inch sections, and I rolled them off to the side.

A couple of hours, two more downed trees blocking the road, and another ten miles later we came to a clearing on the north side of the road. A massive modern log cabin stood proudly in the center, the golden amber stain shining in the afternoon sunlight. Huge solar panels on a tall automated sun tracker stood behind a chicken coop. The dozen multi-breed chickens pecked at the bare ground, much like at Annie's place.

"It looks occupied. Want to stop in?" Jim asked, stopping at the end of the long, well-kept gravel driveway.

"Can't hurt," I said. "We can always use the same introduction line we used with Annie, about buying eggs. And who knows? They might need help with some chores, or want someone new to talk to. They might even be able to pass along some information we need."

Jim stopped the Hummer a hundred feet from the house and called out. A middle-aged man eventually stepped out onto the long covered porch, rifle in hand.

"What do you want?" the sandy haired man asked, holding the shotgun by the barrel, with the stock resting on the wooden deck.

"We saw your chickens and wondered if you had any eggs for sale or trade," Jim said, keeping his hands away from his holster. I stayed in the Hummer, my Beretta in hand, resting on my lap.

"Not really," he replied, "they aren't laying very well. Too many travelers have them spooked." I saw him scratch his opposite shoulder with his free hand, using three fingers.

"Yeah, that'll happen," Jim agreed, nodding several times. "How long has it been since you've seen anyone on this road?"

"Oh, maybe four or five days. Me and the wife don't take well to strangers." The man kept flicking his eyes to the side.

"Well, good luck to you then," Jim said backing up to the Hummer door. "Be seeing ya." We backed out of the driveway.

Once out of sight of the house, Jim stopped. "Those folks are in trouble, Allex."

"I knew it was an odd conversation, but how can you tell?" I asked.

"First, he was holding the shotgun by the barrel, a sure indication it wasn't loaded and he wanted us to know that. When he mentioned travelers, he held up three fingers and only we could see that, no one inside the house could." Jim was ticking these points off as he talked. "Plus the rapid eye movement said to me we were being watched. My guess is there are three men inside that have been holding him and his wife hostage for the last four days. He knows we'll be back."

"How does he know that?"

"When I said 'be seeing ya' I looked in the same direction he had been. I hope when I nodded he understood that I caught what he was trying to tell us."

"What now?"

"We wait for dusk."

*

It was already late in the day and we didn't have to wait long for the sun to start going down. Jim opened his door, retrieved the rifles from behind our seats, and closed the door silently. The memory flashed through my mind of him spraying all of the Hummer's hinges with lubricant before we left. Now I know why he did that. I tried mimicking his movements, being as quiet as possible, knowing how far sound could travel.

"It's still light enough for them to see us," I whispered.

"That's why we're going through the woods and coming in from the side," he whispered back. "Lock and load, Allex, we don't know what we're walking into."

I was nervous, and ready. If these people were indeed in trouble, we needed to help them.

I followed behind Jim as he made his way noiselessly through the underbrush, the new spring growth of the soft green and gold moss cushioning our footfalls. We came out on the other side of the chicken coop, out of sight of the front of the house. We could hear voices drifting out through an open window.

"Whadda ya opening the windows for?" a gruff voice shouted.

"It's very stuffy in here and Kora's asthma acts up when she doesn't get enough fresh air." The voice sounded like the man who had been on the porch earlier. I could hear a window sliding open opposite from where we were hiding. The rest of the conversation was too muted for me to catch, though shortly after, the back door opened and a young woman stepped out carrying a basket. She looked to be about thirty-five, my height, with pale blonde hair tied in a ponytail, and she was wearing a long, dark skirt. Right behind her was a scruffy looking man carrying a rifle. She crossed the small yard and headed right at us, opening the door to the chicken coop.

"You can collect them eggs in a minute. Lift your skirts, I'm horny," Scruffy laughed.

"Please, not again!" she pleaded.

"I said lift 'em!" We heard a slap and she cried out.

Jim moved quickly to the open door, handing me his rifle and drawing his knife. In almost one movement, he stepped inside, clamped one hand over Scruffy's mouth, and slit his throat with the knife. He dragged him out just as silently while I stepped in to quiet Kora.

I held my finger to my lips, in the universal sign for silence. She nodded.

"How many more are in the house?" Jim whispered a moment later, joining us inside the coop. The chickens cackled nervously, though it was a natural sound and wouldn't draw attention.

"Two more, plus my husband, Lee," Kora whispered back. "Thank you! These last few days have been a nightmare!"

"You need to go back in, Kora, and act like nothing has happened. If anyone asks where this guy is, tell them he stopped to take a whizz," Jim whispered to her. "That might even get one more to come out looking for him when he's gone too long."

"I better collect the eggs or they'll be suspicious," she said, snatching several eggs and putting them in the basket she had been carrying.

"How is your asthma? Will you be okay?" I asked.

"I don't have asthma. Lee wanted to get a few windows open so you could listen in case you were coming back to help. He managed to let me know it was possible when we were in the kitchen together." With that, she slipped out the door and went back to the house. I know that must have been difficult for her to do.

Night fell quickly once the sun dipped below the horizon. Darkness in the woods is very complete and we were ready to move within minutes. The yard was shrouded in heavy shadows with the solar lighting spilling from a few windows and made it easy for us to circle the house once to get the layout. We crept up to the back door, with each of us taking a side.

It didn't take long.

"What the hell is taking you so long, George? You get lost?" The back door banged open and a short, stocky older man stepped impatiently into the dark yard. With the same swift precision as before, Jim came up from behind and dispatched him without so much as a sound from either of them. Jim dropped the body and left it. We circled the house again, staying below the windows. I was beside the open window and could see well enough through the curtains to know if I wasn't careful, from how he was sitting, this last guy would see me. I rested my rifle on the sill.

Jim went back to the kitchen door and knocked. The guy turned to the sound, startled. I saw that Arc Eric and Rayn always talked about, and I took my shot.

*

We sat with Lee and Kora Goshen at the dining room table, enjoying a glass of wine from their hidden cellar. The bodies had been removed and dumped in the woods, which was too good for that scum from what we were hearing about the Goshens' brutal ordeal.

"They showed up four days ago, asking for water," Lee was saying. "I told them where the hand pump was and that they could have as much as they wanted. Even though they had tried to cover those orange jumpsuits with mud and old jackets, it was still obvious they were escaped convicts and I knew we had a problem. After they drank their fill of water, they asked for food, and when I turned them down, they rushed the house and took over. We've been their slaves since." He reached over and took his wife's hand. "Kora has suffered the most."

Kora took a sip of wine, straightened her back, and lifted her chin defiantly. This was one brave lady. "They took turns with me, sometimes four - five times a day, insisting I always wear a skirt to make it easier for them to rape me," she spat out. "It'll be a long time before I wear a skirt again!" She had since showered and changed into jeans and a sweater.

"I guess we came along just in time then," Jim was saying. "We would have been down this road sooner, but we've had our own mishaps." His glance slid over to me.

"I fell in the river," I confessed, "and almost drowned. We were delayed an extra day while I fought hypothermia."

"Better late than never," Lee said. He stood, raising his glass of ruby wine. "A toast to our new best friends! I don't know how we will ever thank you enough." He looked over at his wife and she nodded ever so slightly. "Will you stay and be our guests tonight? And for as long as you care to."

"Thank you," I said. "At least for tonight so I can dry out some of my clothes."

"Wonderful! Then tonight we have steak and potatoes for dinner," Kora said.

"Steak?" Jim asked. "*Beef* steak?"

"Yes, we butchered one of the cows two months ago while it was still cool. That solar array runs a big freezer. Those three were eating beef twice a day, we were hiding the good steaks," Lee grinned.

*

After retrieving the Hummer from down the road, Jim brought in our duffels and set them in the guest bedroom. My still soggy boots were set in front of the fireplace where a roaring fire warmed the spacious living room and my still damp clothes went into a clothes dryer.

While Lee and Jim brought out and lit the grill, Kora and I visited their wine cellar and selected two wines for our steak dinner, a Cabernet and a Zinfandel.

"You two work together very well," Kora said. "How long have you been together?"

"I met Jim a year ago when my son and granddaughter arrived unexpectedly at Sawyer and I had to vouch for them," I replied, thinking back to those days. Had it really only been a year? "Then he showed up at my house in early August, crashing my wedding. Our friendship was a bit rocky to start, but eventually we became good friends." Kora gave me an odd look, like she wanted to say more.

"Wedding? Forgive my nosiness, but where is your husband?"

"He died from the flu in December. This trip is Jim's idea of therapy for me. Enough about me, how are *you* doing, Kora? I have limited medical supplies, is there anything you need?"

"As a matter of fact…" she trailed off momentarily, looking away. "With the repeated rapes, I'm really sore. I've tried using aloe, but it stings."

"I've got some hydrocortisone in my bag, I'll get you some. How are you doing…otherwise?" I asked delicately.

"You mean emotionally and mentally?" Kora went silent for a few minutes. "To keep my sanity, I would put myself in a different zone while it was happening, and to keep my emotional balance I got angry. I never let the anger show, they only saw indifference. I think the indifference confused them and defused some of their lust. Now I can be angry though and that pile of wood out back that needs splitting will be a good outlet!" She smiled again, this time more easily.

*

Dinner was incredible.

"I can't remember the last time I had such a perfect steak," Jim said. "Thank you, Lee, Kora." He tipped his newly filled wine glass at them. The ribeye steaks were done medium rare over the hickory smoke fire and could have been cut with a fork. There were small red skinned potatoes roasted in garlic and olive oil then garnished with fresh parsley, plus a small side salad.

"Yes, thank you, especially for the salad!" I said. "I have a greenhouse back home and manage to have enough greens for a salad once a week. It's been awhile though. What was that dressing?"

"A specialty," Kora said. "It's yogurt, cucumbers, and wasabi. I was hoping you liked it."

"How do you grow the fresh stuff?" Jim asked. "I didn't see a greenhouse."

"We have a part of the basement sectioned off for hydroponic growing. Here in the woods, a glass house is too vulnerable to damage and is too easily covered with heavy snow. The solar array originally was for all the grow-lights, although we quickly realized that with enough panels and batteries for storage, we didn't have to do without many of the conveniences we were leaving behind," Lee answered.

"With a bigger system, Lee was able to put in an on-demand hot water unit for me. When we first made the decision to move off-grid, hot water was my biggest obstacle," Kora said.

I had a flashback to the time my ex, Sam, told me we didn't move to the woods for *me* to have conveniences. After seven years I still never had running hot water. These people seemed to have found a way to make it work. I shook off my sour memory of a former life.

"Once the ash clouded the sun for days on end, the larger battery bank was a life saver. We might not have had direct sun, but even ambient light is enough to keep a charge. We shut down a few systems to keep the hydroponics going and once the sun came back out, even on a limited basis, we got everything working again," Lee said.

"How long have you been here?" I asked.

"Five years now," Lee said. "We both needed a complete change after we found out we couldn't have children. I sold my software business and we built this. We took on a ninety-nine year lease with the feds so we wouldn't have to put up with neighbors." We all laughed.

"Any regrets?"

"None," Kora answered quickly. "Other than not having children. It is what it is though. What about you, Allexa? Any kids back home?"

"I have two sons and two grandchildren, a boy and a girl, and another due this fall."

"What about you, Jim?" Lee asked.

"No kids and never married. Military life isn't kind to relationships. I've always moved around too much," Jim answered honestly.

CHAPTER 10

April 20

"Are you sure you won't stay another day?" Kora pleaded.

"We can't. Even though they don't know we're coming, we're overdue meeting up with Jim's unit," I said while we were packing our things into the Hummer. "I promise, though, that if we get back this direction we *will* stop to see you!"

"I want to warn you about a group of convicts up the road," Lee said. "I heard those three talking about them. Seems that there are quite a few of them holed up at a summer camp about twenty-five miles from here. I don't know exactly where, all I know is they're a mean bunch, maybe twenty of them, led by some guy with lots of tattoos. Even those three scumbags were trying to get away from him. The smart thing to do would be to get out of the Hiawatha as soon as possible."

"I'll take that into consideration, thanks. How much further is it to I-75?" Jim asked, looking at the laminated map from Major Kopley.

Lee looked over Jim's shoulder at the map. "We're about here," he pointed, "and we're fifty miles from I-75. From there the roads are still fairly good, even after the quake. Once you get to that point, Sault Ste. Marie is a half hour away."

"I put an ice pack in the cooler for you," Kora said with a mischievous grin. "So don't forget to check it tonight."

*

The drive was uneventful with the exception of a few more small trees across the road, and we made good time.

"We've come forty miles, Allex, I think we're safely past the area Lee warned us about," Jim said, stopping the Hummer. "Ready for a break?"

"Yes! Sitting for so long has my hip stiffening up."

"You should have said something, Allex. We could have stopped sooner."

"No, Jim, I'm fine and I'd rather be away from the danger. I've had enough excitement these last couple of days." I walked a few feet back the way we came, stretching my muscles. I stooped down, brushing aside some leaves. "Morels!"

"Are you sure?"

"Trust me. I know my mushrooms!" I said gleefully. "Now this is the kind of excitement I like." I felt giddy and started looking around more. I found an overgrown logging trail on the opposite side of the road that held promise. "We're going to eat well tonight!"

"Don't go any further until I come back. I'm going to move the Hummer off the road and out of sight first," Jim said. He backed the big vehicle into another trail. The saplings he backed over sprung back up in front of the Hummer as soon as they cleared the under-carriage as good as a natural camouflage could ever be.

We wandered a hundred yards up the old road, filling a cloth bag with this wonderful spring delicacy.

I heard Jim grunt and turned to see him lying on the ground, a short man standing over him with baseball bat! Suddenly a large sack was slipped over my head and I was picked up over someone's shoulder. I tried to scream, but who would hear me?

"Don't waste the bullet on him, Carl. He's dead!" someone else said as we started to move. *Jim is dead??* I felt an emptiness crush my chest at the thought.

CHAPTER 11

I was jostled around for ten or fifteen minutes, and then dropped on the cold, hard ground. The bag was pulled off my head and I saw a dozen or so men staring at me, one of them covered in inky tattoos. *Oh, shit!*

"Oh, looky what we have here," the tattooed man said. "A fresh playmate for me!" He grabbed my arm and yanked me to my feet. "Who is the idiot that left her with a gun?" he screamed, pulling my Beretta from the holster. "What's your name little girl?"

I was silent. I took the moment to observe this… person. The blue and black tattoos started just above his shaved eyebrows and traveled across his equally shaved bald head and down his neck. What skin was visible on his arms was covered in graphic etchings. This had to be the leader Lee had warned us about and the camp we thought we were safely past. We had inadvertently stumbled into a hornet's nest and it had cost Jim his life.

"I *said* what's your name?" he growled.

"Allexa. What's yours?" I snapped back.

"They call me Tat," he said proudly, walking around me. "Strip!"

"No."

He reached out and slapped me across the face. It stung and my first reaction was to retaliate. I slapped him back. The crowd went silent as Tat grinned, and he hit me again, hard. I landed on the ground, the sharp gravel digging into my soft hands. I tasted the coppery tang of blood in my mouth and spat it out. He yanked me to my feet again.

"You're a feisty one! We're gonna have some fun!" He dragged me toward one of the cabins that circled the open area.

The two room cabin stank of mildew and unwashed bodies, and something else I couldn't quite pinpoint. Perhaps it was fear. The one room held a bed, a dresser, and a desk with a chair, with a small bathroom off to the side.

"Now, strip," Tat leered at me.

"No." I repeated. He lunged at me, yanking my jacket off and tossing it on the floor. I pushed him back.

"Yeah, fight me, bitch." Since that was what he wanted, I stopped. I didn't care what he did with me. With Jim dead, I didn't care about anything.

*

April 21
Regardless of the face it wears, rape is still an ugly thing.

April 22
There was a great deal of muffled commotion going on outside. Tat put his belt around my neck like a leash. He did that every time we left the room. The only time I was free of him was when I had to join the other two captive women in the cooking cabin. We stepped outside and I came to a halt, my heart pounding. The relief that filled me made me dizzy and I staggered.

Colonel James Andrews was standing in the center of the compound. I don't know which a better sight: him, or the three dozen armed soldiers that had all of the escaped convicts surrounded.

"I said *where is she?*" Jim yelled at the man kneeling in the dirt. The man tipped his chin in my direction and Jim spun around. "Allex!" He took several long strides and stopped in front of us. "Take that off her," he snarled at Tat.

"I got my bitch on a leash, soldier-man," Tat snickered even as Jim leveled his gun at him.

"Take. It. Off." Tat dropped his hold on the belt, and I limped forward on my stockinged feet, removing the belt from around my neck and dropping it to the ground. "Now hand me that gun. Butt first."

Tat complied. "I suppose you want me on my knees too?" he said and dropped to the dirt, crossing his ankles before Jim could answer.

I stood near Jim, afraid to speak. I wanted to hug him to make sure he was really there.

"I believe this is your sidearm, Lieutenant," he said, handing me the Beretta. I ejected the magazine, checked the loads and slammed it home, chambering a round. I turned to face my captor. My tormentor.

I placed the barrel of the gun to his forehead and saw a flicker of fear in his eyes just before I pulled the trigger. I stuck the gun in the waistband of my tattered and filthy pants and limped back to Jim. "Get me out of here." My knees buckled. Jim caught me, cradling me in his arms, and marched me back to the Hummer. I felt his heart beating against my cheek as I breathed in his scent. Yes, it was really him and I felt a surge of emotions that I'd neglected for far too long.

"Sergeant, execute every last one of them," he barked out when he passed his second in command.

Jim set me down on the tailgate of the Hummer. "I'm so sorry it took me this long to get back, Allex." He brushed a lock of hair away from the fresh bruises on my face. "Are you okay?"

I looked up at him. "No, I'm not okay." The tears started running down my face. "I've been held captive by a violent, sadistic psychopath who tortured and beat me. All the while I had no hope of being rescued because I believed my best friend was dead! When they captured me, I heard them say to not waste a bullet, you were already dead. All my hope was gone in that one statement. I believed you were dead, Jim, and my sorrow was overwhelming. Plus, with you went any possibility of me ever seeing my family again.

"*And* I just killed that psychopath in cold blood. You know the worst part is? I don't feel anything, no regret, no sorrow, no remorse in shooting him. So *no*, I'm *not* okay!"

Jim pulled me into his arms for a reassuring hug and I clung to him. "It will take more than a conk on the head to kill me," he said, trying unsuccessfully to get me to smile. "I came to with a serious headache about a half hour after the attack. I followed their trail back here. It wasn't hard, even a blind man could have followed them. I waited and watched for another half hour. I never did see you. I counted fourteen men; fifteen including Tat." He took my hand. "Allex, if I thought I had even the remotest chance of getting you out by myself, I would never have left, but fifteen to one is not good odds. I'm sorry." He sat down next to me. "I got back to the Hummer just as some of them were starting to search for it. It was too well concealed for them to find. As soon as they were gone I hightailed it for the Soo. I had to stop a couple of times to clear my head. I think I had a concussion. Once I got there though, I must say I had more volunteers for the rescue mission than I could use."

I took a deep breath and winced.

"Ribs still hurt?"

"Tat liked to inflict pain; it's what he got off on: Pain and fear. When I was indifferent to the fear, he started hitting me, and then he started punching on my existing bruises, adding a few of his own. I think one or two ribs might be cracked now. And when I grew numb to that pain, he started on my feet."

"I noticed you limping. What did he do?" Jim asked quietly.

"He started breaking my toes," I bit back a sob. "Rape has many faces, Jim. When he couldn't rape my body he tried to rape my mind by beating my body. Even when he whipped the soles of my feet with his belt, and then started breaking the toes, I remained indifferent to him."

"Y-you mean he n-never...?" Jim stammered.

"Tat was impotent. At least with me he was," I said. "I do think though, that with time, he would have broken me, or killed me trying. Either way, I was still violated and I can barely walk now."

"I brought the medic with me. Maybe he can help." Jim stood right as the firing started. This nest of vermin was history.

"I want to take a shower first, and put on clean clothes, if that's okay."

"Where are the showers?" he asked.

"This was a summer camp once, and each cabin has a passive solar unit on the roof. There isn't much pressure, but the water is usually warm."

He picked me up again, and took me back to Tat's now empty cabin. I opened all the windows to get the stench out, then hobbled into the bathroom and used up every bit of that warm water.

*

When I came out of the bath, a towel wrapped around me, Jim was sitting patiently, with a pile of clean clothes for me: a khaki shirt, BDU's, the blouse and hat with my false rank. I looked at him questioningly.

"Please, Allex, I'm asking you as a personal favor to me to wear your uniform. The men need to see you in it. When I got to the Soo and explained what had happened, the men rallied because they believed this was a mission to save one of their own. They would have come anyway, but that belief, that camaraderie for a fellow soldier and officer, has done wonders for their morale. Please don't take it from them," Jim pleaded. "I'll leave you to get dressed while I get the medic in here."

I found my belt with the holster still attached under the desk, and stoically threaded it onto my clean BDUs and added my Beretta.

*

I sat on the bed with my left shoe and sock still off. My foot was so swollen and painful I couldn't put that shoe on anyway. Jim sat behind me, my back against his chest, his arms wrapped loose, holding me upright. The medic sat on the single chair facing me, looking at my foot and my bent toes.

"Damn! That must hurt, Lieutenant. You're one tough lady. I'm sorry I have to inflict even more pain on you, however, it's the only way I know to maybe fix this. Are you ready?" he asked. I nodded. He pulled and straightened one toe, and I passed out from the pain.

When I came to, my foot was being wrapped. It was over.

"Luckily only one toe was broken. The other three were dislocated and probably more painful. They will heal much faster now that they're back in place," the medic said. "It will be painful to walk for a few days, and the sole of your foot is completely black and blue. Can you lift your shirt so I can check your ribs, please, ma'am?" I did, and noticed the sharp intake of breath and the way he glanced over at Jim. He pulled a wide ace bandage from his bag and wound it around under my breasts. The compression initially hurt, and then I felt relief.

"Are there any... other injuries, lieutenant?" the medic asked tactfully.

"No," I said. I wanted the details kept between Jim and me.

"Let's see if we can get this shoe on you," Jim said, holding up my soft walking shoe that he had cut to accommodate the bandages. He slid it on gently. I stood, testing my weight on the foot. "Here, this might help." He handed me a walking stick.

"Okay, I'm ready. I want out of this room!" I hobbled to the door and we stepped out into the fading afternoon sunlight. Thirty soldiers were lined up at parade rest, waiting for me.

"Atten-*tion!*" the Sergeant yelled, and everyone stood straight.

I took a few steps forward and stopped. I looked at both sides before I spoke. "Gentlemen, thank you." My voice hitched on the last two words. I saluted them and limped forward, each of them saluting me as I passed by, Jim following close behind.

*

The bivouac was being set up and the grounds were a flurry of activity. We wouldn't be staying long, but everyone was tired and hungry. The mess tent was the first to go up and no one questioned when tents went up for Jim and me to be side by side. Only the two other captive women stayed in cabins; no one wanted to go near those buildings, especially me.

"We need to get Andrea and Patsy back to their families, Jim. They've been missing for a very long time," I said.

"Let's go talk with them and find out where they're from." He stood and started walking at his usual fast pace. He stopped, then turned around to find me ten feet behind him and waited. "Sorry."

I limped to catch up, leaning heavily on the walking stick.

Andrea was a young girl of maybe eighteen, brown hair, brown eyes. Scared eyes. This I understood. Patsy was a bit older, though not by much. She was twenty-two and married, with a baby at home. She had long blonde hair that Andrea was trying to finger-comb the tangles out of when we found them by the food cabin. They had both showered and found cleaner clothes.

As I watched Andrea struggle with Patsy's hair I had a thought. "Jim, would you get me that trade bucket from the Hummer, please?" After he left, I turned to the girls. "How are you holding up?"

"Much better now, thank you," Pasty said. Andrea stayed quiet while tears started running down her cheeks. "We thought we would die here, and never see our families again."

"I know that feeling," I said mostly to myself.

"I don't know how to thank you for getting us out of here," Pasty said.

"It wasn't me, Patsy, it was the colonel. He drove half the night with a concussion to get to his men and organize our rescue," I informed them. "That does bring up some things I want to mention before he comes back. He's going to ask you questions, painful questions, about your abduction and your time here. Please answer him as honestly as you can, it might help someone else." Jim came within earshot, carrying the bucket that held all those small items I thought would be good for trading, none of which I had used yet. I twisted open the lid and dug to the bottom. I handed each of the girls a comb. Andrea burst into a huge smile, and started combing Pasty's hair with renewed enthusiasm.

Jim sat beside me. "I think they're ready to answer your questions," I said to him. He nodded.

"Who was taken first?" he asked gently.

"I was," Andrea said. "My home is, or was, in Newberry where the prison is. My dad was a guard there. After the big quake and the power went out, a group showed up at our house, led by Tat. I don't know how they found out where we lived. They killed my dad, and then my mom. When Tat found me hiding in a closet, he raped me right there. Then they burned down the house." Her lip quivered. "I have nothing to go back to."

"What happened next, Andrea?" I prodded.

"They found a motel in Hulbert and we stayed there for a couple weeks while they ransacked the area. I 'belonged' to Tat. The men were afraid of him and left me alone, until they found Patsy six weeks later." She paused for a minute, and I could see the struggle in her eyes. "Tat was mean and slapped me around a lot, until he knocked me out for over an hour once. After that he stopped hitting my face, then the rest of me suffered." The tears started again as a memory surfaced. "Once I was given to the men, they never let me … at least they didn't beat me like he did."

"It was how Tat did things. He got the new girl for himself," Patsy said. "When you showed up, Allexa, I was given to the men, too, for them to share. Had another girl come along, you would have joined us." Her tone was bitter, as it should be. "He treated me much the same. The beatings, the terror – every day. There were times I hurt so much I couldn't get off the floor."

"Where is your home, Pasty?" Jim knew we had to keep the questions rolling, so these two didn't have time to dwell and clam up.

"We have a small farm outside of Yardley," she answered. "For some reason, when they took me from the yard, they left my husband and son alone, which was a blessing and has kept me going. I miss them so much." Patsy cried for the first time.

"We *will* get you back to them, ma'am, I promise you that," Jim said emphatically. He looked at Andrea, young, scared Andrea. "With your family gone, where do you want to go?"

Patsy flipped back her now combed hair. "She's coming with me. She is more of a sister than I could have ever hoped for and she will always have a home under my roof." Patsy took Andrea's hand and gave it a squeeze.

A corporal came up behind Jim and whispered something to him.

"Ladies, lunch is ready."

Since we were only allowed one small meal each day while in captivity, we were all really hungry. Senior staff was ushered to the front of the line. Andrea and Patsy stayed with me and I stayed with Jim, although my false rank of lieutenant allowed me the front courtesy anyway. The meal put together in the mess tent was simple and delicious. We picked up our mess trays and utensils and took the offered scoops of canned green beans with corn, cubed potatoes and carrots floating in meatless gravy, and a roll. The server gave us women two rolls each. The available coffee was thin but hot, and felt good going down. We all ate with relish, mopping up every drop of gravy with the bread. The adrenaline of the day had stoked my metabolism into high gear.

*

"If you ladies are ready, we'll take you home," Jim said after our trays were cleared away.

"I was ready months ago!" Patsy exclaimed.

The troops had come in two transports, one mostly gear and supplies. The Sergeant in charge and the medic had come in a Hummer, while the colonel had arrived in our vehicle with a driver. With his concussion, he was advised to not drive yet. Since we had removed the back seats from our vehicle, we took the other Hummer to accommodate the two women, with me driving, at least at first.

The Sergeant was nervous with me at the wheel. "Are you sure about this, Lieutenant Smeth?"

I gave him my best mom-look, which sent him scurrying. I put the vehicle in gear and gave it some gas. Using that foot was excruciating! I didn't let it show though. I turned west on the access road to get back to Hwy 123 that would lead us to M-28 and to Yardley. Since we had already cleared any downed trees, the going was easy. As soon as I turned onto 123, I stopped.

"What's the matter Allex?" Jim sounded grumpy.

"You didn't really expect me to drive with my foot in bandages, did you?" I stated flatly. Jim got out his side and I slid over across the radio console so I wouldn't have to walk. He got behind the wheel. I certainly didn't mind relinquishing control to him, even with a concussion. I trusted him with my life; I did, I do, and I would again.

With directions from Patsy, Jim arrived at the village limits of Yardley less than an hour later.

"Can we sit here a minute?" she asked, drinking in the sight of the colorful painted houses and buildings along the main street. Then she said, "One more block and turn left. It's the last house on the right, with the white fence in front."

Jim pulled into the long driveway and stopped near the house. A young man of maybe twenty-five stepped out, rifle in hand, a little boy of perhaps two clutching at his leg. Jim stepped out first, came around to the passenger side where Patsy sat and opened her door. As she stepped out, the little boy let go of his father's leg.

"Mommy!" and he went running to her. Her husband dropped the rifle and followed his son. She scooped the little boy up and her husband wrapped his arms around both of them. It was a tear-filled and wonderful reunion and it choked me up. I hoped for the same when I returned home.

As briefly as he could, and leaving out most of the painful details, Jim explained what Patsy had endured for the past two months, adding a stern word of warning to her husband to be patient with her.

The young husband shook Jim's hand repeatedly. "I can't thank you enough, Sir, for bringing her back to us!"

I slid across the seats again and climbed out of the high profile vehicle to open the door for a reluctant Andrea. We both stood quietly beside the Hummer until Patsy was ready to introduce her.

"Honey, this is Andrea. She was kidnapped right after the quake by the convicts that killed her parents and burned their house down. She's been my friend, my only friend, for the past two months and I promised to take care of her. She has no home and I said she could live with us as long as she wanted." Patsy's husband walked over to Andrea and gave her a hug. They now had a family of four.

"Patsy, Andrea, we can't stay. We have to get back to our unit," I said. They each gave me a hug, and then thanked Jim again for rescuing us. "Oh, before we leave, I have that bucket full of fun things. Please, look through it and take whatever you want or need."

It was good to see their happy faces as they selected the sewing needles with colorful threads and fishing line with hooks, small bottles of shampoo and conditioner that Sister Agnes had stuck in there, aspirin, and yeast.

"Can we take some for the other women in town?" Patsy asked tentatively.

"Of course," I replied gently, and they scooped out more of my practical goodies.

CHAPTER 12

"I think those two will be okay now," Jim said as we sped south on 123, looking for that side road to take us back to the troops.

"In time, yes. They suffered a great deal of trauma though. Being home is a good start," I said, gazing out the window at the passing trees.

"Thinking about home yourself?" Jim asked tentatively.

"Of course, aren't you?"

"I don't have a home, Allex," he replied, his mouth in a firm, straight line.

I reached over and put my hand on his arm. "Yes you do, Jim, with us. Moose Creek is your home now, and will be for as long as you want." He glanced in my direction with a very strange look in his eyes. It was as if he was experiencing some kind of pain. I wanted to ask what was bothering him, however, I know him well enough now to understand he will say something when he's ready. If not, then he doesn't want to share.

*

We had been gone for over three hours and during that time the compound had been transformed into a small military base. All the tents had been erected, most for sleeping, one with a red cross on the front that I presumed was the medic tent, and of course the mess hall, with its adjoining space for tables. This was to be a short excursion and only enough seating was brought for the men to eat in two shifts. A large fire pit now graced the center of the large yard and it looked like the men were settling in for days instead of hours.

I had retreated to my tent for a short nap and to elevate my foot when I heard Jim call my name.

"Are you in there, Allex?"

"Yes, come on in." He loomed large in the doorway. These military tents were designed for two people and were smaller than the four man tent we had brought with us that was still in the back of the Hummer. Jim stooped to enter, and then sat on the floor across from me.

"One of the men took down a deer while we were gone, so there's going to be a feast tonight," he said. "Do you feel up to finding that morel patch again? The cook is excited about having morel gravy with steaks tonight."

"I think that would be great fun, Jim, and would certainly give me something productive to do. I feel pretty useless right now."

"No one is expecting you to do anything, Allex. You've suffered a good deal of physical and emotional trauma and you need to recover from that."

"Thanks. I'd rather be doing something though. Help me get my shoe back on please." When I emerged from the tent I saw three young soldiers waiting beside the Hummer, each carrying a basket or a bag. Jim placed his big hands around my hips and lifted me into the front seat so I wouldn't put pressure on my foot or ribs. I must admit I ached everywhere from the beatings I endured and it felt good to be taken care of for a change.

"Pull over here," I said to Jim not long after we turned onto the dirt road. No wonder we caught the attention of those creeps—we were less than a half mile from the entrance to the camp!

We emerged from the Hummer, the young soldiers anxious to find the first morel. "Do you know what you're looking for?" I asked.

"Not really, ma'am," one of them admitted.

"Then just be careful where you step while we find a few to show you." The warm weather of the last three days had done wonders for the growth. Soon the mushrooms were obvious everywhere and the boys were busy cutting and filling their bags. I found a log to sit on while the others were busy and Jim joined me on my perch.

"Done picking already?" I teased him. He held out his bag to me. It was nearly half full.

"I want to save some for us for after we leave here," he said, lowering his voice and putting his bag in the front seat.

*

Dinner was exceptional. The cooks grilled steaks for those that wanted one and had a batch of venison stewed with morels and served over pasta for those who didn't. I opted for the pasta.

Later, after everyone had eaten, Jim brought out our cribbage board and we settled into a quiet game in the mess tent with some evening coffee.

"Care for that fortified?" he asked, producing a flask. I pushed my cup toward him. Our game was interrupted by the medic.

"How are you doing?" he asked. "Are you having much pain?"

"My ribs are uncomfortable to say the least, and my foot throbs. All as expected," I replied with a shrug.

"Let me give you a Darvocet for the night; it'll help you sleep." He placed a single pill by my coffee cup.

"I didn't realize you had medications," I said.

"I used quite a bit of our stock right after we got to the Soo. The fighting was brutal and we lost many of our men. The Canadians suffered heavy losses too. The injuries on both sides were… disturbing. After the quake hit, the Canuks high-tailed it back to their side leaving their wounded behind." He shook his head over such an unmilitary action. "I'm glad I had the medicines I did, thanks to Dr. Robbins."

My head snapped up at the mention of my husband.

"You two spent time in Moose Creek, do you know him?" the medic asked.

"Dr. Robbins died from the flu in December," Jim said quickly so I wouldn't have to.

"What a loss, he was a good man," the young man said, then left the tent.

"Are you okay, Allex?" Jim asked me softly.

"I'm fine, Jim, thanks. Mark's been gone longer than we were married. I will always miss him, but I know I have to start living my life again. Can I have a bit more of that bourbon?" I washed down the Darvocet, hoping for a dreamless sleep.

April 23

"How soon do you want to get going?" Leave it to Jim to get right to the point.

"Are we continuing on to the Soo?"

"Yes, I need to debrief those left in charge. We can take our time, though, there's no hurry now," Jim said.

"You never did tell me why you wanted to find this unit. Are you planning on staying with them?" I asked. The prospect was making my chest hurt and it had nothing to do with the cracked ribs.

"No, Allex, I'm not." He set a fresh cup of coffee in front of me. "I'm still the senior officer and I need to check a few things before we head back to Sawyer. We'll have to spend a few days there while I make a full report to send to Washington and then we can finish our trip and head for home." He looked up as the tent flap opened. "Sergeant," Jim said, "please join us. I need to speak with you."

Sergeant Michael Pitchner helped himself to the coffee that was always available and sat next to me so he could face the colonel.

"Your men looked settled in. Are you planning on staying here for a while?"

"Yes, sir, if that's alright. I thought it would be good for the men to practice some maneuvers in a real woods setting," Pitchner said.

"I think that's a wise decision. I don't know what your orders have been, Sergeant, but I've got new ones for you. I want you and your men to scout the area from Lake Michigan to M-28 and eradicate any more of these escaped prisoner settlements. Protect the civilians, Michael. However, if you find civilian compounds that are as sleazy as this one, take care of them. Understood?"

"Yes, Sir! The men will be pleased to be doing something worthwhile, Sir."

"The lieutenant and I will be leaving this afternoon for the Soo and I will make your orders official when we get there. From there we're headed back to Sawyer. Get back to the Soo whenever you need to resupply. Stay out as long as you need though. You're ranking officer, son, do me proud."

At that Sergeant Pitchner stood and saluted Jim. "Yes, Sir!"

*

There wasn't much to pack in our Hummer, since we hadn't unpacked anything besides some clothes and our sleeping bags. I did notice Jim slipping his bag of morels into the cooler. We were ready to hit the road at three o'clock. As we started to roll, all of the soldiers stood and saluted us. It was a very touching farewell.

*

"If it's okay with you, Allex, I say we spend one more night on the road before arriving at the Soo," Jim said.

"Sure. Any particular reason why?"

"I think one more quiet night would be good for you. Once we hit the next camp, I'm going to be busy for a few days and we won't see much of each other," he told me. "It makes me nervous leaving you alone with a bunch of men. I'm serious, Allex! You're a beautiful, strong woman *and* an officer – the ranks will be hitting on you, guaranteed."

"I'll have to practice being aloof and disinterested then," I reassured him. He still looked concerned.

*

By seven o'clock we were setting up our tent in a vacant National Forest campground. The tent was up, our sleeping bags were on top of the air mattresses, and I had the camp stove set up.

"Let's build a campfire for tonight," Jim said. "It's looking like a clear sky so the stargazing should be good later." We both hunted around for wood and piled it around a ready-made pit.

"What would you like for dinner?" I asked. "We still have plenty of what we started with. What with finding that house behind Walstroms, the kids, then the Goshens, we've hardly used anything."

"You might want to check the cooler," he said. "Kora left us a surprise." I pulled out the bag of morels, and found two still chilled, very large ribeye steaks!

"No wonder you wanted one more night on the road! Beef steaks, sautéed fresh morels, and wine. I think this calls for that 1996 Cap d'Haute," I said. "I wonder if that house we stayed at is still secure."

"Well, we will certainly stop there on our way back. With the 695 bridge out and the hairpin blocked, we have no other route. Besides, we left a great deal of food there that we need to take back to Moose Creek," Jim said. "Here, let me open that."

I took my fresh cup of dark red wine and surveyed the fire pit. "If we can tip three of these rocks up on end near the center, we can build a fire in the middle and I can balance the fry pan across them to cook the mushrooms and then use the grate from the stove on top to grill the steaks over the open flame."

*

The steaks were rare and juicy and the morels delicate. We opened a second bottle of wine and watched the stars into the night.

"I've been all over the world, and I've never seen the stars look like this," Jim said.

"It's the absence of ambient light. Most places are plagued with what's called 'light pollution', which makes it impossible to see the night sky as it truly is. It's one of the reasons I moved up here twenty years ago." I sighed, remembering my first days in the Upper Peninsula woods. "Beautiful, isn't it?"

During the night I was awakened by strange sounds outside the tent. I reached over to nudge Jim, and found his bedroll empty. He was already up and I could feel his presence near the door.

"Any idea what's out there?" I whispered, a bit nervous. Most animals didn't bother me, not even bears. Wolves, on the other hand, I know can be vicious.

"Just some raccoons after the meat fat that dripped on the fire pit rocks," he said, closing and securing the tent flap. He doused the flashlight and I heard him zip his sleeping bag. I had seen the flash of his Beretta before the light went out and felt reassured.

CHAPTER 13

April 24

The morning sky hung heavy and gray with impending rain. We broke camp quickly to get our gear and the tent packed before it could get wet.

I heated some soup on the camp stove and served it in our coffee mugs. "Not exactly the breakfast of champions, but it's hot and should last us until lunch."

"It's still more than I've had some mornings," Jim commented.

"You seem distracted, Jim. Is there anything wrong? Anything I should know about or that I can help with?"

"Nothing is wrong, trust me. I've got some major decisions coming up in the next few days, is all, and I need to concentrate on them. As for anything you can help with," he hesitated, "we'll discuss that after we leave the Soo. While we're there, please be careful, and if you need me, I'll be easy to find."

*

We drove in silence for another hour before coming to the outskirts of Sault St. Marie. Not much further was our destination, a large two-story office complex.

"That doesn't look much like a military base," I remarked.

"It wasn't, but it is now," Jim said. "When the troops showed up, they took over this empty building as housing, mess hall, and command center all in one place. From what I saw during the few hours I was here, it seems to be fairly efficient, if a bit disorganized." He parked near the entrance, and we showed our IDs to the guard.

"Ah, lights! Must be generator time," Jim said. When I looked confused, he said, "Much like Moose Creek, the base generator is running only a few hours a day to conserve fuel. At least we'll have the elevator for you to get to the second floor without having to use the stairs." My feet throbbed at the thought of climbing a flight of concrete steps and my claustrophobia woke up at the thought of getting in the elevator with questionable power. I was torn.

The doors slid open on the second floor and I breathed easier. Jim led me down a hall to a desk manned by a Corporal Donna Cook.

"Colonel Andrews!" She stood and saluted. "We didn't expect you back so soon. Major Hogan will be pleased." Corporal Cook lifted her phone to announce his arrival. "Please go right in," she said with an unasked question in her eyes as I limped past, following Jim.

Major Daniel Hogan was a large man, slightly shorter than Jim and a bit overweight. With jet black hair and dark blue eyes, he was an attractive man and had an air of command about him.

"Colonel Andrews, it's good to see you again." The major stood and shook Jim's hand. "I take it the rescue mission was a success?"

"Yes it was, Dan. Your men performed admirably," Jim replied. "I'd like to introduce you to First Lieutenant Allex Smeth."

I saluted.

The major was stunned. "I thought Lt. Smeth was a man, Jim." He saluted me back. "I can't say I'm disappointed though." He gave me a warm smile. "Please, have a seat." We both sat in the comfortable wing chairs across from the major. The former business office was spacious and decorated with fine furniture.

"My name is actually Allexa, Sir, however I go by Allex," I said, returning his warm smile.

"What's your AOC, Lieutenant?"

"Public Affairs, Sir, with a specialty in civilian Emergency Management." I knew this would come up at some point and I had practiced my response. If I was asked to work, I would at least know what I was doing.

"Is there a spare office I can use for a few days, Dan?" Jim asked. "I need to formally issue Sgt. Pitchner's new orders and do some debriefing before we head back to Sawyer. And we'll both need temporary quarters."

"Certainly. With all the space we have here, most offices come with quarters attached. Female quarters are located on the main level, as well as all male enlisted personnel," the major said.

"Where is the EOC located, Major?" I asked. When he looked confused, I clarified, "The Emergency Operations Center?"

"Well, it was down the hall. Without anyone to run it, we closed it down."

"Then it needs to be re-opened while we're here and the adjoining quarters given to Lt. Smeth," Jim said.

"That office doesn't have quarters."

"Then find an office that does, Major Hogan," Jim insisted. "Lt. Smeth was just rescued from being tortured by a psychopath, who took sadistic pleasure in breaking her toes one at a time. She can barely walk and I will not have her subjected to traversing flights of stairs. Is that clear?"

*

"You were a bit hard on him, Jim," I said when we were alone.

"Not really. Besides, rank has its privileges, and even though this is his command, I still outrank him. A little push now and then reminds everyone of that."

"Well, thank you. I wasn't looking forward to the walk. Plus I didn't like the thought of being so far away from you." When I realized what I had just said, I looked away, feeling a blush coming on.

"Do you really want to reactivate the EOC?" Jim asked.

"Why not? It'll give me something to do while you're busy and I might as well do something useful."

We had been assigned offices on the same floor, at opposite ends of the hall. Two privates had brought up our duffels and set them in the corridor outside the rooms.

"I think the first thing I'm going to do is find the laundry facilities and wash all of my clothes. My jacket still has river mud in the seams and it's itchy," I said to Jim. I left him in his rooms and made my way to Corporal Cook's desk to make friends.

"Corporal Cook, hello, I'm Lt. Smeth."

She looked at my outstretched hand in shock, and then shook it. "*You're* Lt. Smeth? We thought you were a man."

"So I gathered," I laughed. "I was hoping you could help me with a few things. May I call you Donna?" She nodded. "Thanks. Where is the laundry, Donna? I really need to clean my clothes."

I had checked the power schedule and saw I still had a couple of hours. I dragged my duffel to the elevator and descended to the first floor, and following Donna's directions, found the facilities. I loaded two washers, then slipped into the restroom and changed into a sweater and jeans, putting the clothes I had been wearing into the wash. I sat in one of the metal chairs, propped my feet up on another, and leaned my head back, closing my eyes. It had been an exhausting day and it was only early afternoon.

"Hey!" someone shouted at me, slapping my feet off the chair. I almost passed out from the pain. "Are you a civilian or are you out of uniform? And keep your feet off the furniture!" the angry voice continued.

I stood on my good foot and looked at the soldier in front of me. I checked his chevrons and then his name tag. "Sergeant," I said, putting my hat back on so the rank was clearly visible.

He had the decency to look embarrassed. "My apologies, ma'am! I didn't know we had guests."

"I'm here with Colonel Andrews, Sgt… Wilkes," I said, glancing again at his tag.

"*You're* Lt. Smeth?" he said in awe. "We all thought you were a guy."

"I keep hearing that."

"Is there anything I can do for you, ma'am?" he asked with a complete reversal of attitude.

"As soon as I finish folding my uniforms, I'm going up to my office. I'm reopening the EOC and I'll need to staff it. Do you have access to the service records?" I hobbled over to the dryers.

"Oh, yes, ma'am!" he stared. "You're limping. Did I hurt you?" I heard the concern in his voice; technically, he had assaulted an officer.

"No, Sergeant, I was already injured." I stuffed my folded clothes into the duffel, leaving out one set. "Why don't you meet me in my office, 11B, in forty-five minutes, with some of those service files?" He scurried out the door, and I stepped into the restroom to change.

*

After hanging my few clothes in the closet, I opened the adjoining door to my new office. What a disaster! There were two desks and only one chair, which looked very uncomfortable. The one file cabinet had a drawer missing and there were papers on the floor and dust on everything else. And not one computer.

Sgt. Wilkes knocked and entered. "Wow, this is a mess," he said looking around.

"It sure is!" I agreed. "Any suggestions? Like a broom and a few trash cans?"

He set the files he was carrying on one of the desks, and said "I'll be right back."

I picked up a few of the papers off the floor and looked through them. Apparently they were all from the office's previous tenant and nothing military. I continued to pick them off the floor and stack them on the desk. A few minutes later Wilkes was back with two privates, a trash can, several rare plastic bags, a broom, a bucket, and some dust cloths. How he got all that in such short time, I didn't ask. We set to work.

Inside of an hour the place was clean, all the trash had been removed, and I had a new chair.

"Let's take a walk, Wilkes, down to the old EOC and see what was left there," I said to my new right hand.

"I can't believe I smacked your injured foot, Lieutenant," he mumbled.

"Don't worry about it, just don't do it again. I may hit you back!" I said. I opened the door down the hall that was closed as the EOC three months ago. There sat three silent computers. "Why aren't these in use?"

"Maybe because there's no internet," Wilkes responded.

"They're still good as word processors." I turned them on, one at a time. "They all have the latest operating systems. Can you get them moved to the new office?"

*

I sat with one computer on, the monitor blipped with balls bouncing as the screen saver. Wilkes had also retrieved two printers and some paper. I started going through the files he had left and made notes on who might be likely candidates for a new job. I was interrupted by a knock on the door. Jim opened it and stepped in.

"Looks like you're settling in," he said.

"Not really, only cleaned up a mess and moved the computers down. How's it going on your side?"

"Paperwork, paperwork, and more damned paperwork," he said, sitting in the other chair. "Dinner is in fifteen minutes in the officers' mess. Care for a cocktail?" He produced our liquor bottles and two glasses.

"Are officers allowed that, or should you lock the door?" I asked.

"We're allowed. Besides, if I locked the door someone might think....you know."

"Is the major over the shock that I'm not a man?" I asked with a chuckle. "And why is it everyone here thinks I'm a guy?"

"That's my fault, sorry. When I was organizing the rescue I referred to you as Allex, and that's more a masculine name," he informed me. "I must admit that since we showed up, *you* are the hot topic of the entire base." I frowned at him, sipping my drink. He leaned on the desk. "Allex, everyone knows what you've been through, and they are all amazed at your resilience. Quite frankly, so am I." He looked at me for a bit then looked away.

"These drinks need ice," I said, clearing my throat. "I think tomorrow I'm asking Wilkes if he can find a small fridge for my room. I'm finding he's the 'Radar' of this base." I smiled thinking of the TV series *M*A*S*H*.

"Wilkes! He is so enamored with you he would steal it from Dan's office for you," Jim chuckled. "Come on, Lieutenant, let's go to dinner, then we'll come back here for our evening cribbage game."

CHAPTER 14

JOURNAL ENTRY: April 25

I set aside five files that looked promising. Wilkes had agreed to meet with me at 10:00 after his usual rounds to help me with the selection. Major Hogan, Jim, and I had a pleasant, leisurely breakfast earlier of ham and eggs. Real ham... I wonder where they got it.

~~~

"Good morning, Lt. Smeth," Sgt. Wilkes said, announcing his arrival in my new office. "Did you find the mess hall alright this morning?"

"Good morning to you, Wilkes, and yes, I dined with Major Hogan and Colonel Andrews. It's been a long time since I've had ham that wasn't canned."

"Rank definitely has its privileges," he replied without any rancor. "So what do you have for me today, ma'am?"

"I was hoping you could help me narrow down these possibilities," I said, sliding the file folders in his direction.

He picked up the first one. "Lost in battle," he said and set it aside. "He was with the rescue mission," he said of the second and set that one aside as well. He took the remaining three and sat, flipping through the pages. "Pvt. Toth... now there is one strange dude. He seems really smart, however, he does dumb things that get him in trouble and demoted. I don't know Cpl. Ki very well. She sticks to herself, not much of a team player. And this one," he said, picking up the final file, "is bad news. He's in the brig right now." He dropped it in the first pile.

"Where would I find Toth and Ki?" I asked.

"Toth is sweeping floors somewhere and Ki is in the kitchen."

"They both have strong computer backgrounds and they're doing menial jobs?" I asked.

"Like I said, neither one is a team player."

"Can you have Toth report to me at 1100 hours? And will you show me the way to the kitchen? I'll talk to Ki on her own turf," I said, standing with Kimberly Ki's file in hand.

*

"Cpl. Kimberly Ki?" I asked a young Asian girl.

She looked up from chopping vegetables. "That's me. What did I do now?" She wiped her hands on her soiled apron.

I looked her over. "Do you enjoy working here in the kitchen, Corporal?"

"It's a job. One I'm actually appreciated for. Why?"

I opened her file. "It says here you graduated from college at the age of seventeen with a degree in computer science. How did you manage to do that?"

"I had a really good counselor in middle school who let me skip a couple of grades. I was already in high school when I was fourteen and started taking college classes along with my regular ones. When I graduated from high school at fifteen, I doubled up my college classes and was done two years later."

"Isn't chopping onions a waste of your education?"

She sighed. "Permission to speak freely, ma'am?" I nodded. "Yes, I know more about computers and programming than anyone else on this entire base, but nobody wants to hear my ideas and nobody wants to take a chance on this *kid*. This is the Army, ma'am, and this is the good ole boy branch of it." She went back to chopping.

"Report to the EOC in room 11B at 1300 hours. I will have your new orders ready," I said, then I turned and walked out. I sure hoped I wasn't overstepping my bounds!

*

At 1100 hours I heard the door open and looked up. Sgt. Wilkes was ushering in a scrawny, gangly young man. If this was Pvt. Toth, he looked fifteen— a lot younger than the twenty-five his file said he was.

"Thank you, Sgt. Wilkes. Can you come back at 1400 hours? I will have a list ready of supplies I need." I turned to this sullen boy. "Have a seat, Private. I understand you have a knack for computers." He snorted. "I'll take that as a yes. How would you like the opportunity to do some real work? Something besides pushing a broom?"

He looked up. "Like what?"

"Like getting all these computers running as a unit, maybe even trying to get us back online. Think you could handle that?" I crossed my arms while we stared at each other.

"What happens to me when I'm done?"

"That will depend on you," I said. "What do you prefer to be called, Private? Toth? William? Bill? What?"

"What do you care?"

"Stuff the attitude, Pvt. Toth," I snapped. "I need you to make my job easier, and if I can make your life easier at the same time, we both win."

He looked on the verge of tears. "Billy, ma'am," he finally answered.

"Well, Billy, I want you to report back here at 1300 hours and I'll have your new orders ready. Be ready to work."

*

I knocked on Jim's office door and peeked inside. He was on the phone and motioned me to come in. I limped over to a chair and sat, waiting for him to finish.

After he hung up, he said, "Good to see you, Allex! What can I do for you? I'd take you to lunch but I'm swamped."

"Me too. Jim, I need some advice," I said. "I've got two new assistants, and I don't know how to get them transferred to me, or even who I should ask."

"I could do that, although I would suggest you go through Major Hogan, this *is* his command."

"I want to get started as soon as possible." I paused. "Do you have any idea how long we'll be here?"

"I was hoping for only a few days, though now it's looking closer to a week. I'm sorry, I know how much you want to go home." He stood and came around the front of his desk to sit on the edge. "Are you doing okay?"

"I'm doing fine," I said, pushing back the memories of my time as a captive. "I don't know if I will do much good in the EOC, but I think I might help two lives." He looked askance. "I'll explain later. Say, is there a chance to sneak our wine in? I hate the thought of it closed up in a hot vehicle."

"I will attend to that right now!" He stood as I did. "I'll come by to escort you to dinner at 1730 hours."

I did a quick mental calculation: that was 5:30pm. I'd get the hang of this yet.

*

I stopped at Corporal Cook's desk to make an appointment with the Major. She wasn't there, although the door was open and I could hear her voice. So I gently knocked, and waited.

She stepped out, steno pad in hand. "Good afternoon, Lt. Smeth. Are you here to see the major?"

"Yes, if he has a few minutes to spare, thank you." I nodded knowingly at her, she looked flushed.

"Come on in, Allex," the Major called out from behind the half opened door. I walked in with only the slightest limp. "You're moving around better. Have you seen our medic since you arrived?"

"No, sir, I haven't. I think just not being used as a punching bag has helped a great deal." The major winced when I stood with the two files in my hand. "I have a request to make, Major. I'd like these two soldiers transferred to the EOC." I handed over the files for Ki and Toth.

"These two misfits?" he asked, looking at the names.

"Yes sir, those two *misfits* are geniuses when it comes to computers. I believe their unique skills could be utilized - in a monitored situation - and they are exactly what I need right now. If they don't work out, they don't work out, and they can go back to sweeping floors and chopping onions."

"Donna!" he called out to his secretary. She stepped in immediately and Major Hogan handed her the files. "Please type up new orders for these two, transferring them to the EOC." He looked back at me. "As soon as I sign them, I'll have Donna bring them down to you. Anything else?"

"No sir, thank you." I turned to go.

"Good luck with those two, Allex, you'll need it," he snickered.

His attitude made me a touch angry. Whatever happened to 'be all you can be'? These two kids weren't being encouraged to stretch their minds. I had to remember, though, that I was going to be here for only a short time and to curb my *civilian* attitude.

*

Promptly at 1300 hours, Pvt. Billy Toth and Cpl. Kimberly Ki entered the office. Their new orders had been delivered and were sitting on my desk.

"Have a seat," I said and they each leaned against a desk, arms folded. "I'm going to spell a few things out to you two. It's only the three of us in this office, you work with me and I'll work with you. No goofing off, no being late, understood?" They both nodded. "What we're after here is simple: information. Billy, do you think you can get us any kind of internet connection?"

"Probably. The satellites didn't fall out of the sky, ya know. It's just a matter of reaching out and grabbing it," he said, looking a bit interested.

"Okay, and how would you do that?" I asked. When he gave me that 'are you dumb' look, I said, "Bear with me, Billy, I have reports to submit, and I need a simplified version."

He reached behind him and powered up that computer. "See here?" he said as the three of us gathered around the glowing screen. He typed a few commands and moved the mouse, typed again. "This says we have Wi-Fi right here in this building, but the signal is too weak."

"Can you boost the signal?"

"Do I have permission to do whatever I need to?" he asked.

"Within reason, yes."

He grinned like a kid in a candy shop. "I'll be back in less than an hour!"

"While he's gone, Cpl. Ki, you and I will figure out how many of these programs to dump. By the way, what do you prefer to be called?"

"My friends call me Kim, ma'am. Are you really going to let me clean up these programs?"

"Yes, Kim. Once Billy gets the internet connected again, you can download what we need. I want an updated word processor, Excel, multiple search engines, and reinforced firewalls on all of these computers. I want to be able to surf the net in safety. After all, this *is* a military installation. Once we can establish our presence, I'll need you to connect us to Washington. Are you game?"

"Oh, yes, ma'am!"

"Now, we don't know who used these computers before, so no judgement, okay? Dump the games, dating sites, and porno, got it? Once we're all set, if you have a favorite game you can put it on your station if you want. Personally, I prefer Free-cell," I grinned.

"My station? You mean one of these will be for my use?" Kim asked, wide eyed.

"Yes. We will have work to do daily and that will come first. Understand?"

*

Forty-five minutes after he left, Billy barged back into the room. He went to the computer he had turned on and connected to the internet with a stronger, though still weak signal.

"What did you do, Billy?" I asked, impressed.

"This building used to have legal and social services on this floor, and shops and restaurants on the main floor. The businesses installed their own server and their own sat dishes. I got up on the roof and fixed all the connections that had come loose and then realigned the dish. It's also not state of the art anymore, and I have some repairs I need to do. I'll have to reboot the entire system when I'm done and I can't do that until I have a whole day of power. That generator going down before I'm done could blow the whole thing. And we might need to dump some of their memory."

"Why didn't you do this before, Billy?" I asked, dumbfounded.

"Nobody asked me to," he said simply.

"I knew I picked the right two for the job. Billy, will you need any help from the IT guys?"

He frowned. "No, they'll just get in the way. I can do it faster without them, mainly because I won't have to fix what they screw up."

"You don't like them much, do you?"

"No, ma'am, I don't. The only thing they do well is bully." He pushed his glasses further up on his nose, a nervous gesture with him.

"Why did you join the army, Billy?" I asked. "Forgive me for saying this, but you don't seem like soldier material, you seem better suited to the private sector."

"I joined to go to school. Initially, they let me take all the further ed I wanted, which did get me..." he mumbled the rest.

"What was that? Got you what?"

"My doctorate," he said, embarrassed.

"You have a *doctorate* and you're sweeping floors? That is the most ridiculous thing I've heard yet. Okay, so you don't need IT, what *will* you need?"

"I keep my own repair kit, so there isn't much more I need, except maybe a dozen high capacity thumb drives. If you let Kim give me a hand downloading the memory, that will save a lot of time tomorrow when I do the actual repairs and reboot."

"How will you save the files that are on there?"

"We'll use my laptop and do a GIGO," Billy replied.

"What's a GIGO?"

"Garbage In, Garbage Out. The laptop becomes a port and will take it in and immediately transfer it out to a USB stick. No information stays in the laptop. It's really very simple," Billy assured me.

*

Wilkes came by at 1400 hours and I gave him a list that contained the usual office supplies, plus the thumb drives, a couple more chairs, and a small office refrigerator, with a note next to it to *not* take it from the major's office. He walked out chuckling.

Billy, Kimberly, and I worked the rest of the afternoon in relative silence, with a few expletives thrown in from Billy. Soon I saw Jim standing in the doorway. I looked at the wall clock. It was 5:30pm already!

"Okay kids, your day is done. Good job! I'll see you at 0900 hours tomorrow."

"Dan warned me you asked for the two worst soldiers on the base, but those two looked like they wanted to keep working," Jim said once they were gone.

"Those two are amazing. Geniuses, both of them. The right people, with the right skills and the right motivation, can do amazing things."

CHAPTER 15

April 27

I woke to the humming of my new little refrigerator. After dinner last night, Jim and I found the unit in the office on my desk and moved it into my quarters. The generators start at 0700 and shut off at 2100 hours, from seven in the morning to nine at night. There are ice cubes freezing right now.

*

"Is it true, Lieutenant?" Major Hogan asked with a scowl as he came into my office at 0830.

"Is what true, Sir?"

"That you allowed that insolent troublemaker access to a restricted area and allowed him to tinker with the machinery?"

"No one has informed me that there were any restricted areas anywhere here, Sir. As for *tinkering* with the machinery, Pvt. Toth made some major repairs and has the internet running again. Limited, but running."

"What? We have internet back?" The major looked stunned. "How did he do that? Even my best IT guys couldn't do that."

"If I may say so, Major, you *didn't* have the best. Pvt. Toth is geeky, clumsy, and lacks social skills, but he has a brilliant mind and is proving to be a tremendous asset. Did you know he has a *doctorate* in computer technology? I asked him to fix a problem and then let him do it his way." I stood to face the major so he wasn't looking down at me, a tactical stance. "I gave him a job to do and *trusted* him to do it. He didn't let me down. I'm lucky to have him, and so are you." I gave him a sincere smile. "Today comes the mainframe repairs, for which he will need uninterrupted power to do the systems reboot. If the generator even hiccups during this, it could blow all of it."

"I will make sure the generator doesn't even *burp* today, Lieutenant, if it will get the internet back for us."

"Thank you, Major. When they're done, would you like to borrow my staff to get your office back online? After the colonel, that is. Jim has already asked for them."

Major Hogan stared at me, and then smiled. "You're an enigma, Lieutenant. I'm not sure what to make of you. You look military, you act military, yet you don't *feel* military. And yes, I'd like to be next on the list."

"You already are. Oh, and I did want to run something else by you. Billy says the matrix that is the brains of the server is also the information storage. It is clogged up with old legal and business files and is slowing us down. He can download the information onto memory sticks without losing anything. With your permission, of course."

*

"You're turning this base on its head, you know," Jim said, sitting at Billy's console. "And thanks for letting me use part of your office while Pvt. Toth and Cpl. Ki are doing their magic in mine."

I looked up and smiled. "It's good to have you close by, Jim. And the only thing I've done is to give two smart kids a chance to prove themselves." When the kids had returned from their lunch break, I sent them down to Jim's office, after they had spent the morning repairing and rebooting the entire system. It didn't take as long as Billy had thought, and having Kim do some of the work helped. They made a good team.

"You've done more than that, Allex. You bounced back from a horrific experience without so much as a look back. Then you come in here and start organizing what should have been organized from the start. You're putting things back in order that should never have gotten *out* of order. This is the military, and you're not, yet what you're doing is working. Not to mention all the men are in love with you and the women admire you. Except for Donna, she's jealous." He looked down at his keyboard and let out a long breath. "And Dan is making noises about going over my head to have you transferred here to him," he said through clenched teeth.

"He can't do that!"

"Oh, he's going to try."

"Jim, I'm not even—"

"Shh, the walls have ears, Allex," he whispered and stood before me. "You've been cooped up inside for two days now. I think you need some fresh air. Walk with me, Lieutenant," he said louder.

We took the elevator down and were outside in less than five minutes.

"The fresh air does feel good, although I don't know how much walking I can do. My feet are still sore," I said, eying a park bench. "What would happen if Dan discovered our charade?"

"I'm not sure. If he was by-the-book, you could be thrown in jail and I could be court martialed. This isn't a by-the-book situation though, so I don't think they would do anything to you."

"You could still be court-martialed though? Jim, how do we get out of this?" I asked in alarm. I certainly didn't want anything to happen to him because of me!

I sat on the bench and he sat beside me, arms stretched out along the back, his long legs extended with ankles crossed, very relaxed.

"One of our biggest problems could be Donna. She and Dan have had a thing going on for about a month and now she sees you as a threat. She needs to be defused before she starts digging into your non-existent records. Any ideas?"

"Well, you could always take me back to Annie's until you're finished here."

"Running never solves anything. Distraction might be the way to go though." Jim stood and then knelt down in front of me and took my hands. "I'm sure we're being watched; they will think I'm proposing to you and the word will spread. That should cool Donna's jets for a while." My eyes widened. "Just play along, Allex. We'll be out of here in a few days. And please try to act happy about it, you look like you're about to go in front of a firing squad!"

Had I just giggled?

*

I spent most of the afternoon pulling up inventory files from around the base and organizing the information. Knowing what was on hand for supplies and where it was located was vital to a smoothly operating command center. At 1630 hours, 4:30pm, Billy and Kim arrived back in the EOC, chattering away like two fifth-graders.

"What's all the excitement?" I asked, enjoying their animation.

"Nothing really, it's just good to do something... real, ya know?" Kim said. "Colonel Andrews was very pleased with our work. He said what we did was going to make his work easier and he'd be finished in half the time." A girlish grin widened her mouth and she blushed. "And he's so handsome."

I laughed. "Yes, he is an attractive man. Back to business! Are you two ready to tackle Major Hogan's office tomorrow? Or is there enough time to do it today?"

"I'd rather do his and Donna's computers tomorrow, if that's alright," Billy said. "It will be easier to link the computers all at once if those two can do something else for the morning."

"They are welcome to use these stations if need be," I said. "I've noticed you haven't personalized them yet, so it's not a problem, right?"

"I was going to do that now," Kim said. "I guess I can wait though."

"Well, then why don't you two take off early? You've done a great job today." When they hesitated leaving, I asked, "Is there something on your mind?"

"Um, we had to test things out on the computers, ya know? Make sure the search engines could do what you want, and we, um, had to t-test the hookup to the m-military site," Billy stammered.

"We did a simple search, ma'am, to test it," Kim picked up. "So we searched… you…"

"Oh?" I said. This could be trouble. "And what did you find?"

"Nothing. Well, we did find that you really are an emergency manager, which explains why you're so good at this, but you don't have any military records," Kim finished, looking down at her feet.

"You do now," Billy said proudly.

"What?"

"Well, we figured you had to have a really good reason to be doing whatever it is you're doing, and we like you, so we created a file for you so you wouldn't get into trouble," Billy said.

"What kind of a file?" I asked cautiously.

"If anyone searches for you in the military archives, they find an encoded file marked 'Classified' and won't be able to get into it," Billy crowed. "If they have the clearance though, they get to the next level, a file marked 'Special Assignment', and then the next level is 'Covert Operations' with a link to 'Operation 87264' which will take them to a room that flashes 'Security Breach!'. Backing out of that one takes them back to the beginning. It's a continuous loop, and all dated a year ago."

Billy and Kim laughed, delighted with the scam.

"I don't know what to say, except thank you," I said to them. "And yes, I have reasons to be doing this, reasons I can't share."

"We understand, ma'am," Kim said, "and we're having fun being part of it."

"However, I do have to ask you to make a change," I said to Billy. "Operation 87264, I think should be Operation… Boy Scout."

"I can do that," he replied. "But why?"

"That's classified," I said and both of them grinned. "Oh, and if it ever comes up, I ordered you to do this, okay?"

*

With them gone, I turned on my computer and started surfing, trying to find some news. I was more than curious about what was going on downstate. I hadn't heard from my sister in so long… The first thing I found was some maps of the flooding. It was staggering. Michigan is shaped like a hand with the fingers closed: a mitten with a thumb, and that's where my sister was, in the thumb. That area didn't fare as badly as other parts, although the tip was gone, from Bay City to Port Sanilac. Thankfully she was further south, not by much though.

The tip of the mitten, Mackinaw City, I already knew was flooded, and although the Mackinaw Bridge was still standing, it wasn't attached to dry land on either side now. I wondered if sealing up the rift would help that water subside.

Chicago was a holy mess. The entire shoreline was under a couple of feet of water and mud, and because of all the concrete there was no place for the water to go except further inland. Highways 90, 94 and even 55 and 57 were flooded or compromised.

It was interesting and frustrating to read how the rest of the nation was reacting to our calamity. Simply put, they weren't. So what was a foot or two of water? It was that attitude again, that if it didn't affect them directly it wasn't real and couldn't be bothered with. Of course, the rest of the nation had its own problems. Half of Florida was lost, the Yellowstone Volcano was still spewing lava, and the East Coast was overwhelmed with all the refugees and no place to put them. The one new thing I found out was that the San Andreas had let go. A 10.5 on the Richter Scale had ripped a big hole in California. Maybe up here wasn't so bad after all.

I shut down the web and pulled up the word processor. I still had a report to file on the convicts we'd encountered. It would be deeply sanitized before any other eyes read it.

"Earth to Allex!" Jim said. I hadn't even heard him come in. "Ready for a pre-dinner cocktail?"

"More than ready," I said, shutting down my station for the night.

*

I sipped my spiced rum, doubly enjoying the tinkle of ice cubes in my glass. "I need to think of an appropriate gift for Wilkes before we leave."

"Speaking of which, how does the day after tomorrow sound? With a working computer and being online, my reports are filed ten times faster. I'm about done. How about you?"

"The supply inventories are complete and there's just a little polishing on the convict-situation report and I'm done too. Could we leave tomorrow?" I asked hopefully.

"An extra day is called for here, Allex. I think we should host a small cocktail party tomorrow night to say goodbye. We certainly have enough booze to donate and we can restock on the way home."

*

"I'm glad Hogan agreed to the party so quickly," Jim said as we stepped out of the elevator after dinner. "Tomorrow morning we can discuss a menu with the kitchen staff." We were standing at my door when the elevator dinged again.

"The major and Donna just got out on this floor, Jim," I said in a whisper, catching the movement from my peripheral vision.

He looked down at me and smiled, sliding his arm around my waist and pulling me closer. I gazed into his dark, smoky gray eyes and I felt a heat that spread from the inside out. His cheek grazed mine and my heart started thudding in my chest when his other hand reached behind me, opened the door, and he seductively backed me into the room. Jim closed the door and turned the light on. I thought my heart was going pound right out of my cracked ribs.

He turned to me with his lips set in a sly grin and with a touch of mock innocence said, "Cribbage?"

JOURNAL ENTRY: April 29

I'm trying very hard to act like nothing happened last night, which is easy because nothing did. My reaction to what *could* have happened has me flustered and on edge.

~~~

"Good morning, Kim, you're here early," I said looking at the clock reading fifteen minutes before nine.

"Is it true?" she blurted out.

"Is what true?"

"That the colonel asked you to marry him! Everyone is talking about it but no one knows who saw what so they want me to find out since I work for you," she said, barely pausing for a breath.

"Why would anyone think that, Kim?" I said with feigned innocence.

"Well, someone saw you two outside yesterday and said the colonel went on 'bended knee' in front of you and that can only mean one thing, ya know!"

"It could also mean he was tying my shoe. I suffered some nasty injuries not that long ago, and my feet are still pretty damaged." I wasn't sure which line of thought I should encourage. Jim started and has perpetuated this charade, and it's only for another day so maybe I should play along with the way he started it. She looked crestfallen. "What if he *did* propose?" I said with a secret smile.

"I knew it!!" Kim jumped up and clapped. "He's such a great person and so are you and you're perfect for each other!" She threw her arms around me for a hug. "Oh, I'm sorry, ma'am, I didn't mean to get so familiar, I was just excited."

"That's okay, Kim, just try to curb your enthusiasm in front of others. And let's keep this between you and me, alright?" I hadn't admitted to anything; Kim had jumped to her own conclusions. "So others asked you to find out? I gather your fellow soldiers are treating you better?"

"Oh, yes, they are much nicer to Billy and me now that we're working for *you*," she said. "It's made life here a lot easier."

Kim was still grinning ear to ear when Billy came in.

"Now that both of you are here I have a special assignment for you before starting on the major's office." I sat on the edge of my desk facing them. "Can you sweep this office and my quarters for bugs?"

"Sure," Billy said dumbfounded. "You think someone has bugged you?" Funny how he immediately knew I meant an electronic-bug not a critter-bug.

"I think it's very likely anything is left over from the last tenants, *if* you find anything that is," I put my finger to my lips, drawing them into a conspiracy. "And since this is now a government installation we want to be sure nothing is leaking out." Both kids got a big, big smile at being trusted with this project.

Jim stopped into the office shortly after 0900 hours. "We need to talk with the kitchen as early as possible for tonight. Are you ready?"

"Just another minute, Colonel." I turned to my two assistants. "When you're done with this project, go over to the major's office. Oh, and I want the two of you at our party tonight!" I left with Jim, leaving those two stunned over the invitation.

*

"I think that was a very wise move to invite those two kids to our party, although you do know it's going to be mostly officers," Jim said once we were at the elevator. I'll sure be glad when I can run down the steps; it's always so much quicker.

"I suppose we're going to have to submit a guest list, right?"

"Pretty much, yes. I suggest you get with Donna about it. I think she's going to be very different toward you now, after what they *think* they witnessed last night." He let out a hearty laugh. I have a different view of what they *think* they saw, it felt very real to *me*.

"The only ones I want to invite are my two staff and Sgt. Wilkes. Those three have made my life a lot easier here and I want to thank them. Do you have anyone specifically you want to attend?"

"I've been too busy with reports, I haven't gotten to know anyone," he said, thinking. "This does bring up something else. I'd like to hold out some of the liquor we're donating for tonight. A bottle of Gray Goose and Captain Morgan's for our trip home, a bottle of bourbon for Hogan, and a bottle of scotch for Kopley for when we get back to Sawyer."

"Would it be appropriate for me to give Wilkes a bottle too? He seems like a Jack Daniels kind of guy."

"Absolutely. I'll make sure those bottles are withheld before the case is delivered to the dining hall prior to the party, which I believe will begin at 1730 hours, followed by dinner at 1830 hours." We had arrived at the kitchen and were met by the supervising officer.

"What would you like for appetizers, Colonel Andrews?" the sergeant in charge asked.

"I will leave that up to the lieutenant."

"I'm sure supplies are limited, Sergeant, so I will trust you to make the decisions. I hope that makes it easier for you," I said. "Though we do have some gourmet treats we managed to scavenge on our way here to add if you don't mind. We'll be here prior to 1730 hours in case you have any questions and we'll bring them then."

*

Jim left to sort the liquor and I went back to the office to a surprise: a small pile of wired bugs on my desk!

"I really didn't think we would find anything to be honest," Billy said. "After the second one though, we looked harder. There were four in here and three in your quarters. I suppose the good news is these are really old and outdated, so they've probably been here awhile."

"Thank you. This makes me feel better. You know what they say, just because you're paranoid doesn't mean they're *not* after you!" and I laughed to relieve the tension. "Now you two get on over to the major's office. If I don't see you later, I better see you at 1730 hours in the officers' mess."

*

Donna was a different person toward me. Instead of bordering on hostile, she was friendly and helpful. She came up with an invitation list of fifteen officers to invite and quickly formatted an invitation on Kim's computer, printing them out in short order. The small stack waited for Wilkes to return from an errand to hand deliver.

"Oh," Donna half whispered to me, "and congratulations. The colonel is a wonderful man."

I smiled and simply said thank you. How long would we have to keep this up?

*

At 1700 hours I shooed my two workers out to get ready for the party. I took a quick shower and re-bandaged my foot. After a glance in the mirror I added a touch of makeup. When I opened my closet, I found that all my spare uniforms had been expertly pressed, and I wondered who to thank, probably Wilkes.

Jim arrived at 1715, looking fresh and every bit the senior officer. "I know it's only a casual uniform, but it sure looks damn good on you, Allex." He stepped closer and kissed me on the cheek. "Are you ready?"

We arrived ten minutes before the scheduled time to find my three assistants already there and arguing with the head of the kitchen staff.

"Ma'am, these three don't have invitations, and I was told by Major Hogan's assistant that no one gets in without one!" he protested.

"These three are the exception since I personally invited them," I said, and he backed right off.

Promptly at 1730 hours our guests began to arrive. Everyone was delighted to have real alcohol instead of what some were brewing in the basement. The kitchen provided canned apple, orange, and grapefruit juices as mixers, though most took their drinks on the rocks or neat. Appetizers of deviled eggs, cheese, and smoked oysters with crackers were offered by a circulating staff.

"May I have your attention please?" Major Hogan said, tapping a spoon on his glass of bourbon. "I know this is not my party, however, I'm going to take the occasion to make an announcement." He paused long enough to take some papers from Donna. "Private William Toth, please step forward." Oh, poor Billy looked stunned and nervous. "For your exemplary service these past few days, I'm reinstating your rank to Corporal." The applause was long, and he waited for it to die down. "And now I can promote you to the rank of Sergeant." More applause and I could swear Billy was going to cry.

"Corporal Kimberly Ki, please step forward. For your exemplary service these past few days, I'm promoting you to the rank of Sergeant.

Congratulations, Sergeants!" Major Hogan saluted the two speechless kids. Kim elbowed Billy and they returned the salute.

"I'm so proud of you," I told them. "I had no idea this was going to happen!" I gave them each a hug and Jim shook their hands. Billy and Kim were besieged with well-wishers.

It was now 6:15pm with dinner scheduled in fifteen minutes, 1830 hours. Major Hogan again tapped his glass and the room hushed.

"I'd like to propose a toast to our hosts, Colonel James Andrews and Lieutenant Allexa Smeth... the happy couple. Congratulations! May you have a long and happy life together!" There was another round of applause.

Jim put his arm around my shoulders and whispered in my ear, "Smile, damn it!"

CHAPTER 16

April 30

There were a few last minute items to clean up before we departed. My duffel was packed and waiting by the door. The case of wine was already in the Hummer, except for one bottle.

"Donna, I want to thank you for helping me with the cocktail party last night," I said, handing her the bottle of wine.

"Oh, thank you!" she said graciously. "I'm afraid I wasn't very nice to you at first and I'm sorry about that. It's just...."

"No need to say anything. I really do understand," I smiled at her, and I really *did* understand, I'd felt jealousy before. "Be well, Donna, and I hope that things with the major continue to make you happy."

"The major asked me to make sure you got these. He thought you would like to personally deliver them." I opened one of the yellow envelopes and looked inside.

"Oh, yes. I sure do," I said, a warm tingle surging through me.

*

"Kim, Billy, I have something for you," I announced when I was back in my office. "Sergeant Toth, Sergeant Ki, I'm so very proud of you." I know I had a tear in my eye as I handed over their new chevron pins, plus their promotion orders. "It's almost lunchtime. Why don't you go back to your quarters and put those on? The colonel and I will be down to the mess hall in a half hour, and I want to see them on you."

*

"Sergeant Wilkes, I'm pleased you could come by on such short notice." I glanced at the clock, knowing Jim would be by soon. "You've made my stay here so much more pleasant and productive than I had expected, and I want to thank you for that, and for everything you've done that you didn't have to do, like ironing my uniforms." I smiled warmly at his embarrassment. I handed him the bottle of Jim Beam.

"How did you know I was a Beam guy?" His look told me I made the right choice.

"A lucky guess, Wilkes. May I ask one last favor? Will you take my duffel down to the Hummer? It's parked right out front."

"Anything, ma'am, anything." He hesitated and turned back to me. I held out my arms to give him a hug. That was the one thing he really wanted.

*

Lunch was over and it was time for us to leave. The Hummer was parked out front and our duffels sat beside it, waiting. What I wasn't expecting was that literally everyone was outside and waiting too. I looked up at Jim in confusion.

"You've made more friends than you realize, Allex, and they all want to say goodbye."

"I hate goodbyes," I choked out. Jim put his arm around my shoulders and I slid my arm around his waist. He flinched, so I whispered, "Smile, damn it. Act like you enjoy it."

He laughed out loud, and leaned down to give me a quick kiss on the mouth. The crowd roared with approval. He tossed the duffels in the rear and we climbed in.

"Which way, navigator?" Jim asked in a great mood.

"The only way we can go is west on M-28," I replied.

We traveled in companionable silence for about a half hour.

"So how did it feel being deep in military life?" Jim asked.

"I must say I learned a lot. I don't know if I could keep up the pretense for very long though."

"Which pretense?" he asked and I noticed his jaw tighten.

"Stop the car!" I turned in my seat to face him once he had pulled over. "Look, Jim, I know what you're thinking, it's been obvious from the start. You think I'm offended at the thought of us – you and me— being a couple. Well, you're wrong. I have feelings for you, some pretty strong feelings, in fact. The pretense, though, was like jumping from point A to point D missing out on all the joy and fun and excitement that B and C might bring. It left me… flustered and frustrated because I know to you it's just a game, a sham."

He grinned. "You really do have feelings for me?"

"Yes, now just drive, Andrews. We need to make miles before finding a campsite."

*

"Do you see the flashing lights ahead?" Jim asked a while later.

"Yes. I wonder if there's been an accident. We should be getting close to Hwy 123." Jim slowed the vehicle as we got closer and could see a barricade manned by the military. He pulled up and stopped.

"What's going on, Sergeant?" Jim asked the young man.

"There seems to have been a problem in Yardley, Sir. May I see some ID, please?" the sergeant requested. We each reached for the visor in front of us and Jim handed both laminates over.

"Colonel," the young man saluted. "I could pass you on through if you like, sir, but you're ranking officer here. Our highest rank is only a lieutenant." He leaned down to look at me. "No offense, ma'am. We're not quite sure what to do here."

We both stepped out of the Hummer and followed the flashing lights to the scene.

"We were on our usual patrol when we saw this man stagger out to the road here and collapse," the sergeant told us.

"Usual patrol?" Jim asked.

"Yes, sir. When the kidnappings started happening, Major Kopley sent a squad of us from Sawyer to bivouac in Munising and patrol this corridor. There are only a dozen of us, so we go out three at a time. We saw this man and stopped to investigate. He was covered in blood and had several deep gashes on his arms. That was about a half hour ago. He died shortly after saying 'stop her'. We followed his blood trail into Yardley. There was a young woman standing in the middle of the street holding a machete. She and the blade were soaked in blood. She looked catatonic, until we approached her, then she lunged at us with that blade. Corporal Jones shot her."

"Self-defense, Sergeant. What else?" Jim prodded. I was too shocked to speak.

"There are fifteen dead, Sir, and there are also a few survivors. Do you wish to speak to them? They said the girl went berserk and started slashing anyone who came near her."

"No, that won't be necessary. Where is the girl's body?" Jim asked and then turned to me. "Please, Lieutenant, stay here." I didn't argue; I didn't want to see, and I didn't want to know. He walked away with the sergeant. Maybe fifty yards down the road, near the first building of the town, they stopped and I could see Jim stoop down and lift a sheet. Beyond them I could see the rest of the quiet picturesque buildings of

Yardley, looking the same as they did when we dropped off Patsy and Andrea a week ago. Jim and two others walked back in my direction. Jim was doing all the talking until they got close to me.

"Jim?" I asked, afraid of the answer.

"Get in the vehicle, Allex. We're leaving." He pulled around the barricades and sped west on M-28.

*

We drove in silence, making really good time. M-28 was cleared of any trees or debris, likely from the regular patrolling, and the broken pavement was minimal. In the small town of Antenborough, Jim turned south and stopped near a small clearing. He got out of the Hummer and walked down the road a short ways. I sat on the bumper, waiting for him.

I stood as he came back.

"It was Andrea, Allex. Andrea had hacked fifteen people to death." He took a couple of deep breaths. "Patsy is fine. She told the sergeant that Andrea just snapped. She slashed Patsy's husband - don't worry, he's okay. When Patsy stepped in between them, Andrea ran. She attacked every man she saw plus a few women who tried to stop her."

The sun was starting to set. It would still be an hour or two before dark, but we made camp anyway.

I opened the cooler to find bags of ice, ham and cheese sandwiches, and a container of carrot and orange jello, one of my favorite salads. There would be no need to cook tonight. Jim was building a fire when I handed him a tin cup filled with ice and vodka. He looked up at me and thanked me. I set the bottle down beside him, returning a moment later with my bottle.

"It must have been difficult to identify her," I said softly.

"Patsy had already ID'd her. I didn't let on that I knew who she was." He looked over at me sitting on an adjacent log. "I'm glad *you* didn't have to see that. She was a gory mess. Not a good way to remember someone."

"Thank you for keeping me from that. I really didn't know her very well though. During my captivity, our time together in the food tent was limited, and we were *discouraged* from talking to each other." I took a long sip from my cup and let it burn all the way down. "It's just so sad."

We sat by the fire drinking, watching the woods grow dark. Clouds had moved in again and obscured the stars and that was okay. It fit the mood.

CHAPTER 17

JOURNAL ENTRY: May 1

    The clouds from last night hung around all morning while we both nursed a hangover. Early afternoon they opened up, dousing the campfire and saturating everything else. We spent the day talking, playing cribbage, and trying to stay dry in the tent. Dinner was cold Spam sandwiches and two bottles of wine.

~~~

    "Allex, wake up!" Jim barked in my ear from a distance. I could feel I was being shaken and all I could see was Tat pushing me around the small cabin. I stumbled on my bruised and swollen feet and I pushed him back. "Allex, wake up!"

    I jerked awake sitting up, disoriented.

    "You were thrashing about and moaning in pain. Are you hurt or were you having a nightmare?" Jim asked, concern filled his voice in the dark.

I was still breathing hard. "Yes, a nightmare. Tat was beating me again and stepping on my feet. It hurts so much, Jim." I shuddered.

"He's gone, Allex. He will never hurt you again," Jim said, soothing my jangled nerves. "The nightmares may continue for a while though." He pulled me close and we fell back asleep.

May 2

Sometime around midnight the rain stopped and a warm southern breeze picked up. By daybreak the tent was dry enough to pack. We headed north on this back road until we came to M-28 and once again turned west and toward the rift.

"We've made such good time Jim, even with the rain day, what do you say we stop in to see Annie and the kids?"

"That's a good idea. I know they mean a lot to you. I got kind of fond of them myself," he said. East of Munising he turned off onto 94 that would lead us to the new road along the rift and away from the first access bridge. The gravel and dirt road that paralleled the rift was muddy and slippery and slowed us down.

"Do you notice anything different about the new river? It doesn't look as high as it did two weeks ago," I observed. I had the chance to watch it more intensely than Jim, since he was concentrating on driving and avoiding water filled potholes.

There was a high spot in the road and grass was growing on the shoulder where Jim brought the Hummer to a stop. We both got out to look closer at the river. Jim hooked his fingers into the back of my belt, and I laughed.

"You're right, it does look lower. With all the rain we had yesterday, one would think the river would be higher. I wonder if they've managed to finally slow the flow some."

"It will be worth checking out after we cross back over," I said. He let go of my belt when we backed away from the river's edge.

The first pass we missed the narrow dirt road where Annie and Glenn lived and we had to backtrack. Pulling into the familiar driveway was a shock. The house was a smoldering pile of rubble with only the brick chimney standing. The lovely porch had half a charred railing and the front shrubs were scorched black.

As soon as Jim stopped, I jumped out of the Hummer. "Annie! Glenn!" I turned in a circle. "Jared! Jodie!" I started shaking.

"Annie! Glenn!" Jim bellowed. If they were anywhere around they would hear him. The only sound came from the chickens clucking inside the coop. By some miracle that building was spared and the chickens wanted out.

As we neared the coop, the door opened and a little redhead peeked out. "Allex?" said a tiny voice.

"Jared!" I almost wept with relief. Jodie rushed past him and threw herself at my legs. I bent down and picked her up. Her tiny arms circled my neck in a death grip. Jared looked up at Jim, his lip quivering, and raised his arms. Jim quickly picked up the little boy who started sobbing.

We set them down on the back bumper of the Hummer, facing away from the ruins, and got them some cool water to drink.

"Jared, can you tell us what happened?" I asked gently. It occurred to me that I had never heard Jodie utter a single word.

"Yesterday we were playing upstairs because it was raining. Annie called us down and told us to go hide in the chicken's house. She was really scared and worried. I thought maybe the bad men came back. After we were in the coop, Annie came carrying the burpy and told me to keep it safe. She was showing me how to use it to make clean water since you left last time."

"Oh, the Berkey," I said aloud, not meaning to interrupt him. That she was teaching him young meant she learned that lesson well.

"Yeah. Annie said there was a fire in the wood stove and Glenn was putting it out and she had to go help him. She said we were to stay here until she came for us," his little lip quivered again. "She never came back."

I looked up at Jim, pleading with my eyes. He nodded and stood. While I stayed with the twins, he went to look through the still hot rubble. By the time he came back, the twins had wolfed down a half sandwich each and another cup of water.

"I have to talk with the colonel for a minute. You two stay right here, okay?" I stepped away from the Hummer and met Jim halfway to the house.

He put his arms around me and said, "You don't want to go any further. It's still hot, but it looks like Glenn died right at the woodstove. Annie was near the back door, and may have been trying to get out." I leaned my forehead against his chest.

"What are we going to do, Jim? We can't leave the twins here, they're just babies!"

"Why don't we all go to the Goshens'? It will get the kids away from here and maybe Lee and Kora can help us decide what to do."

*

"We're going to visit some friends, okay?" I told the twins, trying to smile even though it was hard.

"We have to take the burpy. Annie said I had to keep it safe," Jared protested. Jim retrieved the water filtration unit from the coop and left the chickens penned up.

Jared sat on the empty radio console and Jodie stayed on my lap. The trip took less a half hour and she had fallen asleep almost immediately.

When Jim drove the Hummer up the drive and close to the log house, Lee and Kora came out immediately, happy to see us return. That changed to concern when they saw the children.

"Who are these little angels?" Kora asked, getting down on one knee while I set a now awake Jodi down.

The little girl eyed Kora, then reached out and stroked her loose blonde hair. "You look like my mommy. Annie said she's in heaven now. I think Annie's in heaven now too."

Kora flashed her eyes up at me

"We need to talk," I said to the Goshens.

*

Inside the big house, Kora led the children to the living room and gave them a puzzle to play with, while the adults went to the kitchen out of earshot. As quickly as we could, we explained what we had come upon. A tear ran down Kora's pale cheek.

"They have no one now and I don't know what to do with them," I said. "We're not going straight back to Moose Creek so we can't take them with us."

Lee was the first one to speak. "They can stay here. We've always wanted children, right, Kora?"

She smiled then, and said, "Looks like we have a pair of them now." I could see the relief on Jim's face and I closed my eyes and sighed in gratitude.

"They have nothing, Kora, only what they're wearing," I said.

"I'll make them some clothes!"

"Jared insisted on bringing the Berkey," Jim said. "Even if you don't need it, he won't part with it. It's the one thing he has of his big sister."

"Jim, what are we going to do about... Annie and Glenn?" I asked.

"Lee, you have a couple of shovels and maybe a cage for the chickens?" Jim asked. "No sense in letting the birds starve to death." Lee nodded and they left the kitchen. Soon we saw them pull out in Lee's pickup truck. When they returned two hours later, Annie's chickens were turned loose in the yard, much to the pleasure and excitement of the twins. It was a familiar thing for the twins to hold on to.

*

"You will stay the night, won't you?" Lee asked.

"Thank you, I think we should. We can't just drop a couple of kids on you and leave," I said, smiling at the absurdity of my statement.

"Good," Kora said. She turned to the twins. "Come on you two let's go see your new bedrooms!" Jodi grabbed Kora's hand; she had made the transition very quickly, perhaps because Kora had blonde hair like her mother. Jared took my hand and the four of us climbed the wide wooden steps to the upper level of the big log house.

*

We had dinner early so the twins could get a bath and go to bed.

"They sure fell asleep quickly," Kora noted.

"It's been a very traumatic couple of days for them," I said sadly. "They do seem to be resilient, though, which is in your favor – and theirs." I paused, thinking. "They are really sweet kids and very well behaved. I want to thank you for taking them in."

"It's us that should be thanking you!" Lee said. "We've said before that we always wanted children, now this house can be a real home for all of us."

The four of us took our drinks out to the large, wide porch to enjoy the evening breeze. The peepers set up a chorus to compete with our casual chatter as we talked into the night. A few early mosquitoes finally drove us in. We said our goodnights and went to our rooms.

"Okay, now comes the awkward moment," Jim said, running his fingers through his short gray hair. "Would you prefer I sleep on the floor?"

"It's a big bed, Jim, I think we can share it like adults."

"Like adults," he repeated with a sigh.

CHAPTER 18

JOURNAL ENTRY: May 4

The bright morning sun coming through the lacey curtains woke me early. Jim was still sleeping, breathing steady and deep, with his back to me. At least he didn't snore. I slipped quietly out of the big bed and went into the attached bathroom. We would be doing a lot of traveling today.

~~~

"Good morning," he said when I came back into the room, showered and fully dressed.

"Good morning. Sleep well?" I asked. When he gave me a look that said I shouldn't ask, I turned away.

"I slept, thinking about those points B and C that we've missed," he replied with a slow smile.

Yeah, me too, I thought.

*

I helped Kora clear away and wash the breakfast dishes. Lee and the children were playing catch out in the dusty yard, and Jim was packing the Hummer.

"You know you're always welcome to stay as long as you want, Allex," Kora said.

"I know, and I appreciate that. It's been four weeks we've been on the road, though, and I'm anxious to see my family again. *And* we still have a stop to make at Sawyer. Jim hasn't said how long that will take us." I put the last dish away in the cupboard. "I've been meaning to thank you for those steaks you put in our cooler. I fixed them with morels," I said, smiling to hide my discomfort at remembering what else happened at that time.

She smiled back brightly at me. "Then you won't mind if I give you two more?"

"That's very generous, Kora. Beef is a very rare treat for us. Ever since that first quake eighteen months ago, nothing has been the same. My family has had more fresh venison than anything else. My boys don't mind though, they enjoy the hunt."

Jim came in right then and said we were ready to leave.

*

"I promise to bring Allex back another time for a longer visit. For now, though, we really do have to go," Jim said. He turned to the children. "I know you two will be safe here. We wouldn't leave you if we had any doubts. And Jared, you take care of your little sister, okay?"

"Yes, sir, I will," the little redhead stated. Hugs and handshakes went all around and we left them behind, one more time.

*

As we once more approached the dirt road that followed along the river, Jim said, "Which way, Allex?"

I looked at him in question.

"This may be our last time for adventure," he stated. "I vote for us going south and taking the lower bridge across. It's only a different route."

"That's a really good idea. It will give us a new view," I agreed. "And quite honestly, Jim, I've had enough adventure these past three weeks to last me awhile."

Jim scowled. "I had hoped this trip would bring you happier, more pleasant experiences, Allex. I never should have let my guard down before. I honestly thought we were beyond the danger zone. It never occurred to me we would walk right into it. I'm sorry, Allex, I really am."

I reached over and put my hand on his arm. "Jim, we can't anticipate everything. And let's face it, my capture could have turned out worse, a *lot* worse. Instead of being brutalized by an impotent sadist, he could have given me to his men. As it was, I was only beaten and not raped." I sat in silence for a minute. "Which also brings up something else. When we get back home, I don't want this discussed. Eric and Jason are never to know about this incident. *No one* is to know. Promise me."

Jim stopped the vehicle and turned to me. "I promise, Allex."

He brushed a lock of hair away from my face and gently kissed me, then put the Hummer back in gear and followed the road.

*

"I can see the bridge ahead, Jim, it's maybe a half mile," I said excitedly. Crossing back to the other side put us that much closer to home.

The Hummer skittered in the mud and Jim slowed to keep control. We were almost at the bridge when it became obvious we were having another earthquake! I know that aftershocks can continue for quite some time when there is a major quake such as the one that opened this rift, or was this a new one?

Jim swerved hard and put us onto the now swaying structure. "Hang on, Allex!"

This bridge wasn't built as strongly as the one further north. I guess that would make sense, since this was for local traffic only and not heavy equipment. The massive wooden boards that extended from side to side were rippling as Jim sped up. The Hummer bounced over the unevenness with ease and Jim delivered us safely to the other side just as the tremor stopped. I gasped for breath.

"I never thought I would have to cross another bridge during another earthquake," Jim said, emerging from the Hummer. "I really am getting too old for this shit." He was breathing hard and seemed a bit shaky. "Are you okay?"

"Yeah, I'm fine. That was scary…" I said. "I never doubted that you wouldn't get us across though."

"I couldn't let us get stranded on the wrong side, Allex. I'm sure in time we would have gotten across, though, even if we had to get a chopper! I didn't want to wait for a ride," he laughed. "Hopefully, there's no damage to the roads on this side."

We drove north on the uneven gravel service road for almost an hour. Another time that hour would have put us all the way to the dam construction, however, we were only about halfway there. The recent rain had washed away some of the gravel, leaving patches of slick mud. Even though it wasn't anything the Hummer couldn't traverse, it did slow us down.

"What in the world?" Jim hit the brakes and brought us to a stop. There, at the beginning of what appeared to be a long driveway, was a "yard sale" sign with colorful balloons dancing beside it in the breeze.

"Those balloons are new," I said quietly. "Someone is having a yard sale. I bet they don't have many takers." During my online research at the Soo, I found out that out of the three hundred thousand residents of the Upper Peninsula, there were fewer than a hundred thousand left.

For being one third the land mass of the state of Michigan, we now had fewer people than a medium sized city. Losing two-thirds of our population to the flu, violence, and the natural disasters sat heavy on my heart.

"That means people, Allex. Do you want to investigate?" Jim asked cautiously.

"Yeah, I do, Jim. I love yard sales. More than that, I'm curious about what they would be selling. We all know money isn't worth much anymore." He turned up the long poorly maintained and rutted road.

A half mile up the road we came to a clearing. There was a large, older clapboard house with a wide covered porch, a barn, a chicken coop—which seemed to be ever popular and accepted now—a few smaller buildings of questionable use, and a very large garden with people working in it. The house itself was sided with a yellow-green vinyl, and the porch hadn't seen a paintbrush in many years. On the porch sat a couple of women and in front of the porch was a long table. A hand drawn sign that read "for sale or trade" was taped to the edge.

All of the women stood as we pulled in. Jim made his usual turn, faced the Hummer outward and we stepped out.

"Welcome!" one of the women called out. "Come on closer!" The work in the garden had come to a halt. I could now see there were three men doing the hard hoeing and the fourth was a woman with a shotgun. The men quickly got back to work.

We stepped cautiously forward.

"What are you looking for?" the same woman asked pleasantly. As she stepped closer to us, I could see she was in her late forties and graying early. The other two kept a few steps behind her; she was the alpha female of a dominantly female household.

"Oh, we're not looking for anything in particular," I said. "I will admit we stopped more out of curiosity. Yard sale signs are not exactly common anymore."

"Got that right!" she giggled. "We haven't had a sale all day." She seemed friendly enough, and wasn't armed. "Say, how about a trade? Anything on the table for some simple labor. Our men aren't what they used to be and are having a difficult time swinging an axe. Could your man split some wood for us?" she asked, giving Jim a long look.

The request seemed innocuous. I looked at Jim.

"Is there anything on the table you want?" he asked. I stepped over to the table while Jim hung back and let my gaze slide over the meager items. A pair of earrings caught my attention, as did a bayonet. I like pretty things as much as the next woman, but I'm a practical person at heart.

"Those are real diamonds," the woman said in my ear. "Worth more than a half hour of splitting wood, but we can dicker."

Jim took off his shirt and picked up the axe.

"Johnny!" the woman called out. "Get your ass over here and stack the bolts!" Out in the garden a middle-aged man stood, stretching his back and rolling his muscular shoulders in a very familiar way, his bald head shining with sweat. When he turned my heart stood still.

John???

Was this why he never came back? Had he been abducted by some amazon wannabees and held in captivity? The man turned fully and I could see it wasn't him. My heart was still beating hard as I chastised myself. I was actually glad it wasn't him. John had left me so many times before I couldn't have him back in my life.

While Jim split wood, a light sheen emphasizing his muscles, this alpha, Lois, invited me to sit. I noticed the others watching him too.

"It's good to see more dominant women," Lois said. "We got tired of being pushed around and forced to do all the hard work while our men sat around drinking beer. Even before the big quake we were organizing to revolt." She sniggered. "Now the men serve *us*."

"I see." I really did. We had stumbled into a female dominated society and the women were taking revenge on the men for all the suffering they had been through. If they wanted to live their lives that way, that was their choice. We would be leaving soon enough.

"Your man… he's strong and easy on the eyes. How much do you want for him?" Lois asked. "Maybe those diamond earrings?" Her grin wasn't evil, it was delusional.

I looked out at Jim, admiring the fluid movements of his body. "Oh, he's not for sale. I'm going to keep him," I said, playing for time. I stood and stepped off the porch, picking up the bayonet. I would rather have the only weapon on that table in my hands, not theirs. "Jim!" I called out. "That's enough." He sunk the axe deep into the block and grabbed his shirt.

"Think about my offer," Lois said.

"Will do," I lied.

"While you're thinking, why not let us keep him for the night and give him a test drive?" she smirked. I noticed how the other women were now closing in.

"I don't think so," I said. "Jim, we're leaving now!"

The others were getting way too close to him. I drew my Beretta.

"You touch him, you die," I said calmly. I know they understood I meant it when they all froze.

*

At the end of the drive Jim turned north.

"What the hell was going on back there, Allex?" he asked, maneuvering around a pothole.

"They wanted to buy you and I wouldn't sell. Now please, don't stop until we get back into the restricted area!"

I couldn't believe I wasn't shaking. Maybe it was knowing that I would indeed have shot to save him that was keeping me so calm. That or the anger I was still feeling.

CHAPTER 19

It had only been a couple of weeks since we were here at the dam, and what tremendous progress they'd made. We arrived in time to see them install one of several concrete slabs.

"Welcome back, Colonel Andrews, Lieutenant Smeth," Captain Argyle said. We found him near the new structure on a walkie, giving directions to a hovering Chinook helicopter. A large slab of concrete hung suspended underneath, secured by guidelines trailing down to the dam framework.

We watched in awe and fascination as the Chinook winch lowered its load to within inches of the water, men on either side guiding it into place. It vanished beneath the waves. A few minutes later the winch retracted, and the copter landed behind us.

"What just happened?" I asked Argyle.

"In the past two weeks we've built an underwater scaffold that these foot-thick ten by ten foot sections slide into. It seemed the best way to make the strongest blockade to stop the water. There is a team of divers down there right now securing that piece. These slabs we're using are about the only thing available to withstand the pressure of the water. Each one weighs about seven tons. We started with six inch sheets at three and a half tons each, however that wasn't even phasing the Chinook's maximum sling-load capacity, which is thirteen tons, so we made them thicker. They're holding up exceptionally well. Without being able to divert the water, a poured concrete dam wasn't practical. These pre-poured slabs are doing the trick and quickly."

"I gather you found the bottom, Captain?" Jim asked.

"Ah, yes, we were almost there before. The rift bottoms out at two hundred ten feet in the center. The chasm is like a wedge, so we're not dealing with all of it at two hundred feet. As it is, we need over six hundred of these slabs to completely cover the opening. Fortunately they can be manufactured just a few miles away," Argyle said. "That little tremor we had earlier was a good test of the framework. It never budged."

"How far along are you?" I asked.

"We started with the insertions a few days ago. That was number three hundred you saw go in. When they are all in place and the flow is either stopped or slowed enough, we will start backfilling the southern face with rocks and boulders, whatever we can get that will fortify the wall."

"You're making good progress. Have you run into any other problems?" Jim asked.

Captain Argyle said, "Yeah. Fish."

"Fish?"

"Monstrous fish. Have you ever seen a sturgeon, Lieutenant?" he asked.

"Yes, many years ago at my aunt's cottage on the St. Clair River. It was almost five feet long," I replied.

"These seem to be rising from the depths off of Munising where it was over fourteen hundred feet deep. The first one we got pictures of was eighteen feet long, and was guessed to weigh close to five *thousand* pounds! It scared the crap out of the diver when it got curious. They are relatively passive fish with no teeth, but they look enough like a gator with their bony plates and back ridges to be intimidating," Argyle said.

I was stunned. "How many have been spotted?"

"At least ten have gone down the river now. Our resident ichthyologist believes the ancient sturgeons are looking for deeper water now, and a new feeding ground. This species has changed very little since prehistoric times."

Ten? Was that what had bumped me closer to the tree when I fell in the river?

"The sturgeons are huge, however, the Muskellunge are a bigger issue. They're aggressive," Captain Argyle said.

"The what?" Jim asked.

"Most people know them as Muskies. The Tiger Muskie is a cross between the muskellunge and a pike. They are almost thirty percent head and all of that is teeth. When that migration started, the divers went down in mesh cages. Those fish are often four feet long. These have been coming in at five and six feet. Muskies have been known to snatch small dogs that are swimming," Argyle said. "Looks like they're getting ready for the next drop. You'll have to excuse me."

We watched in fascination as the Chinook rose and hovered. On the ground, men scrambled to attach the giant hook to a waiting slab of concrete. The helicopter rose slowly, taking up the slack, and then lifted the seven ton section with ease.

*

"That was amazing to watch, Jim. I'm glad we stopped," I said when we were once more on the road and heading toward Sawyer.

"I am too," he said sullenly.

"What's up, Jim? You have an edge to your voice. What are you worried about?"

"This stop at Sawyer has me concerned. I have a major piece of paperwork to take care of and I can't be around to fend off questions about your service record. I know Hogan was starting to dig and now that he's back online I've no doubt he's already been in touch with Kopley about you," Jim stated. "It won't take much to find you don't exist."

I couldn't help but grin. "I don't think you need to worry about that. Kim and Billy took care of that."

"What do you mean 'took care of it'?"

"Now, keep in mind they were only trying to help me," I said, defending my duo. "They created a file for me. A classified file. If anyone tries to access it, they need a very high security clearance, and even then it directs them to a file that says I've been assigned to a covert operation. The files are empty, of course, and if further search is done it just loops. I thought it pretty clever of them."

Jim glanced over at me in disbelief, and then started laughing. "I told you you made a lot of friends there! How did they find out?"

"Quite by accident. They were testing the search engines and used me as the trial. When they found out I didn't exist within the Army, they didn't question why. All they were concerned with was that I was protected. Oh, and the files are dated a year ago, so you're off the hook, Colonel. How long do you think you'll need to complete whatever it is you need to do?"

"I'm hoping no more than two days. It will depend on Washington," he replied, slipping back into an introspective mood. The road smoothed out and we arrived at Sawyer AFB an hour later, presenting our military ID at the security gate.

"Welcome back, Colonel, Lieutenant. We've been expecting you. I have a message for you from Major Kopley," the young guard said, handing over a sealed envelope.

Jim parked the Humvee near the barracks building and opened the envelope.

"He wants to see us as soon as we get settled in," he said after scanning the letter.

"I wonder what's up?"

"My guess is Hogan has been in touch and he wants to congratulate us."

"On what?"

Jim smiled. "Point D. Our engagement."

"Oh."

Ah, yes, the point A to point D remark I made a few days ago when we left the Soo. There hasn't been time to even discuss if we wanted to explore points B and C that we jumped right over.

"Are you ready for a bit more role playing, Allex?" he asked gently and with a touch of humor.

"Now that I know what's going on, I think I can handle it, Jim. Before, it was a surprise and caught me off guard. How far are we going to take this?"

"As far as we need to to keep Kopley at bay," he said, getting out of the dusty Hummer. "Just don't flinch when I touch you." We each grabbed our duffel and headed toward the squat gray buildings that were to be our quarters for the next day or two.

*

"Colonel Andrews! Welcome back, sir." Major Kopley, extended his hand to Jim.

"It's good to be back, Steve, though we won't be staying long," Jim said to his friend and fellow officer. "I need an office with a secure computer to finish some correspondence."

"Certainly, Colonel. You can have my office for as long as you need." Kopley turned to me. "It's good to see you again, Lieutenant. We've been informed about your unfortunate experience. How are you doing?" he asked with sincere concern.

"I'm recovering, Major, thank you. Although there are still a few bruises and broken bones to heal, I'm going to be fine."

"I must say, during your last stay here you two hid your relationship very well," Kopley continued. "Dan told me about that too. Congratulations."

"Thank you. At the time, Steve, there wasn't much to hide," Jim stated. "Allex and I have had a great deal of respect and fondness for each other the entire time we've been acquainted."

"The kidnapping changed things. It was an awakening to how we really felt toward each other," I interjected, which got a surprised look from Jim. "Initially I was told Jim was dead. I hadn't felt that much grief since my husband died. When he rescued me, well, like I said, things changed." I smiled up at Jim and said, "Point B." He looked stunned.

"If you don't mind, gentlemen, I will leave you to work, and I'm going to find the medic and have my bandages changed." I walked away with only the slightest limp.

*

The field hospital was easy to find on the base, since it sported a large banner with a red cross on it. Captain Josh Marley looked up from his desk.

"Yes? Can I help you, Lieutenant?"

"Good afternoon, Captain. I need some bandages changed," I said.

He stood and stepped closer, looking at my face. "By the looks of it, you have a few bruises and contusions also. What happened, Lieutenant? It looks like you've been in a fight."

"I was kidnapped and beaten by a gang of escaped prisoners," I replied, as matter-of-factly as I could.

"You're Lt. Smeth? Everyone here has heard about what happened. Please, come in the exam room and have a seat."

I sat in the chair opposite a rolling stool, which I rightly assumed the medic used. After removing my shoes and socks I sat up on the

THE JOURNAL: RAGING TIDE

papered exam table so he could check the healing of my feet. With gloved hands, he cut away the bandages that held my toes together.

"What was the full extent of the injuries?" he asked, not looking up while he turned my foot to examine the bruised soles.

"One broken toe and three dislocated."

"And the bruising?"

"The soles were whipped with a belt buckle," I said, straining to maintain my calm.

He glanced up in shock. "How long ago did this happen, ma'am?"

I thought a moment. It seemed like forever, yet not. "About eight days now. I've lost track."

"The bruises on your soles are a fading yellow, which is a good sign. The small toe which was taped I will presume was the one broken. The other three are still bruised, otherwise I'd say we don't need to wrap those anymore." He re-taped the broken toe and looked at my face, pressing on the faded spots. "That hurt?" I shook my head. "You have remarkable healing. Is there anything else?"

"Only my ribs," I lifted my shirt so he could unwind the ace bandage.

"Holy shit!" he said. "Sorry, ma'am. What happened here?"

"First, I fell in the new river and was swept into a tree. Then while I was held captive, I was punched a lot there because I was already injured. They were pretty sadistic."

"This bruising isn't as healed as the rest. Are you having any difficulty breathing?" Capt. Marley asked.

"Only when I try for a deep breath. One of the ribs feels cracked," I replied while he wrapped a new ace around my rib cage.

He wrote something down on a prescription pad, handed it to me, and wrote again. "I'm limiting you to very light duty, Lieutenant, and suggest you still stay off your feet. Here's a prescription for some Darvocet. That should help you sleep too."

"I won't need the Darvocet," I said, handing the slip back to him.

"Get it filled, ma'am. That's an order."

*

I met up with Jim outside the women's barracks.

"Are you ready for dinner?" he asked.

"Starving!" I said, taking his offered arm. "I hear its spaghetti night. Too bad we can't have some of our wine with it."

"It's the officers' mess, Allex, we can do what we want," he replied, "By the way, that was a convincing speech you gave Kopley. I almost believed it myself!"

"It's all true, Jim," I said softly. He stopped after a few feet and looked down at the empty hall, and then he kissed me, briefly and thoroughly, leaving me breathless and weak in the knees.

"Point B," he said. "Let's stop at the Hummer for that wine."

*

I sipped the remainder of my glass of wine, which Jim and I had willingly shared with Major Kopley. The table conversation had been lighthearted for the most part with just a touch of business.

"Major Hogan tells me you did wonders for his EOC and in a very short time, Allexa. I understand your AOC is Public Affairs, however no one seems to quite get a grasp on what your orders are," Kopley casually commented.

I knew immediately he was fishing. "Major," I chastised him, "if I told you I'd have to kill you." I added a laugh to lighten the mood.

"Steve, you should have seen the way she handled that scumbag that hurt her," Jim said, deftly changing the subject. "After I handed her service weapon back to her, she checked it over and without so much as a word put the barrel to the guy's forehead and pulled the trigger. I was so proud of her."

Steve Kopley snapped his head around to me. "Did you really?"

"It seemed like the thing to do at the time," I affirmed. "He was to be executed anyway. I wanted to be the one to do it after what he did to me."

"Remind me to never piss you off, Lieutenant," Kopley laughed.

"I don't give warnings, Major." At that I stood. "Thank you for a delightful evening. It's been a long and exhausting day and I'm done in. Good night."

Jim caught up to me before I reached the door. "I'll walk you back to the barracks."

*

Outside my room we hesitated and I laughed nervously. "This feels awkward, doesn't it? Things are changing faster than I thought they would."

"I'm not complaining, Allex." Jim brushed my cheek with his soft fingertips. The kiss started gently and quickly became more demanding. Had we not been standing in the hallway of the women's barracks, the evening might have ended differently.

"Good night, Jim." I slipped into my dorm room and closed the door. I leaned against the closed door, breathing heavily.

CHAPTER 20

JOURNAL ENTRY: May 12

We've been here at Sawyer for a week now. I've managed to rest and eat, gaining some of my strength back. Jim is still working on this mysterious correspondence although he says he should be finished sometime today if he can get a stable internet connection. I'm anxious to be on the road again. Even though they stayed frozen for the first four days, I've packed ice into the cooler daily to keep those gifted steaks fresh. Kora Goshen was most generous and I'm looking forward to us grilling dinner tonight.

~~~

"It's really annoying, Allex. Every time I try to send my final report, something interferes with the transmission. It almost feels like someone is intercepting me," Jim groaned in frustration as I sat across the desk from him.

"I wish we had Billy here to help," I lamented. "Maybe we can! I've got Billy and Kim's email addresses. Let me see if I can reach them." I took Jim's seat and started typing. Soon a small window popped up on my screen: an instant message from Billy.

IM: how's it going, Lieutenant?

"I'm getting some needed rest, thanks. We're having some trouble you might help with." I typed in return.

IM: I'll try. What's the problem?

"The Colonel keeps getting interfered with when he tries to send a report. Is it possible he's being remotely intercepted?"

IM: Sure, that would be easy. Any clues?

"This is Major Kopley's computer. He's been in touch with Major Hogan. BTW your loop has done wonders for my reputation☺"

IM: Great! And FYI, that loop has been accessed three times, twice from here, once from there. I've been monitoring it. BRB

Jim was watching over my shoulder all this time. "What's BTW and BRB?

"BTW is computer shorthand for by the way, and BRB is be right back."

IM: I just now disabled a couple of computers… lol … Try sending the report now.

I minimized the conversation with Billy and Jim sat back down. He pulled up his report and was able to send it right out.

"Thanks Billy that worked!"

IM: anytime my lady! TTFN

The instant message conversation disappeared.

Before Jim could ask I said, "That's ta ta for now, a way of saying goodbye."

"So," Jim leaned back in the chair, "Hogan was tapping into my reports. I could have him court-martialed for that. And it's possible Kopley was involved."

"From things Billy told me before, Kopley might not have known. On the other hand…"

"It's moot now, Allex. That last report was my retirement papers," Jim sighed. "All of my adult life has been devoted to the Army and my country. It feels like something is missing now." He stood and stretched.

His announcement had me shocked. "Why, Jim?"

"I'm tired, Allex. I joined the Army at eighteen, went to college, and moved up in the ranks. I'm fifty-five now; that's thirty-seven years of my life devoted to Uncle Sam. I deserve my own time now, and I'm ready to stay put. My papers become effective one month from today. I say we get back on the road right after lunch."

"That's the best news yet!"

I was still bewildered over his decision to retire.

*

We didn't get the sendoff we had leaving the Soo, though we did get fresh ice for the cooler and a thermos of coffee, plus a mail bag with letters destined for Marquette and Moose Creek.

"It should take us no more than two hours to get back to that house behind Walstroms," I said, settling back in the seat. After all this time it was starting to feel comfortable. The afternoon was as cloudy and as bleak as the morning was. The high, thick clouds kept the sun from even making a bright spot in the all gray sky. The biggest bright spot was that we were once again traveling, and this time toward home.

"We left a great deal of supplies at that house to take home. I think we should look for a trailer of some kind," Jim said.

"Good idea.

I know many of the gas stations around here were also Haul Your Own outlets. Maybe we can find something suitable that was left behind when everyone left."

*

Half an hour later we came to a main intersection with a four-way stop. One corner was dominated by a now vacant gas station/party store.

"Let's pull in here and drive around back," I suggested. There were two of the distinctive dark green and light blue trailers, both missing tires.

"Well, there's bound to be more," Jim shrugged. "Let's keep moving."

Just past the silent ski hill with its chairlifts frozen in time was another business that rented moving trailers and this time we got lucky.

"That one is way too large," he pointed to one near the front.

"This one over here might do us," I said spotting a smaller unit, listing to one side. "Darn, it has a flat tire."

"Tires we can change." Jim opened the back doors to the covered unit and stepped inside. "The floor is solid, and it even has a moving dolly." He stepped back out and looked around the yard. "I can switch tires from that trailer and we can be back on the road in twenty minutes."

He jacked up the large trailer with the tools from the Humvee and removed two of the tires. I didn't question him taking two; it's always good to have a spare. Jim left the large, open trailer sitting on its empty axle. He rolled one tire and I rolled the other over to the smaller trailer. He loosened the lug nuts on the flat tire, jacked it up, and removed it quickly. As he was putting the good tire in place, a tremor hit and the jack slipped.

"AHHHH!" Jim screamed. The axle had fallen on his hand! I wrenched the jack out and pumped it up again, and then helped Jim pull his left hand free. There was so much blood it was hard to tell whether he had two or three smashed fingers. He sat with his back against the trailer and stifled a moan. I ran to the Hummer and backed it as close to him as I could get.

"Let me wash it, Jim," I said calmly, and I poured a bottle of drinking water over the wound. It immediately began gushing red again, but I had seen enough. I grabbed one of my t-shirts and wrapped it around his hand. "I'm going to take you back to the base. You need the medic."

"The pain is making me dizzy, Allex, I don't know if I can even stand." He groaned again as he tried.

"Don't try to move." I went back to the Hummer and got my small med-kit. I found the vial of painkiller and filled the syringe. I swabbed his muscular shoulder and jabbed. "I gave you something for the pain and it should act fast. The moment the pain subsides, we have to move fast to get you into the Hummer. I can't do it alone, you will have to help before the meds knock you out."

"Knocked out sounds good," he moaned. "Let's do it." I helped him stand and he leaned heavily on me for the few steps we needed to go. I closed the passenger door and slid behind the wheel, driving as fast as possible back to the base.

Twenty minutes later I pulled up to the gate and the guard stepped out. "ID please."

"Open the damned gate! The colonel has been severely injured!" I shouted, my adrenaline raging. The young man looked inside the Hummer and saw the bloody wrappings. The gate lifted and I barely cleared it in my hurry.

I jumped the curb in front of the field hospital as two orderlies came out with a wheelchair. I was very glad to see them, as I wouldn't have been capable of moving an inert Jim. They managed to get the unconscious colonel into the chair and I followed on their heels.

"I got a call from the gate. What happened, Lieutenant?" Captain Josh Marley asked, unwrapping the bloody shirt from Jim's hand.

"He was changing a tire when that aftershock hit and the jack slipped. I rinsed it off with drinking water only. Two fingers look bad, Doc. I gave him a shot of Demerol," and I told the medic how much. He nodded.

"You two," Marley said to the orderlies, "get him on a gurney. STAT!" Marley turned to me. "You might want to wait out here, Lieutenant. It's going to get messy."

"I'm not leaving him, and don't worry about me. I assisted my husband in several surgeries, including one on my own son after he was attacked by wolves," I stated, following Marley into the surgical suite.

"Lieutenant, I don't need an assistant, and I definitely don't need another patient."

"I'll make you a deal, *Captain*," I said. "I promise to stay out of your way and if I feel the least bit faint, I'll leave."

He eyed me and said nothing, then he handed me a mask and a pair of gloves.

I sat on a stool at the head of the gurney, wiping cool water on Jim's slack face. Captain Marley irrigated the wounds again. "The ring finger is broken and can be set. The small finger is smashed, pulverized, and I'm going to have to amputate it."

"I know he would want you to do whatever is necessary," I replied. "You've got excellent surgical skills, Captain, and it's obvious you have experience. Where have you served?"

"I did three tours in the sandbox, ma'am. I've patched up more young men that stepped on IEDs than I care to think about," he answered without looking up. "Unfortunately, that included a lot of amputations." He straightened and splinted the ring finger. "I don't mean to sound too casual about this, Lieutenant, but the amputation will be quick and relatively simple. The bone is completely crushed and the tissue is totally separated." He sliced the skin to have a flap to stitch over the nub and dropped the mangled digit in a metal bowl. In less than a half hour, the surgery was finished and Jim's hand was wrapped in bandages.

"May I ask where your husband served, Lieutenant?" Marley asked casually as he scrubbed.

"My husband wasn't military, Captain. He was an ER trauma doctor down in Saginaw. He died from the flu last year," I added, knowing that would be the next question.

"Can I assume you will want to stay here, near Colonel Andrews?"

"Definitely," I replied. "How long will you want to keep him?"

"He should be fine to leave tomorrow morning. I'm sure the colonel would disagree with me, but as I said, this wasn't a bad injury."

*

I sat beside a sleeping colonel, my adrenaline dump beginning. I got shaky, then very tired. I rested my head against his bed and dozed.

*

"Lieutenant? Allex?" I felt someone shaking my shoulder and opened my eyes.

"Major Kopley," I acknowledged him and sat up straight, stretching the kinks out of my neck.

"I was notified that Jim had been injured. What happened?"

"He was changing a tire when the jack slipped. One broken finger and Capt. Marley had to amputate the pinky. He should be fine and we'll leave again in the morning," I answered.

"I think you should stay the rest of the week, give Jim time to recover," Kopley said, taking command.

"It will be up to Jim, though I'm fairly certain he would want to get back on the road, Major."

"Even if I make that an order?" Kopley pressed.

Some serious strategy was needed, and a serious lie.

"Major Kopley," I said, standing to face him, "I know you have attempted to access my records, and you have found you don't have a high enough clearance. I'm not at liberty to discuss my orders with you or anyone else, but I will tell you one thing you didn't find in my file. Jim may outrank me, but *you* don't! So don't try to give *me* orders," I said with all the anger I was feeling about our situation. I sat back down.

Major Kopley looked both stunned and chastised. "Yes, Ma'am." He turned to leave, then turned back. "Lieutenant, Colonel Andrews is my friend and I wish only the best for him. I would be honored if you would join me for dinner in the officers' mess at eighteen hundred hours. You still need to eat."

"Thank you, Major, however, I'm having two trays sent down here. I wouldn't think of leaving Jim alone at a time like this," I replied, softening my stance.

*

"Allex?" Jim called out.

"I'm right here, Jim," I answered, moving so he could see me.

"You're so pretty," he said, closing his eyes again.

"That's because you're on some good drugs right now," I laughed.

"Pretty and brave… smart. So strong. I think I fell in… with you… at… wedding. Not a sham," he slurred and dozed off again in a drug induced haze.

Wow, that was a revelation I didn't need.

He struggled to open his eyes again. "What happened? Where are we?"

"That trailer slipped off the jack during the tremor and smashed your fingers. We're in the infirmary at Sawyer." I laid my hand on his cheek. "You've got one broken finger, and … your pinky finger had to be amputated."

His eyes flew open and he lifted his hand. "No wonder it hurts." He drifted away again.

A half hour later, our two dinner trays were delivered: Chicken noodle soup with crackers for the patient and chicken breast on rice for me. The adrenaline rush had left me hungry, and I ate quickly so I could be done before Jim woke.

*

His eyes were clearer and not so drug-fogged when he awakened again. He took a deep breath and yawned.

"I smell food," he said without the least trace of slur to his voice.

"Chicken noodle soup and crackers is all Capt. Marley will let you have. Tomorrow night, though, it's just you and me, a steak, and a bottle of wine." It was good to see him alert. I cranked the bed up to a sitting position and helped Jim have his meager dinner. Then I gave him the Darvocet Marley had left him and Jim went right back out.

April 27

I laid down on the one of the other beds in the infirmary after taking off my boots last night. Someone draped a blanket over me at some point and I drowsily relished the softness that covered me.

"Good morning, sleepyhead," Jim said. He was already sitting up and eating breakfast.

"Hey, you, how do you feel?" I asked, sliding out of the bed to stand by him.

"I've had better mornings," he chuckled around a bite of toast. "My hand hurts like hell. Marley said I was lucky. I've managed my entire life without losing a body part, and now this." He held up his bandaged hand, scooping eggs with his other one.

"It could have been much worse, Jim. I'm just glad we were still so close to the base." I shuddered at the thought of this happening further away. What would I have done?

"That's what Marley said too, Allex. Your quick thinking resulted in the loss of one finger instead of my whole hand." He looked at me and smiled. "Thank you. I can deal with a missing finger." He took a sip of coffee and noticed me staring at it. "There's a tray over there for you."

"Scoot over, Colonel," I said, climbing onto his bed with my food tray. We chatted and ate until Capt. Marley came in.

"Major Kopley was quite adamant that you could leave if you wanted unless I felt that would be detrimental to your wellbeing, Colonel

Andrews. I can see that you are recovering rapidly." Apparently the major had an about face after my mega lie. "Your uniform was laundered by Smitty and will be here shortly, sir. Once you're dressed and fitted with a sling, you're free to go."

*

"Do I really need this sling?" Jim griped.

"Yes you do," I answered before Marley had the chance. "Your hand needs the support and the elevation. If you left it down by your side it would start throbbing in no time. Buck-up, Colonel, it's only for a few days." Marley handed me a small bag with extra gauze for changing the bandages, some antibiotic cream, and a small bottle of pain pills that Jim would need later.

CHAPTER 21

The morning was minimally brighter than yesterday. The gray, ash-filled clouds looked thicker and more ominous as we drove out of the confines of the military base.

"Don't you give me any grief about me driving, Colonel. You've done ninety-nine percent of the driving ever since we left Moose Creek," I snapped at him.

"My lips are sealed. By the way, what did you say to Steve that made him ask me about your rank?" Major Kopley had stopped by the infirmary while I was bringing the Humvee around.

"Oh," I hesitated, "he threatened to order us to stay on base for the week, so I had to lie a bit more." I told Jim what I said and he laughed.

"That would make you a Lieutenant *Colonel*, Allex, the only rank that separates a major and a full bird colonel. No wonder he was so solicitous." He laughed again. It was good to see him in a pleasant mood.

*

I pulled into the parking lot of the trailer rental, where the unit we wanted waited still jacked up. I finished changing the tire, spun the lug nuts on, and consented to Jim tightening them down, one handed. Together we got the trailer attached to the Hummer and were soon on our way again.

I found the entrance to the subdivision easily and wound around the curves cautiously until we came to the long driveway.

"Everything looks the same," Jim commented as I ascended the still smooth concrete. The first thing I noticed was the grass turning green and the towers of dried leaves piled in the corners of the portico. We'd been gone a month. I made a full circle on the oval apron, aiming outward, and then backed up a few feet.

"I've never been very good at backing up a trailer, so if you want it closer, you'll have to do it yourself," I said, getting out of the big vehicle. I retrieved the door key from where we had hidden it weeks ago, and after testing that the door was indeed still locked, I inserted the key. We both drew our weapons and I nudged the door open. Crushing dried leaves underfoot, we entered the house.

We cleared each floor as we had done before. All was as we had left it.

"I think it's safe to bring our gear in," Jim said.

"In a minute. I want to turn the generator on first and get the water heating," I said. "I'm looking forward to a long, hot bath tonight!"

"And ice cubes," Jim joked. "Don't forget the ice cubes!"

With the power back on, the garage door opened smoothly. Jim backed the trailer in and we disconnected it from the Hummer. "It makes sense to keep the trailer out of sight even if there isn't anyone around."

We emptied the Hummer quickly, leaving only the empty cooler, the chainsaw, and the tent in the back. The weather had gotten cooler and we'd need our sleeping bags tonight.

*

"So what's our plan of action, Colonel?" I asked as we sat at the kitchen island with a cup of steaming hot soup.

"I think we should load up the cases of wine and the liquor first, and put the food in last," he said. "Yes, I'm being selfish, Allex, but by God we've earned that booze and we're keeping it. The food we'll decide what we want and give the rest to the community kitchen. Agreed?"

"No argument from me. I doubt many in Moose Creek would appreciate the quality of the wine downstairs. Not that they couldn't learn, but I'm not about to hold a teaching wine-tasting party!" I laughed at the thought, and then sobered when it reminded me of Bob and Kathy and how generous they had been with me, especially with their friendship.

We lit up the basement and started hauling the cases of wine to the parquet dance floor. I selected a couple of bottles for our enjoyment during our stay and we each took a case up the stairs to the waiting trailer.

"This is going to take us a while," Jim lamented.

"It is what it is, Jim. We can't use the dolly. Even two cases are too heavy for me to drag up the stairs, and you've only got one hand for now. Don't worry about it. We will take however much time we need. If it takes two days or a week, that's okay. We're only one day from home."

Once I said that, the reality of our trip coming to an end hit me hard. For all the trauma, the injuries, the sorrow, the good and the bad events, it had been a remarkable adventure, one that I would remember and cherish the rest of my life.

*

A dozen cases of wine were now tucked into the forward most area of the trailer. When everything was in, we'd tie it down so it couldn't slide in case of a sudden turn.

"There are still a dozen cases down there! These people sure invested heavily into their habits," Jim observed.

"That's what Bob and Kathy considered it too: an investment. And one that brought them much pleasure," I said wistfully, thinking again about my friends.

"I've decided to do something I wasn't going to, Jim, and that's clean out the refrigerator. If we're going to be here for a couple days I think we will be more comfortable with that convenience. You might want to open a few windows and then stay outside until I'm done. It's bound to really stink."

I put on a face mask doused with some perfume from one of the guest rooms and cautiously opened the refrigerator. Much to my surprise and delight, it was nearly empty. A bottle of catsup and one of mustard sat in the door, and a hard as rock slice of cheese in the drawer, that was it. I put the two bottles and cheese in a garbage bag and tied it closed. We'd worry about it later. I wiped the inside of the refrigerator down with some cleaner from the bathroom and dragged the cooler over.

"Say, have you found a grill anywhere? We have steaks for tonight," I reminded Jim.

He eyed the plate I set the steaks on. "Those are huge. Why don't we split one tonight and the other tomorrow?" he suggested.

"Excellent idea. I've been organizing the downstairs pantry and found some canned potatoes. I thought those mixed with some rehydrated onions and heated up on the grill in foil packets would go well with the steaks."

"Sounds good to me," Jim said. "While I was outside, I noticed some darker clouds in the west, and the wind was picking up. We might want to cook early."

I seasoned the single steak with salt and pepper and set it back in the now cool refrigerator. The foil packets were ready for the grill, too. I fixed Jim and me a drink and stepped outside where he was starting the grill.

"How's your hand feeling?" I asked, handing him the vodka over ice.

"A bit sore. I think I overdid it today," he said. I noticed he had put the sling back on and was holding that hand close to his body.

"It's going to be that way for the next couple of days, Jim, no matter what you do or don't do, and it's going to take a month to heal. Do you want a pain pill? You can't have any more to drink if you take one though."

"I think I'll pass on the pill." He lifted his glass to me. "This tastes better."

The storm struck during the night with a fury I haven't seen in a very long time. The wind howled through the trees and the rain mixed with hail pounded on the glass. Lightning flashed every few minutes, followed by deafening thunder. The temperature took a nose dive and I snuggled deeper into my sleeping bag.

JOURNAL ENTRY: May 15

I had hoped the storm last night would have washed the ash out of the sky for a while. I was disappointed when all I could see was more dark clouds and a steady flow of icy rain.

~~~

Jim was standing next to me while I stared out into the gloom.

"Well, I suppose the good news is we don't have to go out in that mess," he said.

The hot coffee warmed my still aching chest as I sipped on my second cup.

"And without the temptation of a nice day, we should get a lot of packing done," I concurred.

"Anxious to get home, Allex?" Jim asked without taking his eyes off the falling rain.

"Yes, and no," I answered truthfully. "We've been gone for over a month now, and I miss my family. Yet in spite of all that has happened, I'm sorry to see our trip come to an end. How about you?"

"I wouldn't trade this past month for anything. Especially point B," he smiled and kissed me. I couldn't help but respond.

"That's been a surprise bonus." I returned his smile and went back to the kitchen before the conversation could get too serious.

"I think we should leave one, maybe two cases of wine in the hidden cellar," I said to Jim, "just in case we make it back here someday."

"I like that idea," he answered. "Gives us something to look forward to."

We stacked more boxes of wine in the trailer throughout the morning, and then tackled the liquor. The wine and alcohol took up more than half of the small trailer.

"I didn't realize there was this much to go," I said, gazing into the back of the packed hauler.

"Do we have enough boxes for all the loose cans of food?" Jim asked.

"I doubt it. Maybe we should check out a couple of the houses for more." I opened a drawer in the kitchen and removed the notebook I had so carefully kept of our finds, and thumbed through the pages. Two houses held promise for some plastic bins.

"We better wait until tomorrow, Allex, it looks icy out there," Jim said after opening the front door. All the time we had spent in the basement and packing, I hadn't once looked outside, and now, everything had a thin coating of ice.

"Looks like another early dinner." I wasn't really disappointed, it meant one more quiet evening together before going back to reality. What was reality? Here and now? Or there and then?

With the dinner dishes in the dishwasher, we settled down in front of the fire and played cribbage until dark. I lit a candle by the game board so we could continue after shutting the gennie down for the night.

"Allex, I'm done with cards for the night," Jim said, and blew out the candle. "Let's discuss point C…" His voice was soft and seductive in the dark.

May 16

The day dawned cool and dreary, however, the temps had climbed enough during the night to melt the coating of ice, making it possible for us to do some scavenging.

"Brr! It's chilly out there. I'm glad I brought that hooded sweatshirt and gloves," I said. I took a shower early so my hair could dry, and dressed in jeans with a long sleeved shirt. The belt with the holster had become as much a part of my attire as my shoulder holster once had. And I must admit I liked the belt holster better.

"You look different out of uniform," Jim remarked. "It's going to take some getting used to."

"I don't see any reason to keep wearing the fatigues when the chances are very slim we'll run into anyone." Jim looked disappointed. "In another month you'll be looking at civilian clothes too."

"I know. Still, you look good in a uniform…and out of one, too." He stepped closer and cupped my chin, delivering a gentle and promising kiss. The display of affection caught me off guard. I must admit though, it's kind of nice and something I've missed.

After I changed the tattered bandages on Jim's hand, adding plenty of antibiotic cream, we ventured out. The pavement was wet where the ice had melted and the grass crunched under our feet. Two doors down, where I had made notes of packing material, was almost a quarter of a mile away. The air was crisp and clean and felt good on my skin. Overhead, the clouds had thinned, though I think the grayness was now something that would be with us for a long time.

"Here it is," I said, checking the address against my pad of paper. "All I wrote down was 'packing stuff' and quite honestly I don't remember what I meant by that."

"Only one way to find out," Jim said and pushed the door open. The place was a mess! We both drew our guns.

"Someone has been here," Jim whispered. That was an understatement, considering every house we had been in was neat and orderly, and we left them the same way. This one looked ransacked.

We inched around the doorway, only to see even more disarray. We cleared each room on the first level and went upstairs. In the second room, we found them. Mickey, the young man we met weeks ago when we first hit Hwy. 41, and presumably his girlfriend, were in the bed, quite dead.

"From the dried vomit on their faces and the pillows, my guess is they OD'd from pills, and it has been over a week," I said, walking around the bed to get a better look. "See here, remains of gelatin capsules."

"He seemed so content," Jim commented, somewhat disappointed.

"We don't know what they've been through in the last couple of weeks, and honestly, it could well have been unintentional," I said. "Let's leave them be and get what we came for."

We found six new plastic tubs in the basement, along with several rolls of duct tape. When the home owners departed, they must have had these left over; they were brand new. We loaded the boxes on the wagon we brought along and headed back in silence, picking our way around the branches that had come down in the last storm.

"We may have to do this in stages, Jim. One of these bins filled with canned goods would be too heavy for me to lift, let alone carry up the stairs," I said. "If we fill one maybe a third of the way, then set it in the trailer, we can keep filling it from the next partial box until it's full. What do you think?"

"Sounds like a plan." He let out a long sigh. "I feel useless with only one hand. You're doing all the work and I don't like it."

"You're doing your share, Jim. I'll bring these up once they're filled and you can fill the one in the trailer while I get another. We're just adapting to the circumstances."

The two of us filled all six bins first with enough for me to carry. We set the first one in the trailer and I brought up another, then another, and I took the empty back down with me. By the time I had brought up all six, Jim was unpacking the fourth one. That gave me time to refill the emptied bins. Two hours later we had moved all of the canned goods into the trailer and secured them. We even took a couple of the heavier blankets from the house to tuck around the boxes. Blankets would always be useful.

"This is going to be one heavy load, Jim. Please tell me the Hummer is up to the task."

"More than up to it, Allex. These vehicles haul artillery around like it's not even there," Jim reassured me. "Are you up to driving it? Our next leg is a long haul."

"I'll be fine," I said confidently, even though I didn't quite feel it. "I kept out a box of linguini and a can of baby clams. Linguini with clam sauce would make a fitting dinner for our last night."

"Last night," Jim repeated.

"It does feel strange, doesn't it? We've been gone more than a month and now we'll be back home tomorrow. I know I should be exhilarated, though I'm not. I'm going to miss this. For all the bad that's happened there was also so much that was wonderful." I turned to him, waiting for him to affirm the good we've shared.

"What are we going to do, Allex? About *us*?" He posed the question we both had on our minds yet were afraid to ask.

"I don't know, Jim. Maybe we should let it play out on its own. I have a feeling that if we wait, it will all become clear. The solution is there, I know it. I just can't see it yet."

This was how I really felt, I realized. The solutions to these dilemmas always, *always* presented themselves at the right time. I slid my arms around his waist, resting my head against his chest, and we held each other for a long moment. I have so missed this kind of touch. Initially I felt a wave of guilt, then I reminded myself that Mark was dead, not me, and I was still a woman with wants and needs of my own.

CHAPTER 22

April 30

"Okay, the trailer is attached and secure. Are you ready to roll?" Jim asked, leaning on the Humvee, his hand back in the sling.

"As ready as I'll ever be." I had no problem admitting to myself that I was a bit nervous driving with so much weight behind us.

"Go ahead and pull out. I'll close the garage door, turn off the generator, and then lock the front door." Jim disappeared and the big overhead door lowered. A few moments later he climbed in beside me. "I put the spare key in the same place and turned off the gas at the tank."

I nodded and put the Humvee in gear, easing down the steep driveway.

*

Traveling on US 41 was easier this time since we were aware of the areas congested with abandoned vehicles. We passed through

Negaunee and then Ishpeming where the empty semi-trailer was still parked. It was all passing in a blur.

"It's been over a month," I said, frowning. "I'm not sure I will recognize the entrance to the mining road."

"I've got a GPS in my head, Allex, I'll find it," Jim assured me. And he did. I turned the big vehicle with its heavy payload onto a side road where he indicated and headed north.

"Wow, I would have missed that for sure!" Shortly after, I began recognizing the surroundings. When we came to the rough gravel, I slowed and asked Jim to get the map out.

"Don't trust me?" he asked with a grin.

"With my life! I only want to see how far it is to that wet area I marked on our way through here before."

He opened the side pouch where I had put the map. "Looks like maybe another five or ten miles."

I had slowed to twenty-five miles per hour and chugged along steadily until I saw some shimmering blue a half hour later.

"The pond has grown," I said. I stopped the Humvee when we came to an area where the road was under water. We both got out.

"This really isn't a problem for the Hummer, Allex," Jim said.

"Humor me, Jim. I want to be sure there is road under that water!" I took my walking stick and began to wade through the ten foot wide pool of water, probing as I went. Intent as I was, I didn't realize Jim was walking parallel to me, seven feet away – the width of the Hummer. "Feel anything missing?" I asked. He shook his head. "Me neither." I breathed a sigh of relief and we both trekked back.

"To be on the safe side, I'm going to lead you across on the same path we just checked," Jim said. "It'd be a bitch if we strayed a foot too far only to find the road was gone." Jim took the walking stick, centered himself in between our two paths and waited for me to pull closer. About midway through the deep puddle the Hummer started to bog down.

"It's the trailer, Allex! Stay straight and give it more gas – you're almost through!" He stepped out of the way and I accelerated, sending little waves splashing outward in both directions. The trailer started to slide as the front tires grabbed dry ground. Once completely free of the puddle I stopped and got out.

"Well, that was… exciting," I said, my hands shaking a little.

"You did great," Jim said, catching up to the Hummer. We looked out at the small lakes that had formed in the last month.

"I can see why this could cause road issues," I said. "We had very little snowfall this year. In a normal year, the meltdown of the snowpack would have made this unpassable for us."

We continued on, still moving slowly and cautiously. There wasn't any more water over the road, however, recent rains had made some areas slick with orange mud.

"Not being from around here, forgive my question of what may be common knowledge. What makes this mud orange?" Jim asked.

"There are two factors. The first is the area is iron-rich. Most wells have a lot of iron in them and need filters unless they are really deep. The other reason is the rain and snowmelt run along the ground and travel through fallen leaves, pulling the color. The water is literally stained with organic tannins and that settles into the ground."

We traveled slowly for another hour, when the sky started getting dark.

"Looks like we're in for more rain. Are you okay with the driving?" Jim asked.

"It won't be long, maybe another ten miles and we'll be back on pavement. I'm fine, really," I said as a crack of thunder roared at us and a streak of brilliant lightning split the sky. "Whoa! That came up quick." Another flash of light was followed ten seconds later by a long, slow, very loud roll. The next ten minutes was peppered with sky brightening flashes and far off thunder.

"It sounds like the storm may be moving off," I said hopefully. Then the sky opened up and we were deluged with heavy sheets of cold rain.

I held steady in the center of the gravel road, a white knuckle grip on the wheel. It was getting increasingly difficult to see.

"Hang in there, Allex, we're almost out."

We entered a more wooded area that would lead us to the mine road. Once again on pavement, I stopped to take a few deep breaths. The lightning and thunder were now coming simultaneously. The rain increased as the wind picked up and rocked the solid Humvee.

"I think we should find some shelter and wait this out, Jim. I don't like the idea of us being in a big metal box, pulling another big metal box, during an electrical storm!"

"I agree, but where?"

"The mine is just up the road from here," I said, making a hard left turn.

*

It was late afternoon when I pulled around the guard gates and drove past the administration buildings. In the artificial darkness caused by the storm the entrance to the mine itself sat, gaping like a giant maw. I pulled in and stopped. I got out of the car shaking from the adrenaline surge. Jim climbed out, still cradling his hand, and walked around looking at the structure in amazement.

"This is incredible! How did you know it was here?" he asked.

How did I explain the time I spent there, waiting for word if John was alive and trapped or dead and crushed beneath tons of rock after a cave-in? That felt like a lifetime ago, when it really had been less than ten months.

"The emergency manager got free tours," I said, covering up the painful memories with a fragment of truth. I looked around, noting the chairs and desk were gone, the monitors I had watched were gone too, and only the map was left on the wall.

"How far back does this go? It's too dark to see."

"At this level, another two hundred feet, then it turns and starts to descend in multiple switchbacks."

"I think what I'm going to do then, is pull back out of here and back the trailer in so we have access to our supplies without the chance of getting soaked," Jim stated, climbing into the Hummer while I moved off to the side and out of his way.

The gloom was oppressive as we worked to unload a few supplies from the Hummer.

"The rain hasn't slowed. If anything, it's even heavier," Jim said.

The rain came in gray sheets, and the thunder continued to boom with each flash of lightning, illuminating the recesses of this manmade cave. The intensity and briefness of the flashes left me blinded for a few seconds each time, to the point of having spots dancing in my eyes. I tried to keep my sight on the interior, however, the mesmerizing fury kept claiming my attention.

"We're not going anywhere tonight, so we might as well make camp," I sighed. So much for getting home today.

We turned the tent to face inward, in the event the rain drained into the shaft. "Even though we can't pound stakes into the concrete floor, I think enough supplies and us in the tent will hold it. It seems to stand well on its own," Jim said. He finished threading the final pole in the tent seams.

I set up the camp stove to fix an early dinner since we'd skipped lunch, and Jim lit the kerosene lantern to warm up the tent. It was decidedly chilly inside the mine entrance. While I fried chicken patties for sandwiches, Jim fixed us each a drink, leaning on the tailgate of the Hummer to enjoy his.

"Here's to one final adventure." He clinked his tin cup to mine.

"It was a pipe-dream to think we would make it home without one more happening to write about," I chuckled.

"Have you been writing down everything about our trip?" Jim asked suspiciously.

"Well, not *every*thing. Some things are just too private, and I'm not likely to forget those." I sat down next to him. "How's the hand?"

"Throbbing a bit, but not too bad."

"The initial healing will be less than a week. The severed nerve endings will take longer, as will the broken bone. I keep thinking how fortunate it was that your non-dominant hand was hurt. You can still use a knife, a fork, a pencil, even your weapon as you always did. Even though many things require two hands you'll have use of the three uninjured fingers in a day or so. In time you won't even miss that pinky."

We finished our sandwiches, washed down with a pleasant California red blend, and retired to the warmed tent to listen to the pounding rain.

CHAPTER 23

JOURNAL ENTRY: May 17

The storms haven't subsided. The lightning strikes shake the ground; the thunder is so loud it hurts my ears; and the rain pounding the ground never lets up – it would make a good torture method.

We walked further back into the mine to see if the distance and depth would block out some of the noise. It didn't work. The sound followed us and echoed off the walls, giving it an eerie tone. We did try a bit further, however, my claustrophobia kicked into high gear and I couldn't breathe.

We'll just have to wait it out. At least we have plenty of food, drink, and companionship. Jim now owes me almost a million dollars in cribbage losses.

~~~

May 18

It was mid-afternoon and the storms had finally stopped. There was only a mild foggy drizzle now, though a much heavier, dense fog hung just below the tops of the trees.

"We're less than an hour from home, Allex, I say we go for it," Jim said while he folded up his sleeping bag in preparation for taking down the tent.

"Yeah, let's do it. The rest of the route is all paved, so there shouldn't be any problems."

*

The first mudslide we encountered was ten minutes after we left the mine. We skirted most of it and continued on. The next one was worse.

Jim stood by the front bumper and stared at the eighteen inches of wet mud and sand that covered more than two-thirds of the pavement and stretched for ten feet.

"The Hummer might make it, I doubt the trailer will."

"Then we shovel," I said, getting the small collapsible shovel that was part of the camping gear.

Jim paced out the dimensions and marked where to dig. "We don't have to remove all of it, just enough to reduce the depth by half and wide enough for the left tires of the Hummer and the trailer," he concluded. I started digging. Jim spelled me, however he couldn't do much with the injured hand. He banged it once with the shovel and the pain took him to his knees, though he stoically said nothing.

We dug for an hour. Wet sand is heavy and my back ached so much I fantasized about the hot tub and the steaming, bubbling hot water. It was the only thing that kept me going, that and seeing my sons again.

"I think we can try it now, Allex," Jim said after he walked the length of the digging, kicking at the dirt occasionally.

"Good, because I don't think I could lift another shovel full." I got behind the wheel and drove right through, never hesitating, never stopping. Once I cleared the slide I sped up to a reasonable speed and within twenty minutes we pulled up to the stop sign at county road 695. I turned right, heading for my home.

"I'm just going to let them know we're back, Jim, then we can take the trailer to the lake house." I pulled into my horseshoe shaped driveway and spotted Eric out in the garden working in the late afternoon sunlight. Chivas came running to greet us.

Eric dropped the hoe he was using and followed the dog. "Mom!" He swept me up in his arms for a hug. I winced silently from the pain in my ribs. "It's so good to see you! We have all been really worried! Rayn! Mom's back!" His new wife stepped out of the house and came to us for hugs. Eric stepped over to the large metal triangle I've had for years and banged away on it.

"You're looking well, Rayn, how are you feeling?" I asked. I know it's only been six weeks but I was thinking she would be showing her pregnancy more.

"I'm doing great. Dr. James let us listen to the heartbeat a few days ago!" she answered.

The gonging alerted Jason, and soon everyone was gathered around. I almost wept with joy at seeing my family. They would never know that I had doubted this reunion at one point.

"I guess you will be wanting your house back, eh?" Eric said sadly. His arm was around Rayn's shoulders and she had taken on a blank look. Something was going on here, I could feel it.

Was this that moment when my decision would play out on its own as I told Jim it would? Many things ran through my mind in a space of a second or two.

"Actually, Eric, I've been considering moving into town with Jim and Tom. There's still so much work to be done," I said, like it was the plan all along. I saw Jim's head turn toward the conversation and he smiled. "Would you mind if you and Rayn stayed here?" I could almost see the relief slide off my son. "I'll come back for the rest of my clothes, but I need a few things now. I haven't been able to do laundry in days!" I slipped past everyone and let myself into the house, where I was greeted by Tufts. I picked him up and snuggled him, knowing I would have to leave him behind with Eric. I grabbed a few things from my closet, noting new items hanging there that must be Rayn's.

Eric had followed me in.

"Mom, thank you," he gave me another hug. "Please don't move into town unless it's really what you want to do." He hesitated before continuing, "I want you to know that I really love my brother and Amanda, but living with family in such tight quarters was getting on everyone's nerves. We've gotten along so much better in the last month with us here and them over there."

I was wondering if that was the tension I felt from them.

"Yes, Eric, this is what I want to do," I assured him. "We'll discuss the details another time. Right now all I want to do is get a hot shower and into some clean clothes. It's been a rough couple of days." I kissed his cheek and went back outside.

With assurances that we would all get together tomorrow in the afternoon at the lake house in town, Jim and I drove into Moose Creek.

"Pull over," Jim demanded. After I stopped, he reached across the console and pulled me into a quick kiss. "Couldn't you have given me some warning?"

"No, I couldn't, Jim, I didn't know until that moment. Remember when I said we needed to let the issue of *us* play out on its own? It just did." I put the Hummer back in gear and said, "Let's go home."

*

I drove down the long sweeping driveway slowly and carefully, parking nose in next to Tom's dark blue sedan. Jim would have to back the trailer up later.

Tom came out on the small cement stoop, shotgun in hand until he saw us emerge.

"I'll be damned! I figured if you two ever came back at all it wouldn't be for a couple more months!" Tom said, giving me a hug tight enough to crack another rib, and then shaking Jim's hand repeatedly. He gave up on that and delivered a quick, one-armed hug to Jim. I think he missed us.

"Hey, what did you do to your hand?" Tom asked with true concern when he noticed the bandages.

"Trailer slipped while I was changing a tire. No biggie," Jim said. "If you don't mind, I'm going to back the trailer into the barn and get it out of sight. Then we can empty the Hummer. Give me a hand?" Tom walked up to the barn and opened the big doors while Jim expertly backed the Hummer up and they disconnected the trailer from the vehicle. They unloaded the chainsaw and the camping gear into the barn to be dealt with later.

When we began removing our personal stuff from the Hummer, Tom noticed the cases of wine.

"Wow, what did you do, find a liquor store?"

"We'll tell you all about it when we're done, Tom, and *after* I get a shower and some clean clothes." I said.

*

I stuffed my soiled clothes into the washing machine and headed to the basement with what I brought from my house to shower and change. After days hunkered down in the cold, damp mine, hot water never felt so good. I had to stop myself from using it all and saved some for Jim.

I emerged from the lower level wearing a long sleeved ankle length dress of deep red. I ran my fingers through my short wet hair with a sigh. "Oh that felt good!" Both men were staring at me. For the last month, Jim had seen me only in jeans or BDUs, and I suddenly felt very feminine.

"Jim was telling me that you're moving in with us, Allex," Tom said. "I think that's a great idea." He handed me a drink, the ice cubes floating around in the amber rum.

I glanced at Jim. "Yes, I thought I would take that second bedroom downstairs. I know you use this spare room as an office, and besides, I've always preferred the lower level."

"Excellent! Jim was also telling me you got the EOC in the Soo up and running in only a few days. You'll have to tell me all about that."

"All in good time, Tom. Right now I'm sure Jim wants his shower, and I should put together some dinner for us." I stood. "Oh, and we're having a small get-together here tomorrow afternoon, just family."

*

Dinner was a simple pasta dish. I certainly did not feel like being inventive just to satisfy our hunger and the three of us were more anxious to discuss the road trip. We were all sitting on the upper deck enjoying the mild breezes off Lake Meade and the rest of the second bottle of wine we opened for dinner.

"First, tell me what's in that trailer," Tom said, his curiosity bubbling over. "It looks full."

"It *is* full," Jim answered. "Over half of it is booze and wine, which by the way, we're keeping."

"Jim, I've been mulling over what you said about that, how we've earned it," I said cautiously.

"We have, Allex, especially *you*," Jim stated emphatically.

"Oh, I don't disagree, quite the opposite, actually." I paused, trying to form my thoughts. "I think we should keep *all* of it. I know that sounds selfish of me, however *we* are the ones who risked our lives, literally, to get those supplies. Besides, that food will keep us from needing to tap into the town food pantry, which will mean more for everyone else." I turned to Tom. "How are the supplies holding up, Tom? I know it's only been six weeks, but I was pretty much out of touch long before we left."

"Marsha has done some deep rationing, so it's still okay. Plus, with fewer people to feed it will go further." Tom stopped himself from saying more, knowing my husband was one of those fewer mouths. "How much is out there?"

"We filled six tubs with loose cans and there were several cases of things like tomatoes and vegetables that were still shrink-wrapped," Jim said. "There's a lot of food out there."

"My rough estimate is that what we brought back would feed the three of us for six months," I said.

"Wow," Tom said.

"Much of it is gourmet stuff, which is logical considering where we found it. There are cans of white meat chicken, albacore tuna, clams, olives, capers and artichoke hearts, things of that nature," I added. "Some of it I would like to share with my family and maybe our clergy. For the most part though, it's ours, and I think we should be the ones who decide who gets it, rather than turn it over."

"I think Allex has a good point, Tom, and as she pointed out, we won't be taking anything from the community this way." Jim leaned back, took a sip of wine while leveling his gaze at me.

"Okay you two, what went on out there?" Tom burst out. "How is it you risked your lives?"

Jim and I exchanged glances.

"I don't even know where to start..." I said.

"I know you didn't want it discussed, Allex, however, I think Tom should know," Jim said softly.

"Perhaps," I said, turning to Tom, our close friend, "on the condition you never say a word to anyone. My sons must never know."

"What happened?" he asked gravely, concern etched deeply on his face.

"Promise me first, Tom," I said.

"Of course I promise, Allex." He looked from me to Jim and back to me. I looked at Jim and gave the slightest nod for him to start.

"To keep it as brief as possible, the second week out Allex was abducted by a gang of escaped cons and I was left for dead," Jim began.

"When they told me Jim was dead, I felt a grief second only to what I did when Mark died. After that, I didn't care what they did to me," I said.

"After I came to, I followed their trail only to find I was outnumbered twenty to one. I hated leaving her there." Jim stood. "I need something stronger than wine for this." He came back out with a tray, three glasses filled with ice, and our preferred liquor.

"Jim had traveled half the night with a severe concussion to bring back a troop of soldiers from the Soo," I continued the story.

"During that one day, though, she was beaten and tortured. Her toes were broken and dislocated, the soles of her feet were beaten with a belt buckle, and she suffered a cracked rib. She couldn't even walk," Jim said angrily.

"I still think that cracked rib came from hitting the tree," I said to Jim.

Tom was listening intently, stunned, looking from me to Jim as we spoke.

"When Jim showed up to rescue me, I felt more than relief. I feel that's when things changed for me. I was completely liberated from my past."

"Wait, back up. What tree?"

"I fell in the new river and almost drowned. The current, and something else, slammed me into a fallen tree where I held on until Jim pulled me out."

"She bounced off rocks, slammed her chest into a tree, and suffered severe hypothermia. This is one tough lady we have here, Tom," Jim said, smiling warmly at me.

"This was before the kidnapping?" Tom asked, still stunned.

"Yes, so she suffered bruises on her bruises." Jim took another swallow.

Tom turned to me. "Allex, were you…?"

"No, I was not sexually assaulted, but the rest of it was just as bad."

Tom leaned back in his chair. It rocked on the heavy duty springs as he thought. "You two certainly have been to hell and back. My vote – if I get one – would be for keeping what you've found. You've more than earned that right."

Jim and I silently nodded.

"What happened to those convicts?" Tom asked.

Jim snickered. "That is my favorite part! When I handed Allex her gun back, she walked up to the guy without a word, put the barrel to his forehead, and pulled the trigger. Then I had my next in command execute the rest of them."

Tom stared at me for a long moment. "I understand why you don't want the family to know about this."

"I'm exhausted, and we have a lot to do tomorrow. I'm going to bed," I said, standing.

"Can I ask one last question?" Tom stood also. "Are you two …?"

"Yes," I said and went inside.

CHAPTER 24

JOURNAL ENTRY: May 18

I slept late. I guess I needed the rest. I got up at nine and took another shower. I need to discuss filling the hot tub with my roommates. Once heated, the small spa wouldn't take much electricity to stay warm, but the startup drew a lot of power.

~~~

"Good morning," Jim said when I came up the stairs. "Coffee?"

"Does a fish swim?"

"Sleep well?"

"I did. I was exhausted. How did you sleep?"

"A real bed felt good, but lonely." He looked at me through the steam off his coffee. "I'm surprised you admitted to our new relationship so quickly, Allex."

"Why? Is it something to be hidden like we're ashamed of it?"

"No, of course not. I thought you might want to ease in to it though."

"Jim, if a relationship needs to be hidden, it's neither a good nor healthy relationship and should be dissolved. I'm certainly not going to be broadcasting the news, as there are some, like my sons, who would think it was too soon for me to be moving on. Not that I really care what others think as long as *we* are happy between us. The only ones that matter to me are my family, and some of them might not be completely understanding. Tom, on the other hand, needed to know. Since we all will be living together it would be difficult to hide and I wanted to be up front with him."

"Do *you* feel it's too soon for you to move on?" Jim asked cautiously.

"In another time, another life, perhaps it would be. This is a brutal world we now live in, and relationships are forged quickly. Look at Eric and Rayn. When someone is fighting for their very survival, it's a common, *normal* thing to seek out the comfort and companionship they need. To find that in someone I already know and care for is a wonderful, reassuring thing," I said honestly, reaching for his hand. "So, no, it isn't too soon for me to move on. If it weren't, I wouldn't have."

"Could it be that you're grateful to me for rescuing you?" he sadly.

"I'm certainly grateful that you did rescue me, although that whole situation merely brought the feelings into the light for me."

"That's very logical, Allex." He smiled and squeezed my hand, and then stood to refill our cups. "So what is on the agenda for today? Tom went in early to take care of some lingering paperwork so he could take the afternoon off for this shindig you're planning."

"The first thing we need to do is tackle the trailer and start bringing some of the wine and liquor inside. We can restock Tom's bar up here, and the bar downstairs, and most of the wine can be left in the barn until we have help that can use the dolly." I made some notes on the pad of paper he slid over to me. "Which reminds me, how is your hand feeling? Perhaps you should have Dr. James check it over."

"I'll do that. You do know that word is going to spread like wildfire that we're back, right?" Jim raised his dark eyebrows at me.

"Yes. I'm wondering if we should hold something like a press conference," I laughed. "Then again, I doubt the town would find our adventures very interesting, and I'm certainly not going to share our *mis*adventures."

"I think we should invite the clergy to this party today," Jim suggested offhandedly.

"Great idea, that way some of the stories we *can* share will have another outlet," I agreed. "I think we need to decide what is kept between us, though. Like the kidnapping and the pretend proposal."

"Why not share the proposal? It was one of the more amusing things on the trip and it will keep people distracted from what we're leaving out. I think we should keep it as honest as possible, Allex. We'll leave out the kidnapping and Point B, and especially Point C, how's that?" he said with a mischievous grin.

"Okay, I can live with that." I leaned across the island and gave him a quick kiss. "Time to get busy, Colonel."

*

We brought in two cases of mixed liquor and two cases of wine, one red, one white, and then divided it up between the upstairs bar and the lower one. I really had no idea where everyone would congregate.

Next we went through the first tub of mixed cans.

"I think some crabmeat salad on crackers would be tasty, and the crab would mask any staleness in the crackers," I said, setting aside a couple of cans.

"Sharing the crabmeat?"

"There's another whole case of it, Jim. Remember, this is family and close friends." I handed him two cans of salmon to put in the box we had already set on the dolly.

"Are you going to make more of those fishy pinwheels? They were really good," Jim said.

"I think I have enough time to make a batch of tortillas, so yeah, probably. If there isn't enough time, it'll be on the crackers.

One of the residents of the wealthy subdivision had thought ahead to buy a case of crackers, not realizing they would all go stale within a year. I remember hearing they could be freshened by heating them for ten minutes in a 350 degree oven. I'd have to try that and see if it worked.

Jim pulled the dolly one-handed into the attached garage, and then I pulled it up the two steps into the house. We unloaded everything onto the kitchen island.

"Why don't you have your hand looked at while I get started on this? I won't need any help for hours."

Jim silently nodded and left. From the cupboards I pulled out bowls and the hand mixer. Over the many years we were friends, I'd gotten to know Kathy's kitchen almost as well as I knew my own. Of course, now my kitchen is Rayn's kitchen. I need to talk to Eric about that more.

*

The tortillas were cooling and the two spreads were mixed and chilling. The crackers were set next to the baskets they would occupy. There was very little left to do, so I grabbed a bottle of red wine and went up the hill to visit with the nuns next door.

*

"When we saw the Humvee leave this morning, we were all hoping you had returned!" Sister Agnes said after giving me a welcoming hug. "How was the trip? Did you learn anything new?" she managed to ask before Father Constantine arrived from his quarters. I handed her the wine and turned to the priest. Of all of my new friends, I think I missed Connie the most.

"Allexa! I'm so relieved you're back," he said, giving me a bear hug. "Everyone in town has been worried about the two of you."

"Well, we're back, safe and sound, more or less." When they looked concerned I added, "We're fine, really. In fact, we're throwing a small welcome home party for ourselves, just family and close friends, and I'd like for you to join us, this afternoon, around three o'clock?" They agreed, and I said "Great. I can't stay, I have things to get ready." What I really wanted was a few minutes alone.

*

I found a chair on the lower deck and sat with a glass of water, trying to empty my mind. So much had happened in the last six weeks and I hadn't had time to absorb it all. I felt like I was still caught up in a whirlwind with my toes – my bruised and broken toes – barely touching the ground. Was moving in here such a good idea? I could have asked for any housing and gotten it. I could have insisted on my home back and Eric would have moved out. I really didn't know what the right thing to do was.

Being with Jim felt good. I didn't know yet if it was right or not, but it did feel good. He made me feel safe, and that said a lot to me. I hadn't felt safe for a very long time. Yet, him telling me that he felt lonely last night without me in his bed put pressure on me I didn't want. This was something we would have to discuss, and soon.

I sipped my water and watched the chilly blue water of Lake Meade lap at the shore fifty yards away. It was blissfully quiet. Too quiet, I realized. There are no boats on the water, no skiers, no children playing in the sand at the park's beach. There aren't even any of the annoying seagulls lofting about, and only one lonely goose. Wait. *A goose?* I stood for a closer look, almost spilling my water. I suddenly felt a surge of hope that things just might get back to normal for us one day. One day starts with one goose. It wouldn't be soon, this I knew, maybe not even in my lifetime, but some day it would.

And this was all I needed.

*

At two forty-five, I opened the can of black olives, drained them, and dumped them on the divided tray. I added a jar of green olives, and then some sliced pickles, both dill and sweet. It was a simple condiment tray that was rare food these days.

The crackers were in baskets beside the two dips, and the pinwheels would come out of the fridge when the first guest arrived.

Glasses were lined up above the bar, and the ice bucket was full.

"Table looks good Allex," Jim said, his hair still glistening from his recent shower. He gazed at me. "May I ask a favor? Would you wear that red dress you had on last night? It looks so good on you and as much as I've liked seeing you in BDUs and tight jeans, I really liked seeing you in a dress."

I could do that for him, for me. I grinned and scurried downstairs to change before anyone arrived.

*

"Mom, you didn't have to make food for us," Jason said eying the olives and then popped one into his mouth.

"Enjoy them," I said when I saw his delighted expression. "They are the only thing that can't be replaced. If we don't eat them soon, they'll go bad."

Rayn scooped some crab meat onto one of the oval crackers. "You mean there's more crackers?"

"Some, but we can make saltines, wheat, and cheesy crackers, and graham crackers, too when these run out. We'll do some baking classes soon."

I left them at the food table so I could talk with the nuns who had just arrived.

"I'm so happy to see you could make it," I said to the clergy group.

"We wouldn't have missed it," Father Constantine replied for all of them. "I must admit that we are all curious about your adventures."

"We'll do our best to entertain you," I laughed. "Sister Agnes, while we were at Sawyer I was given a bag of mail that was destined for Marquette and Moose Creek," I said. "You four are the ones who know best who is here, so I thought you would be the most logical to sort through it all and deliver it."

"We would be delighted to," she replied. "Will there be regular mail?"

"I doubt that, unless we set up a regular run to the base. It's highly unlikely they will be coming here just to bring mail." A regular run to Sawyer. Now that was an interesting thought.

*

Everyone had a few bites to eat and with a glass of their chosen drink, they all began to congregate in the large living room, settling into the comfortable leather couches or sitting on the floor. Tom had thoughtfully started a fire in the large fireplace to keep the chill away. A stiff breeze had picked up and the outside air had cooled significantly.

"I'll be the first to say that it's good to be home," I said, looking around at the faces of my family, my friends. Of course Jason, Amanda, and Jacob were here, as well as Eric, Rayn, and Emilee. Ken and Karen stood near the door, ever vigilant, and Joshua stood near the back, trying to stay out of sight. With the nuns and priest, and Art and Clare Collins, it made for eighteen of us, a tight and supportive group.

"So start at the beginning and tell us everything," Amanda said gleefully.

"Well," Jim started, "we took the new mining road all the way to Hwy. 41 and it took most of the first day."

"Now that county road 150 is open, getting to 41 will be easier," Tom said.

"Open? There was that rock slide, how did you get past it?" I asked.

"Keith Kay brought one of his earth moving bulldozers in from the field. It took him almost a week to move all the boulders, and then a crew to deal with the small stuff, and it's now open," Tom informed us. "You could have come home that route if you had known, but of course there was no way to let you know."

And had we known we wouldn't have had three extra days sheltered in the mine portal avoiding the electrical storms.

"Anyway, Walstroms had burned and collapsed, and the Shopmore store's roof caved in, likely from the big quake. There is no way to salvage anything further from either place," Jim continued. I noticed Tom taking notes.

"We found a house in a nice subdivision to stay in overnight," I said, "and we stayed for two days, checking out the rest of that neighborhood for anything salvageable."

"It was our first encounter with bodies," Jim stated flatly. "A family of four; we put all of them in one room, so they would be at rest together." The room got very quiet.

"Were there more?" Art asked solemnly.

"The next day we found a murder-suicide in one of the other houses," I said. "After that, we headed to Sawyer."

"Why go to Sawyer, Mom?" Jason asked.

"I needed information on the rift and on my troops that went to the Soo," Jim told him. "That *was* the main purpose of this trip."

"What we didn't expect was they weren't going to let me, a civilian, onto the base."

"So I made her a lieutenant," Jim laughed. "And no one dares question the top ranking officer when I called her that."

"Do we have to salute you now, Mom?" Eric teased and we all had a good laugh.

"Did you get to see the rift the earthquake caused?" Father Constantine asked.

"First hand," I said quietly.

Jim put his arm around my shoulders. "She fell in." That caused quite the stir of questions, which we sidestepped for now.

"The Army Corp of Engineers built two bridges across the rift, which is about five hundred feet across at Superior and varies in width all the way to what was Gladstone. They are in the process of building a concrete and rock dam to stop the flow into Lake Michigan. It's really quite impressive. We crossed to the other side at the one bridge that's military guarded," I went on.

We spent another hour telling everyone about Annie and Glenn, and the Goshens, including our return visit to their homesteads. As agreed, we left out the kidnapping, so also left out the situation with Andrea and Patsy and the massacre in Yardley.

"Colonel, did you make it to the Soo?" Rayn asked, naturally curious about her fellow soldiers.

"Yes, we did, Sergeant. The battle with the Canadians ended with the big quake, so everything was fairly quiet there," Jim replied. "I had a great deal of inspecting to do, and reports to file, so we stayed close to a week."

"During that time some of the more senior officers kept hitting on me, so the Colonel came up with a plan to stop them," I interjected, letting Jim explain the rest.

"I knew we were always under watch, so I let our 'spies' see what they believed to be me proposing to Allex," Jim said.

Wow, I didn't expect the room to go dead silent. "I wasn't and didn't propose, though if they thought Allex was 'my woman' they wouldn't dare approach her. What we couldn't let anyone find out was that she wasn't really military. It worked."

"Meanwhile I kept busy setting up their Emergency Operation Center, which the ranking major had let close," I said looking at Tom. "It was something I knew I could do and had been trained for, and already having the expertise fit with my new military image."

"Since Allex had gotten two computer geeks to get the base back online, the word of our 'relationship' made it back to Sawyer before we did," Jim continued.

"Actually, it was all very comical, but I guess you had to be there to find it as funny as we did," I added when no one even cracked a smile.

"We stayed a couple more days at Sawyer while I finished some final paperwork, which included my... retirement papers," Jim announced. "In three more weeks I will be officially retired from the Army."

"You will always be Colonel to us, Sir," Eric said proudly and fondly. "May I ask how you hurt your hand?"

"I was changing a tire when a tremor hit and the jack slipped. Allex got me back to Sawyer where the field medic amputated my little finger, which was crushed beyond repair. The ring finger is broken and will be fine," he answered, holding up the freshly bandaged hand.

"After that we went back to the house we stayed in on our way out," I picked up. "We loaded up a trailer we found and came home."

"Not quite," Jim corrected me. "We had just made it to the paved mining road when the storms hit, and we took refuge in the mine. Three days of lightning, thunder, and heavy rain in a cold and damp cave was about our limit. We dug our way through mud slides and here we are!"

"Those storms were bad here, too," Tom said. "We shut down the generator during the storms to prevent it from getting fried."

I was quite pleased that we were able to tell our travels in such a brief yet complete way. After two hours of almost non-stop talking, my throat was dry and I was ready for a drink!

*

I had taken my spiced rum on the rocks out onto the big upper deck for some air, while the others helped themselves to more food.

"Mom," Jason said, following me outside, "I have the feeling you didn't tell us everything about what went on."

"You don't need to *know* everything," I said. "Besides, much of it was a long, boring drive. Give me some time to be home, please. It's been a trying and complicated six weeks, Jason. I can't just dump six weeks of events into two hours!"

*

After everyone had gone home, the three of us cleaned up the few dishes and glasses. It was late, and although I had slept in, I was suddenly very tired. The air outside was once again dropping in temperature in spite of it being May. I think the past several months of a mild winter were now being paid for. Tom put another log on the fire and we pulled up chairs to enjoy the warmth and one final drink before heading off to bed.

"I think that went well, don't you?" Jim said, stretching his long legs out in front of him.

"Yes, it did, and Jason is already asking for more details. He senses we left a lot out."

"Well, you did," Tom said. "I mean I understand you don't want them to know about the kidnapping, but the details of everything else were pretty sketchy. They're going to be curious as well as concerned."

"I will tell them more as it comes up, Tom," I stated. "So much happened that it's hard to talk about just yet. They will have to be patient... and so will you." I smiled at my long-time friend.

"What's on the agenda for tomorrow?" Tom asked.

"I think we need to deal with the trailer contents as soon as possible. And that means getting it inside where we can inventory all of it," Jim said. "What kind of hours are you keeping at the township hall? We're going to need help moving things. With this bum hand I can't do a great deal yet."

"I'm taking tomorrow off," Tom said. "Maybe even the next day." He looked at us. "Damn, it's good to have you back!"

"Now that that is decided, I'm going to bed." I tossed back the water in the bottom of my glass and set it in the sink. "Good night, Tom."

As I came out of the bathroom after having brushed my teeth and washed my face, Jim was there, looking out the glass door of the walk-out basement.

"Jim, we need to talk about our arrangements," I said, broaching the subject gently.

"Yes, we do, Allex. I cherish the time we spend in the same bed, but I've slept alone for so long I don't think I can share a bed every night and get enough sleep," he said apologetically.

I chuckled. "And here I thought I was going to be saying that." I kissed him softly. "Join me whenever you want, and I'll do the same." With that, I went into my room, leaving the door slightly ajar. I heard him running water in the bathroom. A few minutes later, I felt the mattress give beside me as Jim snuggled up and we fell asleep.

CHAPTER 25

May 20

Jim left the house early to meet with his security team. He was anxious to know what had gone on in town during the last six weeks, though he did promise to be back in an hour to start on the inventory.

"I'm going to run this mail bag up to the Sisters so they can start sorting. I'm sure once people find out there is mail, they'll be anxious to know if they have any," I told Tom.

"I'm going to set up some sawhorses and planks so we can organize all of your booty," Tom grinned, "so take your time."

*

I found Sister Margaret at the supply shop after there was no answer at the house.

"Good morning, Allexa. It was delightful to hear about your travels last night. Thank you so much for inviting us," she said.

"I'm happy you could join us. I've brought the mail bag I mentioned. With the meticulous records you kept during the flu sweep, I know you will be able to sift through this quickly. I did notice a certain amount of junk-mail. Maybe those who don't get any mail might enjoy the catalogues and circulars, even if they're out of date and unusable."

"What a generous thought. I'll be sure that nothing is wasted," Sister Margaret said, taking the canvas bag from me.

*

I met Jim as I was walking down the driveway. We continued arm-in-arm, mostly from habit from when he helped me walk on bruised and broken feet, partly just because.

With Tom manning the dolly, he and I moved three twelve bottle cases at a time down into the empty wine cellar. We left the boxes stacked, not seeing any reason to put things away just yet. Next were the cases of liquor. Again, we stacked them out of sight. Moving the tubs of canned goods was proving to be more difficult considering how heavy they were.

"How in the hell did you two get these in here?" Tom grunted.

"We didn't; we filled them in place," Jim said. "Why don't we take two of those plastic crates over there, and partially empty this first tub? That should make it easier to move." We worked steadily for an hour, sorting the cans of food as we emptied a crate or tub.

I was taking an empty crate back to the barn when I noticed Sister Margaret coming down the driveway.

"I'm so glad you're here, Allexa!" she exclaimed excitedly. "You have a letter!"

"Me? A letter?" I took the envelope from her and saw the return address was from my sister! I turned away without saying a word. The emotions that swept through me would be hard to describe: relief, happiness, even dread on what news may be inside. I walked past the garage where Jim and Tom were sorting cans, and into the house. In my basement room I closed the door before I carefully opened the letter.

Dear Allex,

I hope you get this, I really do. We hear so little about what is going on in the Upper Peninsula and what we do hear is all bad. I so want to believe that you are alright.

I can't thank you enough for nagging me into prepping! I know I was a reluctant student, but after that first ice storm when I lost power for a week in the winter, and I had enough food and water and a camp stove to cook on, well, I knew you were right and just looking out for me. Things got a bit rough for a while after the ash cloud, but I'm doing okay.

When that big quake hit in December I was so worried about you. Then when the flooding started, I was worried about ME. You know how I've always wanted waterfront property? I got it now! Well, almost, sort of. I only have to hike a half mile to get to the new shore! I dug out one of Daddy's old fishing rods last week and went fishing. You remember the glass rod we found under the wooden steps at the lake? I thought it might bring me good luck. I didn't catch anything, but at least I remembered how. It reminded me of all the times we went camping. We learned so much back then, didn't we?

I'm going to keep telling myself that you got this letter. I don't know if there is any way for you to write back, but I won't give up hope.

I love you sis!

Pam

"Allex, are you in here?" Jim called out, knocking on my door. He opened it and saw me weeping. "Allex, what's the matter?" He pulled me into a hug and I handed him the letter. "Oh, this is good news, isn't it?" he asked after reading it, still holding me. I could only nod.

I went into the bathroom to blow my nose and wash my face.

"It's wonderful news, Jim," I said when I returned. "I didn't realize just how much I missed my sister. To know she survived the ash clouds fills me with joy! I wish there was some way I could let her know I got her letter and that I'm fine and so are the boys." I sat back down next to him.

"We'll figure something out, Allex, I promise."

*

We worked for the rest of the day sorting and stacking cans. There was so much there.

"You two made quite a haul," Tom said when we were finally done. "What are you going to do with all of it?"

"Most of it will be for the three of us," I said, looking at Jim for confirmation.

"It's not going to the town?" Tom questioned.

"Our primary mission was to find my men in the Soo, and a safe route to Marquette, not to scavenge food for the town," Jim asserted. "That we found some makes it ours."

"I see."

"Maybe you don't, Tom, you weren't here a year ago. I've given this town enough. I gave them my own food and supplies and they gladly took it. I gave them my knowledge and my council, and they refused it. I've done enough." I paused for a moment, looking at Jim for support. "I'd like to give some of this to my sons, though they also are on a tight learning curve to fend for themselves and to be honest, they've got more years ahead of them than we do." I looked at my two best friends. "Jim and I have been to hell and back, Tom. I think we've earned the right to be a bit selfish and to enjoy our lives now and that includes a bit of gourmet food and good wine." I grinned at him, hoping to ease the tension. He nodded thoughtfully.

"I suggest we put it back in the bins, labeled, and take it downstairs," Jim said. "You can decide now or later what you want to give the boys, Allex."

"I'll wait. Maybe Rayn is having cravings for something special."

May 21

The temperature was even colder this morning, almost as if we were entering a second winter, or maybe the winter we didn't have. While at Sawyer, I heard the winter on the Keweenaw was brutal, with heavier than normal snow and subzero temperatures.

"Do you need me for anything at the office, Tom?" I asked. "I need to get with Eric about the garden and the greenhouse. They're going to need most of my seeds, however, I plan on resurrecting these raised beds for us and I'd like to do it soon."

"Do you really think things will grow this year, Allex?" Tom asked, looking up into the ever present dark clouds as he was leaving for the township hall.

"I don't know, but I want to try. I'm also going to ask Jason about doing a plastic dome over these raised beds to help magnify and retain what sunlight we do get."

*

I left Jim a note telling him I took the Hummer and would be back within an hour. I didn't like taking his vehicle without his previous knowledge, but I didn't know where to find him. On the outside chance he might be having a security meeting at the offices, I stopped there first.

"Yes, they're in a private session right now, Allex. What did you need?" Tom informed me.

"I just wanted him to know I took his ride. Part of my going to see Eric is getting *my* car back."

I found Eric and Rayn in the greenhouse watering the foot high seedlings.

"Those are looking great. I see tomatoes, peppers, and that's squash – what kind?" I asked my son.

"Summer and winter both. The zucchini should fruit quickly once it warms more," Eric answered. "And the pumpkins will need all the time we can give them."

"I'll be back to talk more about it. Right now though, I need one of you to drive my car over to the township so I can give Jim his Hummer back. It should only take us a few minutes," I said. "Oh, and can you help me get my bicycle down from its hooks? That will be so much easier for me to use around town than the car and faster than walking." We removed the peach colored bicycle from the barn and put it in the back of the spacious Humvee, along with the matching helmet and a tire pump. It had been a long time since I'd ridden it, though they say you never forget how. Having Eric drive my car over would give me a few minutes to talk with him privately when I took him back.

I left the keys in the Humvee and we drove back to the house. As soon as we left the office parking lot, I asked Eric what was going on.

He sighed. "I'm not really sure, Mom. Maybe it's Rayn's changing hormones because of the pregnancy, but she and Amanda are constantly bickering, and that's with us living in your house! When we were all together, it was worse. So I wasn't looking forward to having to go back." He paused like he wanted to say more but wasn't sure if he should. "Some of it I can understand, and in part it's because of Emilee."

"Emi? I don't understand."

"Because your house is so small, Emi's been sleeping over there, and… her behavior is changing." He stopped the car on the side of the road and turned to me. "If you are really, really sure about letting us stay there, I'd like to make some changes."

"Like what?"

"I'd like to eliminate the TV room, making that our bedroom, change the bedroom into a nursery, and put in a bed for Emilee to get her back with us," he said. Obviously he'd been thinking this over.

"I think that's a great idea, Eric. If you were waiting for my permission, you have it." How could I say no when there was so much at stake? The look of relief on his face said it all to me. "I'm sure we can find a spare twin bed for Emi somewhere." The Eagle Beach house instantly came to mind. "On another matter, sometime soon I'd like us to take an inventory of my long term storage buckets."

"Why?"

"Because I want some of them." I looked sharply at my son. "You took over my house, Eric, not all of my possessions. Between you, me, and Jason, we will decide who wants what and divide it three ways."

"There will be four of us soon," Eric muttered.

"And there are three with Jason, and three with me," I reminded him. "Plus you have the greenhouse now, and I expect you to share in that because that's what I would do." I patted his hand on the steering wheel. "Don't worry, it will work out, it always does."

*

I took a bucket of rice, several boxes of pasta, some flour, salt, sugar and yeast: basics I need no matter where I am. In the food storage shed I found a bucket dated "y2k". It was hermetically sealed seeds, designed for long, long term storage, all heirloom, and from my brother. This was what I would start my new garden with.

I piled some of my clothes in the back of the Subaru and went home. Rayn and I had gone over what I had, and she kept some of the items that fit her and that would be wearable as she continued to get bigger, like t-shirts and no-waist style dresses. We also arranged a day for me to take her "shopping" at the supply store.

As I drove past the offices I noticed the Hummer was gone. Hoping to find Jim at home so I could get my bicycle, I went straight there.

"I hope you don't mind I borrowed the Hummer for a few minutes," I said to Jim when I found him in the big barn, tinkering with my bike.

"Not at all," he replied. "Nice bike, and it looks new."

"I got it a year before the first quake and just haven't had a reason to use it. I think it will be a great way to get around town."

"I wish we had a half dozen of these for the security team. I don't like having to put them on foot, but we need to start conserving gas." He filled and tested the tires.

"Are we getting low on fuel already?" This was a concern Tom and I knew would happen, though I didn't expect it so soon.

"Not really, but the sooner we start rationing the longer supplies will last."

"Maybe we should put the word out we need bicycles, and have the community check the garages of their new homes," I said. "They could take whatever they find to the nuns at the supply store and you could take your pick. I'm sure there is someone that can make any repairs necessary. The big issue will be tires and tubes."

"The added benefit of the security team on bikes will be the town seeing us setting an example, and it will encourage them to conserve too," Jim finished my thought.

"I'm going to take *my* bike for a spin. See you here for lunch?" After he nodded I headed up the driveway, giddy with excitement.

I headed up Dutch Street and turned at the old post office, waving to a group seated under the shelter at the park. I rode past the school, the cold wind blowing through my short hair. There was a sense of freedom to be moving so fast under my own power. I pulled into the parking lot of the supply store and stopped, slightly out of breath. Sister Lynn was just coming out.

"Oh, my, that looks like fun," she giggled.

"In an effort to start conserving gasoline, the colonel wants to put the security guys on bikes. Can you help get the word out for everyone to check their places and to bring all bicycles here?" I told her of our plan.

With renewed enthusiasm I rode down to the township hall, just in time to see a motorcycle with a trailer pull into the lot.

I leaned my bike against the building. "Hello, can I help you?" I asked.

"Perhaps *I* can help *you!*" the man replied with a smile. He had dark hair and dark eyes, and although he wore a leather jacket and a helmet, he didn't strike me as the biker-type. I quickly chastised myself. I tried not to stereotype others any more. It just didn't work in this new world we lived in.

I held out my hand. "I'm Allexa Smeth."

"Harold Wolfe, purveyor of seeds and tinker, at your service," he introduced himself with a bow of his head and a firm handshake.

"Well, Mr. Wolfe, please come in to our offices and meet the mayor," I said, opening the door. I stepped inside after him and went directly to Tom's office. "Tom, we have a visitor. Mr. Wolfe, this is our mayor, Tom White."

Tom stood, surprised at the new face, and extended his hand.

"Harold Wolfe, seller of garden seeds and tinker," Harold said.

"Forgive me, we don't get visitors anymore," Tom stated. "What can we do for you?"

"For the past year I've been traveling, selling the seeds I've collected over the years, and helping to repair things if I can."

"What kind of seeds do you have, Mr. Wolfe?" I asked. I must admit I was very curious about what he may have brought with him.

"Harold, please. Mr. Wolfe was my father," he laughed. "As for my seeds, everything is heirloom or heritage and grows in the cooler, short seasons. My goal is to spread food that can be grown again and again, by saving the seed. Many of the seeds available prior to the crash were genetically modified with a kill-gene, and either would not grow again, or would not be true to the parent plant."

"I'm a believer in heirloom seed myself," I said.

"Ah, then you know how crucial it is to our future!"

"What is the price of this seed?" Tom asked skeptically.

"It's all negotiable. I ask only for a place to stay while I'm here and one meal a day. Plus some gas when I leave so I may continue to spread the gardens. I like to think of myself as a Johnny Appleseed of vegetables," Harold chuckled.

"What kind of guarantee do we have that this seed will grow?" Tom asked, ever thinking about the good of his town.

"Life doesn't offer guarantees anymore, Mr. White. However, I plan to stay long enough to prove the seed germinates. Growing it is up to you," Harold said.

"Fair enough," I said. "We have a large meeting room you can set up in if you need to display. And quite honestly, I'd like to see what you have. It's still a bit early for us to be planting, and with this current cold spell, I'm not sure when the ground will be warm enough, but I know everyone is anxious to start growing something, anything."

*

Tom and I helped Harold bring in some boxes from the trailer and set them on a table. Harold opened one for us to see a bunch of water bottles filled with seeds.

"That's an interesting way to transport," I commented.

"Oh, not just for transport, it's how I store them. The bottles are air tight and water tight, which protects the seeds from the elements. Back in Virginia I used to keep them all in my 'hidey hole' under the back porch. It worked extremely well."

"How do you get more seeds?" I asked.

"Well, last year at the beginning of summer, I stayed in the community I sold to and helped them grow it. My price was just a couple of plants of each variety, and I processed those seeds, and then moved on. It was a win-win for everyone. Most of my seeds I harvested from the first fruiting, which was before the ash cloud hit." He seemed to drift away for a moment. "Those were some good people and I wonder how they're doing."

"Whose bike is out front?" Jim asked as he came into the meeting room.

"Harold Wolfe, this is Colonel James Andrews, chief of our security force," Tom introduced the two. "Harold just arrived to sell us garden seeds."

We spent some time helping Harold sort the bottles out by type of seed.

"It's a bit late to start tomatoes and peppers, although I might want some for next year," I said, looking at the different types of tomatoes listed on the bottles. "What kind of veggies do you two like?" I asked Tom and Jim, realizing I didn't know their preferences.

"The edible kind for me, Allex," Jim teased.

"Just don't make me eat spinach," Tom added.

"Then slow-bolting Swiss chard is for you, Mr. White. It's sweeter," Harold said knowingly. "Are you the gardener of the family, Ms. Smeth?"

He zeroed right in on the three of us being together. "Yes, Harold, I am." It was best he knew upfront how tight we were. "We're going to leave you to finish setting up however you prefer. This building is quite secure. Tom, Jim, can we go over some business?"

*

"This could be the boost the town needs, Allex," Tom was the first to say once we were behind the closed doors of his office.

"I agree," Jim concurred. "We're starting to have minor scuffles among the residents. Everyone is getting bored. A garden to tend will give the people something to do and pull them closer together."

"I know there are a couple of vacant rooms at the Inn. We can put him up there if that's okay, and Marsha can give him his one meal per day. My guess is that he will seek a second meal from anyone willing to feed him," I said.

"You've got good instincts, Allex, what do you think of this Mr. Wolfe?" Jim asked me.

"I feel he's sincere, although I suggest we keep an eye on him. Why don't we have him for dinner tonight? That way we can get a better feel for him and decide if his motivations are what he says they are."

"I know you can handle yourself, Allex, but I don't want you alone with him, okay?" Jim said. I patted his cheek and agreed.

*

"Harold, as you might have surmised, the three of us make most of the decisions in town, and we've unanimously decided to accept your offer," Tom said. "We'll put you up at the Inn in the center of town. You will also get the one meal per day you've requested. It will be your choice if you want to display your seeds here in the offices or take them with you to the Inn. Tonight we would like you to be our guest for dinner. Colonel Andrews will check you in with the proprietress there, and show you where to come for dinner, say around six-thirty for cocktails?"

"Thank you, Mr. White, cocktails will be a nice treat." Harold locked eyes with me as he left.

As they walked out the door I heard Jim quietly say, "She's mine."

*

I had just enough time to get home and put together a one-rise batch of bread in time for dinner.

By six o'clock, the table was set, bread was baked, and the salmon patties were seared and waiting to go in the oven for the finishing touches. The rice pilaf with mushrooms was done and the three-bean salad was chilling. Jim, Tom and I stepped out onto the deck with a cocktail.

"Any thoughts on how to deal with Wolfe?" Tom said.

"I don't know if there's anything to *deal* with, Tom," I said. "Let's give him a chance. He's either honest or he's not. We'll find out soon enough." I shivered. "It's getting cold. I'm going back inside."

"For being the end of May it feels more like October," Tom observed, once we were all inside again and warming by the fireplace.

"And the clouds are back, darker than before," Jim added. "Allex, are you going to be able to plant anything in this cold?"

"If it doesn't warm up soon, maybe not. I'm going to do root crops first: potatoes, carrots, beets, rutabaga, turnips. And I'll cover the beds with plastic until they germinate," I said. "Tomorrow I'll talk to Jason about some kind of tent or shelter for over that area to help hold in the heat. Eric has tomatoes and peppers in the greenhouse. I could bring some back, though they're better off right there for now."

There was a knock on the door. Our guest had arrived.

*

"That was wonderful," Harold said, wiping his mouth with the napkin. "I haven't eaten that well in ages!" Jim moved to pour more wine, and Harold put his hand over his glass. "One glass is my limit, thank you. So, what are you looking to plant this year, Ms. Smeth?"

"I was telling Jim and Tom that because it's so cold still, I thought I'd start with root crops until we can devise some kind of heat retaining shelter," I answered. "We were lucky this past winter for weather. It was exceptionally mild, considering. It could be because we were on the northern edge of the cloud and that the Keweenaw blocks a lot of our bad weather. I have a feeling our luck has just run out." I gazed out the vast windows, seeing dark clouds accumulating over Lake Superior.

"Tell us more about the last place you were at, Harold. Oh, and where are you from again?" Jim asked.

"I'm originally from a small town in Virginia. After my wife and daughter were taken during one of the flu outbreaks, I had no reason to stay there and decided to travel with my seeds," he said. "The last town I stayed in was Andersonville, just south of Crystal Falls. Nice town and nice people. As I mentioned, I left there before Yellowstone blew, so just before the ash cloud. Once the eruption happened I hunkered down on a farm north of Escanaba with an elderly couple for the duration. Another win-win situation. They needed the extra help and I needed a place to stay."

"Where are you off to next?" Tom asked.

Harold laughed. "I have no idea."

"One last thing to cover," Jim said. "I'm sure you are aware that the country is under martial law, and that includes us, although my security force is pretty lenient. If you have a weapon, please keep it secure. Curfew is ten at night until six in the morning."

"I will keep that in mind, Colonel. On that note, I think I will bid you goodnight and head back to my room." Harold stood. "Thank you again for a wonderful meal and a delightful evening."

After he left, I turned to Jim, "We have a curfew?"

"No, but *he* does."

CHAPTER 26

JOURNAL ENTRY: May 23

Even though the air is still chilly this morning, the winds have died down to nothing. I decided it was as good of time as any to start working on the raised beds up by the big barn. I found a rake and a hoe in the barn and got to work. I will have to find some way to create a compost pile for all the leaves and weeds I'm removing – I don't think my friends did much along that line.

~~~

"That's starting to look good, Allex," Jim said when he came back to the house for some lunch.

"I thought I would start with getting the leaves and debris off the eight beds first. After lunch I think I'll dig up two, maybe three of the beds and try to get at least some potatoes in the ground." I dusted the dirt off my hands on my already dirty jeans. "Raised beds are nice for weeding and harvesting, though not being able to rototill them creates even more work, in my opinion."

*

It was late in the afternoon by the time I finished getting the potatoes, carrots, and seed onions into the freshly turned soil, and I was more than ready for a break. After washing up, I took my bicycle up the steep driveway and hopped on. It was a short ride to the supply shop and I wanted to check with the nuns about when they might start asking the town for more bikes.

"Oh, my goodness! Where did all of these come from?" I was amazed to see over a dozen adult bicycles and a few children's bikes parked in the lot behind the supply trailer.

Sister Lynn looked surprised. "Isn't this what you asked us to do, Allexa?"

"Well, yes. I just didn't expect results so soon!" I said, truly impressed. "How did you manage to get the word out so quickly?"

"Don't forget we also run the school," she giggled. "Many of the parents volunteer and we've created our own 'calling tree', except it's by word of mouth. Some of these bikes showed up overnight and some this morning. Is this enough?"

"I think it's more than enough. Although, this would be a good place for anyone to get transportation if they want it," I said. "I'll let the colonel know he can take his pick. Thank you!" I hopped back on my bike and headed up the street toward the school. Beyond that was Bradley's Backyard, the township community garden.

"It's good to see someone working here," I said to the person raking smooth a section of ground. He straightened up, stretching his back, and grinned. It was Harold Wolfe.

"Good afternoon, Ms. Smeth. Have you come to help?" he grinned.

"No, I have my own gardens to tend," I replied. "Why are you working the ground, Harold?"

"Someone has to," he said, setting the rake aside and walking toward me. "I took a walk around your quaint little town this morning and spotted this area. It was an educated guess that this is the community garden spot, is that correct?"

"Yes. You don't have to work it though, that should be done by the residents. They have to learn to fend for themselves," I said a bit too harshly.

"I understand that, however, if they see someone working in their behalf, they may feel the pressure to assist." He wiped his hands on his trousers. "As a matter of fact, there was someone here earlier. She had to leave to fix lunch for the school kids." Harold looked like he wanted to say more. "May I be candid, Ms. Smeth?"

"Of course."

"The colonel has deep feelings for you from what I can tell, and is understandably possessive of you. I feel quite uneasy around him. Would you please assure him I am not a threat?"

"I will do that, Harold, and please call me Allexa," I said. I heard some loud shouting coming from the other side of the Inn. "Excuse me!" I said, and peddled my bike as quickly as I could, just in time to see two men in a fist fight.

Almost at the same time Ken and Karen pulled up in their car and jumped out.

"Hey, what's going on here?" Ken ran up to the fight as the older man knocked the other one to the ground.

"He's been making moves on my wife!" he snarled.

"No I haven't, and she's not just your wife, she's my …" the younger one said, getting to his feet. The older man landed another punch before the boy could finish. The younger one only pushed back as if he didn't want to fight. Just as Ken started to step in between them the older one pulled a knife and thrust it, stabbing Ken instead of his intended victim.

"Ken!" Karen screamed and pulled her service revolver.

"No, Karen!" I yelled too late. She was already pulling the trigger. The report echoed off the back of the building, the sound ricocheting off the external bricks of the fireplace on the other side, and the man went down.

We both ran to Ken's side. Blood was oozing out of his side and he struggled for breath. "Stay here, I'll get Dr. James!" I sped away in the scout car, leaving Karen crying on the cold ground with Ken in her lap, bleeding profusely. The younger man knelt in the sand and gravel weeping over his assailant.

We returned a few minutes later with Dr. James driving the ambulance. While the doctor examined Ken, I took vitals on the gunshot victim. I couldn't find a pulse or a heartbeat. The shooting was at such close range I would have been surprised if Karen had missed. I left him lying there, mourned by his victim, and helped Dr. James tend to Ken.

Jim wheeled the Hummer in next to the ambulance and jumped out.

"What happened?" he demanded, and then saw me covered in blood. "Allex, are you hurt?" he almost whispered. I looked down at my shirt seeing the red splotches for the first time, my arms also streaked with wet crimson.

"Not my blood, Jim. Help us get Ken on the gurney."

"The wound doesn't look too deep, but I need to get Ken into surgery immediately," Dr. James said. "Allex, can you assist?" I nodded and while Dr. James climbed in back with Ken, I drove the ambulance to the hospital Mark had founded.

*

We spent over an hour in surgery. Dr. James was good, but not as experienced as Mark, and went slowly. I handed over what I remembered Mark asking for in a similar situation, changing instruments quickly when James asked for something different. Eventually he was ready to close.

"Thank you, Allexa. I can see why Dr. Mark had you assist as often as he did. You have good instincts." He let out a big sigh as he stripped off his gloves. "I better go talk with the wife. Will you finish the bandages?" I nodded and left the room. Poor Ken. A perforated lung. He would be laid up for quite a while. There was a great deal of blood loss from the entry site and the slicing of soft tissue; blood which we couldn't replace unless Karen knew his blood type and we could find a matching donor. Nothing was ever simple or easy anymore.

After I finished, I washed and removed my mask and gloves. The surgical drape I used went into the hamper for washing. I don't do that chore any longer... I wonder if Amanda does it now. In the hospital common area, Jim sat alone. James must have had Karen in the office, as I saw the door was closed.

"Hi," I said.

Jim lifted his head. "Is Ken going to be alright?"

"Dr. James believes so." I sat down next to him and took his hand. "What's to become of the other man in the fight?"

"It's an interesting story. Are you ready to leave and go home?"

"Not just yet. We need to move Ken into a bed. Will you help?"

"Of course."

I tapped quietly on the office door. "Jim is willing to stay long enough to help move Ken into a bed. Can we do that now?" I asked when Dr. James opened the door. Karen had her head down on the desk.

The transfer went smoothly with the three of us lifting and pulling. James set an IV in Ken for fluids and more painkillers to keep him asleep for the night.

*

When we got home, I went directly downstairs to shower and change my bloody clothes. The air was still cool, yet not any cooler than this morning. I thought that was a good sign.

Dressed in a dark green long sleeved t-shirt and plaid flannel pants, my hair air drying, I went upstairs to join Jim and Tom in the kitchen. Jim pulled me into a firm hug, holding me close, while Tom fixed me a drink. When Jim let go, Tom took his turn in the hugging.

"Hey you two, I wasn't hurt. What's up with all the concern?" I asked looking from one to the other.

"It's traumatic to see a friend injured that badly, Allex," Tom said. "And then to assist in the surgery to put him back together, well, that takes courage." I hadn't thought about it like that.

"It was something that had to be done. Dr. James hasn't trained an assistant yet. What was difficult to do was to assist Mark when he did surgery on my *child* after the wolf attack, and then again on my grandchild for his appendix. I don't want to ever do that again," I stated, and downed my drink. Tom quickly refilled it. "So what is the 'interesting story' about the other participant in the fight?"

Jim leaned back in his chair, formulating how he was going to say what had developed over the last few hours.

"It seems that this Jeremy Smith, who is now twenty-three, got into his adoption papers two years ago and found out that Lawrence and Loraine Misko are his biological parents. She gave birth when she was only fifteen and put him up for adoption. They eventually married, but Lawrence never knew about the pregnancy. Jeremy didn't know how to approach them so he tried to attach himself to their family instead. Recently, Jeremy told Loraine the truth. Lawrence thought Jeremy's attention toward Loraine was more than it was," Jim paused. "Now Jeremy is consumed with guilt that he's responsible for his father's death, and Loraine is in shock, both from the loss of her husband, and also with the sudden appearance of a son."

"Wow. What a tangled web we weave…" I commented. "If only he had been honest with them from the start things may have turned out differently. What's going to happen to Jeremy?" No wonder the young man didn't fight back, he didn't want to hurt his own father.

"Nothing, he didn't pull the trigger," Jim stated.

That statement concerned me. "So what's going to happen to Karen, then?" I asked cautiously.

"As far as I'm concerned, nothing for her either. A fellow officer had been attacked and she defended him. It's that simple." He sipped his Grey Goose.

"Will the town's people accept that?" I asked, noticing Tom had yet to comment.

"They will have to," Jim said. "We might not really have a curfew here, however, we *are* under martial law."

"Tom, you've been very quiet. What's on your mind?" I asked.

"I think we're going to have a problem with this," he said. "And I don't know what we're going to do about it."

JOURNAL ENTRY: May 24

With things heating up and tense in Moose Creek, the security force was down by three. Ken would be laid up for a couple of weeks, Jim didn't want Karen on patrol, and Rayn's pregnancy automatically took her out of service. That left Sgt. Frank Sanders, Cpl. Ansell Perkins, Eric, and the colonel. Almost half of the force during a difficult time is *not* a good thing.

~~~

"I think I should call a town meeting," Tom said to us over breakfast. "Maybe if we face this head on and clear the air, we can prevent an uprising."

Jim nodded. "Good move, Tom, and the sooner the better. I'll talk with Father Constantine, since he's the other person on our council. Allex, can you get Eric in town for a few days while we get this settled?"

"I can ask him, Jim, though remember he's not military any longer."

*

The meeting was scheduled for tonight and we had a full house, which wasn't a surprise. Even though it was fewer than the first meeting, the attendance was still impressive. This was the first major issue the town had faced as a whole since the flu sweep, and I wasn't sure if the turnout was because of the issue or out of boredom.

Tom led the group in the Pledge of Allegiance and the group quieted.

"We've called this meeting to discuss with you the events that happened yesterday and the results of the ongoing investigation. I'm turning the floor over to Colonel Andrews," Tom said and sat down.

"At approximately 1700 hours, or five in the afternoon, there was an altercation between Jeremy Smith and Lawrence Misko, which took place behind the Inn at the service entrance. During this fist fight, Allexa Smeth arrived, followed shortly by deputies Karen and Ken Gifford. Deputy Ken Gifford attempted to stop the fight by stepping in between the two assailants and was stabbed. Deputy Karen Gifford, responding to an attack on a fellow officer, shot and killed Lawrence Misko. Deputy Ken Gifford underwent extensive surgery to repair a punctured lung and several lacerations and will be off work for an unknown period of time while he recovers from his injuries.

"After questioning everyone present, it has been determined that Deputy Karen Gifford acted within the parameters of her duty and therefore will not face any charges." Jim stopped reading from his statement and looked at the silent crowd. "Now, I know some of you are wondering just who made this determination. I'll answer that right now. I alone made that decision." The crowd murmured. "It's been about seven months since everyone has settled here in Moose Creek, and it's been relatively peaceful. Much of that is due to the fact that we are still under martial law, and my security team, which is made up of military personnel and civilians, has worked diligently to keep all of you safe. Martial law means military rule, and it means that *my* word is law. As long as everyone keeps that in mind it will make this easier to understand. When it comes to involvement of my team, *I* set the rules, *I* make the decisions, and I alone suffer the consequences of their actions." Jim stood there for a moment. "Are there any questions?"

A young man raised his hand and stood. "Colonel, it seems to many of us that Mrs. Gifford is getting a free get-out-of-jail pass for this shooting. Wouldn't any of us have gotten arrested? This seems like police favoritism."

"Yes, you would have been arrested. *Deputy* Gifford is not getting a free pass; she doesn't need one. She pulled her weapon *after* her partner had been stabbed and she shot the assailant in self-defense and in defense of her partner. That's not police brutality. Now, had it been proven that *you* acted in self-defense, you would not have been arrested either." Jim looked around again. "Any other questions?" He sat down when no one responded.

Tom stood. "I hope that settles this matter. On another note, tomorrow will be the first Seed Day at the township hall. Mr. Harold Wolfe has come to town offering garden seeds, of which we are in need. I think you will find his 'prices' more than reasonable. Doors open at ten o'clock tomorrow morning. Meeting adjourned." Tom hit his gavel on the table and we all stood to leave.

I was quite impressed with the way Jim handled the meeting, always referring to Karen as Deputy Gifford and not as Ken's wife. A fatal shooting as the wife could be looked at as an act of passion, not self-defense. This still concerned me. I was the only other one there and I know Karen didn't have to shoot.

*

Those who had sat on the dais, Tom, Jim, myself, Art Collins, and Father Constantine, now sat at the kitchen table, each with a glass in hand. The vodka, bourbon, and rum bottles were left out on the island. Father Constantine was enjoying a glass of ruby port.

"Well, I'd say that went rather well, except that truth and justice should always go well," Father Constantine said.

"Yes. Still, doesn't mean there won't be problems, there should just be fewer," Jim replied. "Karen will need time off, mainly to take care of Ken. I don't want her on patrol and exposed while the town is still upset. That leaves our force pretty lean."

"I can offer a few men to fill in if need be, colonel," Art responded. "And wasn't Lenny one of your deputies before, Allex?"

"Yes he was. It will be up to the colonel to decide though," I said, looking at Jim, who appeared deep in thought.

"I appreciate that, Art, and I'll take you up on that. It makes this next thing a bit easier." Jim looked at me then turned away. "I need to make a quick run back to Sawyer. I'm leaving first thing in the morning and I'll be back the following day at the latest. With county road 150 open the trip down should only take a few hours. I would suggest all of you keep my departure quiet. I'm taking Perkins with me to ride shotgun."

This stunned me. Why would he take Perky and not me?

CHAPTER 27

May 25

"I'll tell you everything when I get back, Allex. For now, please just trust me," Jim said and he tossed an overnight bag in the Hummer. Perkins was already seated and anxious to be somewhere other than Moose Creek.

*

Tom and I opened the doors of the Moose Creek Township office building precisely at ten o'clock. Harold had all of his seeds out on a table for the public to view. It was a nice display, I must admit. He had brought along a small box of plastic snack bags to put seeds in once a person decided on their choice.

"I think I can find you another box or two of those bags, Harold," I said when I noticed his dwindling supply.

"For that, Allexa, your seeds are paid for. These are irreplaceable now," he lamented. "So what would you like, corn, peas, squash?"

"Even before the ash cloud we were never sure if we would have a growing season long enough for corn, so I'll pass on that. Besides, I still have some."

"Perhaps then we can trade like for like to add variety to each other's supply."

"That's worth considering," I said. I selected some Detroit red beets and he measured a tablespoon full into a baggie and labeled it with a marker. "How much pea seed for another, still sealed marker?"

He looked up, surprised. "You are good at bartering! How about a half cup of peas?"

"Deal!" I also took six pumpkin seeds and a teaspoon of radish. "I'm surprised you have flowers, Harold. I would have thought you would carry only edibles." I picked up a bottle to read the label.

"Not just any flowers: marigolds, which are a natural bug deterrent in gardens. Plus the nasturtiums, which are edible."

The townspeople started filing in around ten-thirty. By noon the place was empty again. Everyone seemed in a good mood being able to get fresh seed so they could be ready when it was warm enough to plant. It also looked like the shooting issue was pushed aside in favor of something more positive.

I noticed that Harold was giving growing advice quite freely, and he never gave enough seed for two seasons. I asked him about that.

"It's better for everyone to learn to save their own seeds. By designating a couple of plants out of the many they grow, they can have enough seed to perpetuate their gardens indefinitely. *That's* my objective," he explained. "To feed the world, one garden at a time."

May 26

Jim arrived back home late afternoon, tired and in a good mood.

"Mission accomplished!" he said gleefully.

"And are you now going to share what this *mission* was all about, Colonel?" I pushed, still a bit miffed that he didn't want me along. Tom smirked as he poured us each a drink.

How long had this drinking been part of our evening ritual? Forever it seemed. And what would we do when the booze ran out?

"Well, after the town meeting the other day, the truth and the implications of my words really hit home. We *are* under martial law and likely will be for a very long time. In out of the way places like Moose Creek, martial law is enforced by the senior military leader, and in this case that's me. It occurred to me that my retirement would have changed that."

I hadn't thought about that part. Who *would* be in charge after Jim retired?

"Currently, as a full-bird colonel, I'm in charge of the entire Upper Peninsula. The thought of military troops stumbling into our fair town and taking over bothers me, though that can happen only if I retire," he continued.

"What are you saying Jim?" I whispered, now worried.

"I rescinded my retirement papers." Tom and I were both shocked. "Can they call you back to duty now?" I murmured.

"No. What I also did was to take an indefinite leave of absence by initializing years of back furlough. In effect, I'm still a colonel in the army, with all the rank and privileges, but I have no orders to follow. It's the best of both sides, Allex."

"I can see where you felt the need to do that, Jim," Tom said. "And as mayor, I thank you for thinking of the town."

"So doing that took you all day?" I asked.

"It took a good portion of it, yes. Once I got a chat link with my superior—- and friend— General Jameson, whom I had sent my retirement papers to, asking for them to be held for a month, I kept the link open until we had finished our business. That was my primary objective, but not my only one." He looked at me with a Cheshire cat grin. "Because my other reason would take longer, I initiated that one first and contacted the acting commander at Selfridge, Chandler O'Malley." He took my hand. "He himself went to your sister's house to give her your message. At first she wouldn't even open the door to him, until he gave her the password of 'Tufts'. He told her you received her letter and that you and your sons were fine. Chandler said she broke down crying and thanked him over and over."

I couldn't talk. The tears streamed down my face. I reached out for him and held on tight.

"There's one final message from her. Here's the copy." Jim handed me a sheet of paper.

"'The fishing is getting better,'" I read aloud and laughed.

CHAPTER 28

May 28

Jason greeted me as I dug and turned the soil in another of the raised beds. "Eric said you wanted to see me about some kind of shelter?"

"Yes, thanks for coming over." I smiled at my youngest and wiped my hands on a towel at my waist. I found a small towel easier to wash once a week or every few days as opposed to washing dirty jeans every day. "With some of that plastic we used to wrap the porches from the ash fall, I'm hoping you can cover this area, like a greenhouse. With the cool weather we're experiencing, I'd like to retain as much heat as possible."

Jason paced the diameter of the area and measured the height of the tiered section in the center that was home to all the herbs. "Do you want sides on it?"

"Won't hold much heat if there aren't any sides…"

"You do know that it might get *too* hot in here then?"

"That's why I want the sides to roll up," I answered. "Besides, come September and October it won't be too hot anywhere, and I still want to extend the season as long as possible."

Jason nodded in thought. "Give me a day or two to collect enough posts for the roof support and I'll be back." He gave me a hug and left.

With the way Jason worked he would likely have this done in less than a week. I got back to digging, hoping to get the soil ready for the beet and pumpkin seeds I had pre-germinating in the house.

*

There was a stiff, cool breeze coming in from Lake Meade, making it too cool to continue working in the garden. As necessary as the garden is, I was confident a day or two wait wouldn't affect the growing season. I decided to pay a visit to Ken and Karen.

"How is he doing?" I asked Karen when she answered the door. They were still in the house just down the road from Jason and Eric. For some reason that surprised me and I said so.

"We've discussed moving into town after Ken has healed and is back to work," she said. "We have loved being here and part of your family, Allex, though I must admit it's not the same without *you* here. Being in town will make it easier on both of us and on the gas situation. And before you say anything, yes we are getting whatever diesel we need. However, if we don't need it, it can go toward feeding the generator, which is more important to the community as a whole. Besides, I'm looking forward to riding one of those bikes," she added with a grin.

"Have you selected a house yet?" I asked.

"We loved living on the lake, and I suppose we could move back into our old house. I think that's still too far, so I'd like something on the lake but right in town like maybe the old Johnstone place. I know it's still vacant," Karen said. I could hear the question in her voice, asking for permission.

"That would be a good position for the two of you. I'll mark it off of the available housing and save it. So, how *is* Ken doing?"

"Well, it's been less than a week and recovery is slow. Doctor James thinks he's progressing well, however, Ken is stubborn and wants to be all healed yesterday."

We walked into the room where Ken was sitting in bed, reading.

"Allex, good to see you," he said. "Have you come to spring me from this boring life?"

"Nope! Only Jim can do that once Doctor James says he can. So just get used to it."

*

I stopped at the township offices on my way home to talk with Tom about the housing situation. When I stepped out of my car I was met with a blast of icy air and snowflakes.

"What happened to our nice weather?" I remarked, shivering.

"Have you been watching the sky, Allex?"

"Yes, and I've noticed how dark the clouds are getting again." I frowned, thinking of my new garden. "Has there been any word on the ham radio about the situation?"

The ash cloud produced by the Yellowstone eruption last July was now circling the world, bringing with it an ever diminishing level of sunlight.

"This morning one of our contacts down in Lansing said there were more eruptions in Yellowstone over the past few days. They weren't nearly as bad as the first ones, but it just keeps adding to the ash in the upper atmosphere. Whether that prolongs the cover or just makes it denser is pure conjecture at this point," he replied. "Allex, I'd like your take on something."

"What?"

"I'd like to move the ham setup here to the offices where we can monitor all day," Tom said. "Joshua and Emilee have done a great job so far, especially making the initial contacts. However, they can't listen to it all day and still get chores done. I've noticed that the time stamps

Joshua puts on all the communications are toward the evening. And Emilee has to be in school during the day."

It didn't take me long to think this over. "I wouldn't move the radio, Tom. Everyone needs to feel like part of the community and that they are contributing somehow. This is the only way Joshua does that. He's very much a loner and I'm afraid he will withdraw even more without this. And it would devastate Emi. She's growing and maturing rapidly. The radio is her window to the outside world."

"I'd still like to figure a way of moving it, Allex," Tom insisted. "It would also help to reduce the gas consumption. Which is something we need to have a meeting about: rationing."

"Let me talk to Joshua first, please, and I think I know a way to soften Emilee's disappointment."

"I certainly don't want her to be hurt, Allex, those pre-teen years are tough enough. What did you have in mind?"

"What if we made the radio part of her school curriculum?" I suggested. "Eric can bring her in early and she can have an hour on the radio; then again after school until someone can take her home."

"The school is close enough we could make an hour midday part of her classes and she can bike over here," Tom said enthusiastically. "So far she's really one of the best observers."

"I think that's from being young enough that adults still see those her age as invisible and talk freely around them. Those youngsters pick up a great deal of info that way," I said.

*

I explained the situation to Joshua as gently as I could.

"Well, Ms. Allexa, that really does make sense," he said, looking down at his folded hands on the table. "I'm really going to miss my new friends, though it would give me more time for all the chores I have to do." His disappointment was so thick it could be cut with a knife and it hurt me to see it.

"Joshua, I have an idea," I said. "What if *you* take Emilee to school in the morning and take that hour on the radio? You can monitor and talk to your friends and still have that extra free time for chores."

"I think that is a very workable compromise, Ms. Allexa," he said happily.

＊

After explaining our new solution to Tom, I set out for the Mathers Lake Compound to talk with Art about Adam dismantling the radio setup and moving it to the township hall.

With our new and mutual working relationship with Art's group, the gate was now always unlocked, though it was often still manned.

"Good afternoon, Allexa," Pete said as he swung the gate open for me and waved me through.

"Hi, Pete, is Art on the premises?"

"Yes, ma'am. He should be at the big house."

＊

"I'll have Adam meet with Joshua tomorrow around noon, if that's soon enough?" Art said after I explained the situation to him. "I'm pleased you came up with a solution that allows those two to still have radio contact. They are both very good with it and I've noticed that Joshua is by far less shy when he's broadcasting. And Miss Emilee, well, she's the personality that never ends," he chuckled.

I picked up my cup of mint tea and took a sip. "How is the leg doing, Art?" I asked, remembering how he broke his leg and arm when a tree fell on him.

"Better than the arm," he replied. "I think the type of breaks involved have something to do with that. I just need to be more patient."

"Are you doing your physical therapy exercises that Mark recommended?"

"Yes, I am," he said. "Claire makes sure of it." He hesitated. "How are *you* doing, Allex?"

"You mean about Mark's death?" I asked, though I had no doubt that was what was on his mind. "I'm doing okay, really. He's been gone longer than we were together, you know. I will always cherish the time we had, but I can't and won't stop living. I think the road trip did me a great deal of good in healing, in spite of some of the trauma and mishaps we endured. It was very therapeutic."

We talked for a bit longer and then I stood to leave. "Oh, I almost forgot. Tom wants a meeting of the council to discuss rationing, and now that includes you."

"I still think Doctor James should have replaced Mark on the council," Art protested.

"James is a good doctor, Art, but he doesn't have the wisdom Mark had, and you *do*. You were the logical replacement. The meeting will be in the council chambers on June first at noon."

May 30

I heard the rumbling of an engine as someone pulled into the driveway while I was working in the garden and cautiously ventured out to see who it was.

"Good afternoon, Keith! What can I do for you?" I asked.

"I'm trying to do something for you, Allex," Keith Kay said. "Carron and I went out to the fishing hole this morning and caught a couple of lake trout. They all came in about twenty pounds, big ones for the hole! We thought you might like to have one." He held out a paper wrapped package. "We're keeping one for ourselves, and this one is for our township officials."

I took the package from him. "This is wonderful, Keith, thank you so much! We'll have it for dinner tonight." I looked at my longtime friend and wood supplier. "How are you and Carron holding up? It's been a rough year."

"Now *that's* an understatement," he chuckled. "We're doing well, better than most, in fact. That greenhouse I built five years ago for starting plants has been a true lifesaver. Carron spends hours on the gardening and canning so we don't go hungry." He hesitated before saying anything further, but I could tell he wanted to.

"I can tell there's something else on your mind, Keith," I said.

"I just wanted to thank you for allowing me to supply the town's wood, Allex. I would have died from boredom if I didn't have this to do," he said awkwardly, and then he backed the big truck around, and dumped a load of wood for our fireplace.

*

The fish was already gutted, though I still needed to filet it. I ran cold water in the kitchen sink and washed the large fish again. One filet would easily feed the three of us, so I decided to make gravlax with the other half. I cut the meat off the boney carcass and then carefully felt for any lingering small bones on both filets. I skinned the piece I was going to make into that wonderful cured treat.

Gravlax was really very simple to make by taking equal parts of pepper, salt, and sugar, blending it well, and then applying a thick coating to the raw fish. For the next step I would need dill, lots of dill, so I need to make a trip to my/Eric's greenhouse later. I put the seasoned fish into a plastic bag and set it to chill. Once I could pack the dill onto it, it would chill for three to four days while the seasonings cured the raw meat. I seasoned the other filet with a small amount of salt and pepper, and placed it skin side up on a plate until dinner. Fresh fish would be a wonderful treat for us, and I decided to pick some ramp greens to go with it.

I packed all the bones and skin into a sealable container and headed over to my old house… Eric's house… I didn't know what to call it now. It was still *my* house and I guess I will always think of it as that.

*

I let myself into the greenhouse to pick herbs.

"Oh, you startled me, Allexa," Rayn said, pocketing her gun. I would have to remember to announce my presence in the future!

"I'm sorry, dear. There's no way to let you know in advance that I might be stopping over," I apologized. "I've just come for some of my herbs." I finished clipping the lacy fernlike leaves off of several dill plants in the herb bed and then pinched some fresh basil for another dish. When I reached for one of the ripe tomatoes, Rayn winced.

"I was hoping to have those with dinner," she pouted.

"Okay, I'll take two of the less ripe ones and have them later," I capitulated. "Rayn, I want you to know how much I appreciate you and Eric taking care of my greenhouse." I picked a single green bean and took a bite. "I spent many hours in here, planting and weeding, and I miss it."

I hoped that was a subtle enough reminder to her that this was still *my* greenhouse and that I had every right to harvest what I wanted.

Rayn remained silent.

"Oh, and I brought some fish bones to pressure cook for Chivas and Tufts." I handed her the sealed container.

"Smells are making me sick lately," she said, handing it back.

"I'm sorry to hear that, though it's not uncommon during the early stages of pregnancy," I said. "Tell you what, I can either cook these here, outside, or I can take my pressure cooker with me and just bring back the pet food later."

Eric peeked around the door leading into the house. "Hi, Mom!"

"Hi. Would you do me a favor and help me carry a few things to my car? I would like to take a few of my canned goods back with me,"

I said, stepping around Rayn and into the pantry room. I took a jar of pickled sausage and two of the pickled beets. Eric looked at the beets and then over at Rayn. "Are you craving the beets, Rayn?" I asked.

"Yes, she is," Eric answered for her.

"Then I will take only these two jars. It's a good thing we can grow more!" I reassured them. Why was I feeling guilty about taking my own food??? "And do you have a dozen or two eggs I can have?"

"That we have plenty of," Rayn nodded. Eric set everything I selected into the cooler in the back of my car.

"I think we should talk," I said to the two of them, so we sat at the picnic table under the spreading maple trees. "I can understand how attached you are getting to the house and the gardens. After living here for the last couple of months it probably feels like it's yours, right?" Poor Rayn, she looked sullen and tearful when she nodded. "That's good, and don't worry, I'm not going to kick you out," I laughed. "Please remember though, that just because I was gone for six weeks that didn't mean I wasn't coming back. I did not *give* you all of my stuff. If things would have turned out differently, I would have moved back here. I do want you to treat what *is* here how *I* would, and that means it gets shared with family." Eric understood, however his new wife, with her mixed up pregnant hormones was having trouble. "Rayn, I worked years stockpiling what's here; growing and canning all this food, *by myself*. I'm entitled to take back what I want. I would never take food from you if you needed it. Please remember, I need it too, that's why I did all this."

*

When I got back home, I packed the dill on the salmon and set the jars on the counter. I needed some quiet time. The trip to Eric's had left me feeling like a bully and a thief.

CHAPTER 29

June 1

A cold rain splattered on the windshield of the Hummer as Jim and I pulled into the parking lot of the township office. I had wanted to ride my bike down, however, Jim nixed that idea at the first sprinkle.

"I will not be responsible for you coming down with pneumonia!" he said emphatically. I made a face at him, then saluted, which earned me a chuckle and a hug.

We dashed through the rain and made it under the protective overhang just as the sky opened up. Everyone else was already inside enjoying a hot cup of coffee. Tom sat at the head of the scarred rectangular wooden table, with Father Constantine on his right and Art Collins on his left. I poured myself a coffee and sat next to the priest. I gave an involuntary shiver as a drip of cold rain fell from my hair down the back of my neck.

"Now that we're all here, we can get started," Tom said. These were always informal meetings and no minutes were kept. Tom kept a pad of paper beside him to keep track of our final decisions. "In the seven plus months we've been here in Moose Creek, we've used almost one-third of the diesel fuel, one-fourth of the gasoline, and one-third of the propane. While that sounds good by some standards, it also means we will run out a year from now. Any suggestions?"

"Obviously we need to start conserving these limited resources," Father Constantine said, making a steeple with his fingers. "The Sisters and I keep the heat set at fifty-five. I think we should make that mandatory for anyone on propane: fifty-five or less." Tom jotted that down.

"Our biggest usage seems to be diesel. Is that from the generator use?" I asked.

"Most of it is. There are a few diesel vehicles, like the Passat and the Humvee, though they aren't used as much as one would think – your road trip aside. There's also the wood splitting," Tom said.

"How long does the generator run every day?" Jim asked.

"Ten hours or more a day," Tom said. "It's been difficult to do less when the teachers need to do laundry after classes, and for the men working in the woods to get showers when they're done."

"If we cut the generator time to five hours, which five would be the most efficient?" I asked the four men sitting around the table with me. "Five hours would cut the use in half, effectively doubling our remaining time."

"We would want to have power for the school," Father Constantine reminded us.

"Yes, although they really don't need lights during the middle of the day. Even with the increased cloud cover, there's still enough light to see by," Art chimed in. "In the compound we lined the school desks up next to the windows to take full advantage of any sun. It's an option."

"That's a good suggestion," Tom said, writing it down.

"If the generator ran from one o'clock to six o'clock every day, I think people would get used to the schedule and work around it. It would force them to be more organized about their daily chores, too, plus one to six would cover the off-school hours the teachers need to do whatever they need to," I said. "I know that when I ran the gennie at home, it was only for an hour or two. I would shower, do dishes, and wash clothes. I filled buckets for flushing and for filtering, and would use the electric grinder for making flour. I would turn it off, and *then* make bread, and hang the wet clothes to air dry. The more things that are done needing power while the generator is on makes that time more efficient. It's wasteful to do something not requiring power when the gennie is running."

"There are going to be those who don't get everything done. What do we do then? Extend the hours?" Tom asked.

"I say no. A few times of having the power go off in the middle of something and those people will start to adjust, as long as we don't give in," Jim said.

"What about the hospital?" Art asked. All of us knew that accidents don't keep a schedule, and neither do babies.

"The hospital has its own generator, Art. I'm sure the electrician can rig something where the hospital can operate from the grid gennie while it's on, then be switched to a gas gennie when needed," I said, "Likewise for the township offices. With the moving of the ham radio to here, the idea was to monitor more, not less. It would be practical to run the propane generator from nine in the morning until one o'clock when the big gennie kicks in. That one doesn't need to be rewired since it's an automatic startup and is already wired."

"The master electrician that came out on the buses died in the flu sweep," Father Constantine said. By the look that clouded his eyes I'm sure he also thought of his sister Doris being claimed by the same virus.

"I've no doubt that Jason or Earl Tyler can do just as well," I stated. "Speaking of Earl, how many are now using his new wood burner? Does anyone know?"

"He's done an amazing job, Allex," Tom said glowingly. "He really has. Everyone who needed a wood burning stove now has one. There are even a couple of spares in his workshop in case a house gets opened that doesn't have one."

"And the wood situation?" I asked.

"Keith continues to cut and split. The men working in the woods are his helpers that take the split wood and fill the trucks for delivery.

The pile in the baseball field goes down as people take some, then he fills it back up. For the out of the way places, like where your boys are, he delivers on site. It seems to be working well. Keith is happy to stay busy," Tom answered. "Anyone think there should be a time adjustment for the weekends?"

"You mean for church?" Father Constantine smiled. "No, I think the church should be under the same restrictions as everyone else. We can set a good example. Besides, if we had power during services that would limit everyone's time to get things done. I plan on continuing services from eleven to noon, so the congregation can get home to do what they need to."

"So," Tom looked at his notes, "are we agreed to start limiting the big generator use to five hours each day, from one to six in the evening?"

The ayes had it.

"Now, about the gasoline," Tom continued.

"I think we should encourage everyone to use bicycles whenever possible," I said, thinking of my bike sitting dry in the barn, "and save the gas for generators. There are a few that can't ride a bike, like the elderly, however, if we give them the opportunity and encourage it, they might like it and get enough exercise to help with their physical problems."

"And the propane?" Tom asked.

Everyone was quiet, so I spoke up again. "I think that should be saved for this generator, the Inn, and our two houses," I stated.

Father Constantine crossed his arms and leaned back. "Isn't that rather selfish on our part?"

"Yes, and no, Father," I replied. "The Inn could house many if need be. The township offices need to stay running. Your house is home to four and I know you counsel people in your home. You are the much needed spiritual leader of this town." I straightened my back for the rest, "And we three are needed too. Using the diesel, gas, and propane at *our discretion*, is the price the new residents are paying for our services: the hospital, the Inn for food, church services, and for *our* guidance."

"Allex is right, you know. We descended on this town with no warning, and there is a price that needs to be paid," Tom was quick to agree. "If that price is all of the fuel we brought with us, so be it. Of course, we're using that fuel mostly for the good of the people, so I personally have no objection."

Put that way, the ayes had that point too.

"How is the food holding up?" Jim asked.

"Pretty well, actually. Sadly, what has helped the most is having fewer people to feed." Tom looked down, knowing two of the five at the table had lost someone dear to them when the population was thinned. "Marsha and her crew have done a fabulous job at rationing what's going out and stretching what is left. With the fresh seed from Mr. Wolfe has come renewed enthusiasm in growing more food, which should start as soon as the weather warms up more."

"What if it doesn't warm up?" I asked cautiously. They all turned to look at me. "I'm hoping it does, but what if it doesn't? We're going to be faced with a major problem if we can't grow food, guys, we need to address it *now*."

"Let's table that for one month," Tom said, clearly uncomfortable. "In that month we should know if there is anything to be concerned about." Everyone except me thought that was a good idea.

"The supply shop is a non-issue for us since it's actually grown in inventory," Tom stated. "I think that covers it all. Does anyone have anything else to say?"

"Harold Wolfe mentioned that he would be leaving as soon as the rain stopped," Father Constantine added with a frown. "It would be nice to have one more dinner with him." Father turned to me and grinned. "We five, as the town council, should show him our appreciation."

"I think the five of us, plus Claire, and the Sisters would make a good number," Tom said. "Allex, will you be willing to do a larger dinner party in a day or two?"

"I think with nine of us, an appetizer party would be more appropriate for mingling. I'll start working on a menu."

*

"What is going to happen to the town if our little garden plot does well and the community garden doesn't? Jason is almost done building the heat retention shelter, so I should be getting seeds in soon. If we get green beans and no one else does, will we have to defend our food? Yes, I'm feeling selfish right now, and I think I have a right to," I said to Jim and Tom while we sat by the fireplace having after dinner drinks. The roaring fire felt good and took the chill off the air. A log shifted and sent a plume of orange sparks dancing up the chimney.

My comments were met with silence. "And what about the greenhouse that Eric is tending? He's growing quite a few starter plants for everyone: tomatoes, peppers, squash and eggplant. They will know there's more. Will a cold summer put my sons at risk?" I stood and paced.

"Allex, please sit down," Jim said, his voiced laced with concern. "We're not ignoring this plight. You must admit, though, that we don't even know if there will *be* a plight! What's that old saying? 'Don't borrow trouble?' We have enough issues to deal with, let's not add more just yet."

I sat down on the floor. "You're right. I've always been one to plan ahead, that's all." I paused. "No, not 'that's all'... that's *everything*! That's my belief system and it's what has saved my family from starvation, from attacks, and from all these disasters: planning ahead." I was feeling very frustrated that my two housemates couldn't see the potential problem looming ahead of us.

"I think Allex could be right, Tom," Jim ventured. "Perhaps we should consider some kind of natural shield for her garden, so others can't see it. Remember, it's *our* food too."

"Maybe we should concentrate on making sure *everyone's* garden does well," Tom commented.

CHAPTER 30

June 3

I walked around the plastic sheeted structure Jason had erected. It wasn't very tall, barely covering the central pyramid that was home to all the herbs and a few perennial flowers Kathy had planted in the past. The seams were held together with several layers of duct tape.

"This looks good, Jason, really good," I complimented him.

"There is one panel at the top you can open to let out hot air, and two sides can be rolled up, whereas the other two are anchored tight," he explained.

"For now everything needs to stay closed up," I said, shivering from the cool breeze off the lake. "What's this for?" I asked, spotting a cut-off rusty barrel.

"I thought you might like somewhere to build a fire, just in case it gets colder earlier than you want."

"A smudge pot!" I exclaimed. "Thanks, I hadn't thought that far ahead. I'm guessing that's also why you put an air vent in the top, to let the smoke out, right?"

Jason grinned.

June 5

"How are your plans coming along for the big party tonight?" Tom asked.

"I got a lot of the food done yesterday. There are only a few things that I couldn't do ahead," I answered.

"So what's on the menu?" Jim chimed in, peering over my shoulder.

"There are deviled eggs, cheese and soda crackers, soft pretzels with fresh mustard, smoked oysters from our road trip, an olive, pickle, and spiced beets dish, plus some pickled sausage I found in my pantry. Today I will make up the salmon balls and the Nori rolls. The Nori rolls will be a meatless sushi, though I will have some of the very thinly sliced fresh gravlax available for topping it, along with the pickled ginger also from the road trip."

"I'm getting hungry already," Tom teased. "Is there anything we can do to help besides eat?"

"Sure, the table chairs can go in the living room so there's room to walk around the food table. And you can set up the bar on the island. Oh, and Jim, would you get a couple of bottles of wine from downstairs? Two red and two white should be enough," I replied. "With as cool as it's been, what do you think about a fire in the fireplace?"

*

Our first guests showed up at five thirty, with everyone else arriving shortly afterward. The food was well received, even though there wasn't a lot of any one thing. These were appetizers not a meal. As anticipated, the nuns stuck with wine, while Father Constantine went for the bourbon.

Promptly at six o'clock, the lights went out. The fire illuminated the room with a cozy glow, however, I knew that with the darkening sky we would soon need the lanterns I had set out earlier. I lit the candles on the food table first and that added a nice ambiance. Tom was quick to light the oil lamps and the party never missed a beat.

I was listening to a conversation between Clair and Sister Margaret about children's clothing when I noticed Jim approach Harold Wolfe. I joined them in time to hear Jim ask Harold when he was leaving.

I slipped my arm through Jim's possessively and joined the conversation. "Harold, didn't you mention before that you usually stayed in a community at least long enough for the seeds to start growing? Why are you leaving here so soon?"

"Normally I would stay, yes." He hesitated briefly, then looked at Jim and said, "But I know I'm not welcomed here."

"Has someone been rude to you?" Jim asked cautiously.

"No one has been rude, no. Colonel Andrews, *you* make me very uncomfortable." This blatant statement stunned Jim. "It's so very obvious the two of you care deeply about each other, so I don't understand why you consider me a threat, sir."

Wow, talk about coming right to the point.

"My apologies, Mr. Wolfe," Jim said humbly. "This kind of a personal relationship is new to me and I'm unsure on how to react to… jealousy."

"Jim," I said, "that's very sweet. Please understand, I have no interest in Harold, other than for his gardening expertise. *You* are the only man in my life, sir." I smiled up at him and kissed him on the cheek. "Now, Harold, how would you normally spend your time with a community?"

"I would stay where they assigned me, working the gardens with them, doing whatever I could and in time find a family to take me in for the winter. Then I would help with the canning and any other chores to pay for my keep, and then move on in the spring."

"I know there are families who could use extra help," Jim said, "and I understand many here haven't a clue about canning. Please reconsider leaving." I looked at Jim in admiration.

"Thank you, perhaps I will." Harold stuck his hand out, they shook, and a new bond was formed.

*

As I readied for bed later, washing my face and slipping on my night shirt, I turned to Jim and looped my arms around his neck. "It takes a big man to do what you did," I said and kissed him lightly. "There are some things we haven't talked about yet, but I want to assure you I am strictly a one man woman. You have my total loyalty, Jim, please don't question it again."

He tightened his hold on me.

June 6

"Jason, I need you to look for something for me," I said when he stopped over to retrieve the rest of his tools. "I want a gas stove."

"Don't you have a stove here?"

"Yes, but it's electric, so I can't use it after six when the generator shuts down. I'm trying to think ahead for winter too. If you can find me a basic gas stove, one that has pilot lights and can be lit with a match, it would solve a major problem I see coming. I want it installed in the basement, tapped directly to the big propane tank."

"Why the basement, Mom? Don't you have the grill on the lower deck for cooking down there?"

"Come winter, Jason, we won't be able to heat the upstairs and Tom will have to move down with us. Having a gas stove will let me cook and bake and that will add extra heat to the area. The grill won't do that."

Jason nodded as he contemplated what I said. "I'll get right on it."

CHAPTER 31

June 8

"Are you sure about clearing Ken to return to work, Dr. James?" Jim looked doubtful. "It's only been two weeks since he was stabbed."

"I'm not clearing him for active duty, Colonel," Dr. James said, looking alarmed. "I only told him it was okay to start moving around. It's my understanding that Ken and Karen want to move into town and that would allow him to do desk duty. He needs another two or three weeks of low activity."

"Oh I see," Jim snickered. "Your patient is getting bored."

"Do you have enough paperwork to keep him busy and sitting?" I asked.

"I think that between the three of us, we'll have him wanting to go home early every day!" Tom laughed.

We used the now empty Haul Your Own and a few volunteers to take Ken and Karen's few belongings from their house down the road over to the house on the lake they had selected.

JOURNAL ENTRY: June 9

It appears that knowing Harold would be staying to help with the community garden has revitalized everyone's interest. That plus the warmer temperatures. The clouds are still a dirty gray and there's little actual sunshine, though what there is has warmed the soil considerably.

I've been enjoying my time in the garden, especially now that a few of the early seeds have started sprouting. We'll be having fresh radishes next week, and soon I hope to see the lettuces growing. How I miss my salads. I need to come up with some way of growing lettuce throughout the winter.

~~~

"Allex," Keith Kay said when he stopped by again, "there is something strange going on with the lake, not that there's anything anyone can do about it. I thought you should know: the water is rising." He definitely had my attention. "Last time Carron and I were out fishing, we made a pile of rocks at the edge, by the new water line. The water is up now by about an inch. Maybe that new dam you told us about is starting to work."

"Are you sure?"

"Yes. We set six flat rocks at the edge, out of the water, and then piled more on top in a pyramid. The flat rocks are now underwater."

"This is good news, Keith, thanks! I will be sure to let the mayor and the colonel know."

This really was very good news, especially for Lake Michigan.

*

"I think we should set our own gauge to measure the lake," Tom said when I told them.

"I agree. That way we can keep track too, and I think we should mark it somehow to make sure no one is moving it as a prank," Jim said.

We found a four foot piece of a two by four in the big barn. Remembering how I used to measure snow out in the woods, I drew a line at the one foot mark where we would sink it into the rocky lake bed and then a heavy line every inch. Then I printed a 2 at the two inch line, and a 4 and a 6 at those lines.

"Just six inches? Why not all the way up?" Tom said.

"I can do that. After six inches though, there should be no doubt the water is rising. Besides, it will take a long time for it to get that high. The lake is fed by countless streams, creeks, and artesian wells, and refilling will be a slow process. It's been estimated that the retention/ replacement time would be almost two hundred years! Thankfully they won't be trying to completely replace the entire lake. Still, it should rise only two and a half feet every year, or two and a half inches per month. At that rate it will take over thirty years for Lake Superior to regain the eighty feet lost."

The three of us drove down to end of Eagle Beach where the water edge was closest for access. We moved rocks and dug a hole in the sandy bottom. Once the two by four was in place, Jim packed it down and we piled rocks around it up to the one foot marker I had made. On the back of the new marker I wrote today's date, as a reminder of when we started watching.

*

After the cocktail party we hosted for Harold Wolfe, who had agreed to stay on, the three of us had the rest of the gravlax for ourselves. Tonight I made more Nori rolls for our dinner. I remembered the day I bought two dozen packages of the dried seaweed sheets for storage, and had thought I was being really paranoid going overboard in my buying. I'm glad I did now. Even though these will last a while, I still need to think about what I can replace them with. Nori rolls are one of the few ways I truly enjoy eating rice.

Jim expertly used chopsticks to mop up the last of the soy sauce from a tiny bowl with his remaining Nori roll. "That was superb, Allex, and a great way to celebrate the refilling of Lake Superior!"

"I just hope that in thirty years someone remembers about the river," I commented.

"What do you mean?" Tom asked.

"The St. Mary's River was the main regulating drain for Superior spilling over into Lake Huron, and it was completely blocked during the earthquake in December. The Whitefish River was a secondary outlet. If it stays dammed, Superior will *over* fill, flooding out anyone who still lives on the shore, like Moose Creek."

CHAPTER 32

June 12

"It took some time, Mom, but we did find the right stove," Jason said excitedly.

He and Eric emerged from the big pickup truck Eric had parked down by the doors to the walk-out basement.

"The really tough part was getting enough copper pipe and fittings. Too bad the gas can't travel in PVC pipe, we found plenty of that," Eric said. "And yes, Mom, we made note of where that supply is." He grinned, knowing I would ask. They wheeled the hand-truck carrying the new stove into the enclosed lower deck, and then into the house.

"I'm going to have to turn the gas off at the tank to sweat these pipes, Mom, just so you know... in case you want to do something else," Jason said.

"It's such a nice day I think I'll work in the garden. Let me know if you need anything," I replied. The weather had taken a nice turn with seventy degree days and muted sunshine. The sunshine was always muted or muddy these days.

*

As I loosened the dirt and pulled weeds, dropping them into the waiting basket that would go to the new compost pile, it gave me plenty of time to reflect and think. I knew I was very concerned about the coming winter and our food supply. I feared we would lose even more people to starvation, and there was nothing I could do about it. The more I thought, the more I was reminded of the Survival Creed I learned so many years ago: *"The well prepared are under no obligation to endanger their own survival to assist those who have refused, for whatever reasons, to provide for their own welfare."* I tried to remember this every time I got the urge to give away some of our food. I couldn't feed everyone. I couldn't save everyone. I just couldn't.

What *could* I do to help the people who now lived in Moose Creek to help themselves?

I finished the weeding and cultivating quickly, then headed down to the shore of Lake Meade. The water was very still, reflecting the pale blue sky like a glass mirror. I could see reflections of trees and houses around the lake in the silent water. I followed the shore, becoming more and more interested in the transformation of the houses. Once home to the wealthier of Moose Creek, with multiple boats tied to expensive docks and pristine trimmed lawns of evenly cut deep green, the long yards were now churned up and growing vegetables. I waved to the people working these gardens and smiled when they waved back. The house that caught my attention though, had no one working the ground, no toys on the porch, no bicycles leaning against the door. And that house was next to the one I shared with Tom and Jim. No one lived there anymore.

The closer I got to the house, the closer I got to an idea. This vacant building, with all its huge glass windows that faced the usually sunny lake, could be turned into a living greenhouse that could provide food during the cold winter months that were sure to come.

I turned the doorknob and let myself in. I had issued this place to a woman and her husband, along with her adult daughter and *her* husband; they had wanted to stay together and had wanted a large garden. They had all perished in the flu epidemic. I walked through the quiet house slowly, never having been inside before. The floor to ceiling glass walls could be used as passive solar heating and if we put in well-spaced shelves there would be a great deal of growing area.

The kitchen was massive, with lots of counter space and a large work island: a cook's kitchen. It would be ideal for processing and canning. The large, six burner gas stove made my decision easy. We could turn this house into a food processing center for the entire community to use. I could see us holding classes for those that were unfamiliar with the art of canning. It was a good thing Harold decided to stay, as I certainly couldn't do it all myself.

I wandered down to the basement level. That it wasn't a walk-out was a bonus. Half buried and concrete, it would hold the temperature of the ground plus be spared the icy winds that were sure to arrive in a few months. We could install bins and boxes of soil for those crops that needed that storage method like carrots and beets. I could visualize shelves of wire to hold potatoes; hooks to hang cabbages and onions from...

This could work.

CHAPTER 33

June 15

"Are you trying to keep us busy, Mom?" Jason lamented when I told him of our latest project.

"Is that a bad thing?" I asked. "Besides, I think this is just as important as having a gas stove for the winter, maybe even more. Walk with me, Jason." Eric had stayed home to tend his own garden, knowing that Jason would be making most of the technical decisions anyway.

I asked Harold to meet us at the house since this would be more his project than mine. I talked with Tom and Jim about how Harold could earn his keep during the winter, and they had agreed.

We entered the quiet house through the back door. Harold was waiting for us in the kitchen. The house had an eerie silence that I could almost taste as Jason and Harold wandered the house on their own while I waited in the massive kitchen.

"Nice house," Jason said when he found me standing by the large windows. "Tell me again what your thoughts are." Harold waited silently.

"The kitchen is perfect as it is. The only drawback is the stove is new and has an electronic ignition, which means we can light the burners manually, but not the oven. Baking would have to be adjusted to the five hours of power time; not a big deal. There is more than enough cabinet and counter space for storing jars and the canners.

"These windows let in a lot of light that I want to utilize for growing things during the winter. We'll need shelves for that, which is where you come in. Floor to ceiling would be my preference, though the top shelf might be too high, so could be for storage only. The shelves need to be well spaced so the available sunlight will reach all the plants, and I'm thinking no more than two feet deep. Covering all these windows will still give us plenty of shelves, which I think should be made of wire to allow ventilation, evaporation and more sunlight.

"The very bottom shelf can be wood for stability and will house the earth-boxes I found in the barn. Those are filled with water and will be quite heavy. The boxes for the upper shelves will vary, and mostly will be shallow for growing beans, greens, shallow rooted things. I can also see flats of starter plants." I turned back to them. "Harold, do you have any thoughts or suggestions to add? This will be mostly your project."

"Where are we getting the equipment from?" he asked.

"Some of it will be my private stock, although I thought we could approach it the same way we did the bicycles: ask everyone to check their basements and garages," I answered. "Especially for jars, my supply of that is very limited and already in use."

"And all this furniture," Harold swept his arm toward the couches and tables that took up space in the open living room. "What are we going to do with it?"

"This is a four bedroom ranch. I think we can take down some of the beds to make room for moving the unnecessary items," I responded. "Much will have to go anyway when the wood burner is installed. There won't be any other way to keep the place warm during the winter. I've already arranged with Earl to do that since it's his unit."

"So do you want this going all winter?" Harold asked.

"That's my intension, yes," I answered. "Only if you decide to stay and to live in this house." He raised his eyebrows in question. "Someone has to keep the fire going or all the plants would freeze no matter how good the sunlight is."

"Shelves are no problem, Mom. I can get a couple of guys from town to move the furniture once Harold decides which room he wants to keep as his own. Is there anything else?" Jason asked.

"There is the basement that I think would make a good root cellar, though we first need to know what kind of vegetables we'll be storing. Regardless, we'll need hooks to hang things from and wire shelves for storage, maybe a couple of bins with sand for root crops."

June 25

Joshua had been bringing Emilee to school for a couple of weeks now using the extra four-wheeler. It was charming to see how he waited for her to get inside the doors before he left for the office and his time on the ham radio. As arranged, at three o'clock when school let out, Emi took her turn manning the radio until someone arrived to take her home.

"I'm really glad you suggested this arrangement, Allex," Tom confided in me. "Joshua has an engaging personality when he's on the mike, and we're getting a great deal of information through him."

"Anything useful?" I asked.

"Not anything pertinent to us, but it's been good to hear what's going on elsewhere. There's yet another bridge that's been replaced over the New Madrid crack, and traffic has increased. Those on the east side of the fault line aren't happy about the extra population though."

Joshua burst into the office with a sheet of paper and handed it to Tom. He read it quickly and turned to me.

"The president has died, Allex," Tom said, stunned. "An apparent heart attack. With the VP already missing and presumed lost, that leaves the Speaker of the House as president."

"Disturbing news to say the least. Still, I don't see how that will affect us here," I replied. "We are a forgotten piece of real estate, and for the most part that's not such a bad thing, in my opinion."

CHAPTER 34

July 1

"Have you been out to the water marker lately?" Jim asked Tom over our evening cocktail. "The water is continuing to rise."

"How far has it come up?" I asked. "We set that marker less than a month ago."

"It's up to the six inch mark."

"Wow, it's rising quickly," Tom said.

"That would be six feet a year," I said after some mental calculations. "It would still take over a decade to refill the lake at that rate, so I don't think there is much to worry about. I just hope the increase in water doesn't affect our weather."

July 2

Tom decided the town needed a break. Everyone was working long hours in the community garden, their private gardens, or stacking wood for the winter.

"I think we can forego a parade, however, I think a community picnic for the Fourth of July would be a nice celebration," he said. "I know Marsha just received another deer from Art Collins. Wouldn't it be nice to have grilled burgers for a change?"

July 4

The township park, with playground equipment for the children and a shelter with picnic tables for the adults, took on a festive air with streamers and pinwheels everywhere. I found a couple of bins in the big barn filled with all types of red, white, and blue decorations and nearly everyone came out to help decorate.

Marsha had ground up the venison to make burgers for grilling, and several of the women helped her make buns. There was a gallon container of catsup, one of mustard, and one of dill pickle slices, that she told me privately she had hidden for a special occasion.

"I knew that one day we would have a celebration worthy of something normal. This is it!"

Father Constantine led the town folk in the Lord's Prayer, followed by a very short sermon. He was getting well known for his brevity in the pulpit.

*

Jim and I strolled through the baseball field. I could almost hear voices coming from beneath my feet, reminding me to be careful where I stepped. I knelt down and cleared the sand from the only grave marker, the flat one that I placed there for Bob and Kathy. It had been less than a year, yet it felt so much longer that they'd been gone.

JOURNAL ENTRY: July 14

With having lost so many people, and so many children, to the flu, birthdays are celebrated with gusto. Today Jacob turns eleven. School is running all summer, so Jacob gets to celebrate with his new friends.

Marsha has taken on baking cupcakes when a child has a birthday and delivers them to the school at lunch, which was nice. I dug a couple of potatoes out of the compost in my greenhouse yesterday, and I'm going to make him a big batch of French fries for lunch. I think he'll like that better than a gift.

~~~

July 19

"Mom, you know what today is, don't you?" Eric asked when he found me working in the raised bed garden.

"Do you think I could forget that my only granddaughter is now a teenager??" I laughed. Jacob and Emilee were two years apart in age, and five days apart in birthdays.

"Can I ask what you're giving her?"

"No, it will be a surprise for you too."

I had thought long and hard about what to give Emilee that would be appropriate for a young lady in this new world of ours. I found it behind the township hall, and with Tom's approval, I cleaned it up and had it readied by Earl Tyler.

*

All of us showed up at the school for the now traditional lunch cupcakes, to help celebrate Emi's thirteenth birthday. She had grown into a beautiful young lady and had matured way too fast, though that was expected these days. This was a true milestone for the town.

Eric and Rayn "purchased" a leather satchel from Art Collins that was similar to mine, though a bit smaller, as their gift, and Emilee was overjoyed with it. Everyone turned to me, especially an expectant Emi.

"I bet you're waiting for my gift, aren't you?" I said to my granddaughter. She solemnly nodded. "We will have to take a walk outside for it." The entire school poured out the doors behind Emilee when she spotted her very own new, metallic purple, four-wheeler that was parked at the curb. She was speechless. She turned to me with tears in her eyes and wrapped her thin arms around my neck in a fierce hug. Then of course she bolted to the curb to sit on her new ride.

*

"Mom, I'm not sure about this," Eric said. "Those things can go really fast!"

"Not this one," I assured him. "I had Earl fit it with a governor. She can't go more than twenty-five miles per hour. Once she has proven herself on it, he can remove it, but only at *your* request."

Eric grinned. "I can deal with that." He watched his daughter for a moment. "Did we grow up this fast?"

"*All* children grow up faster than their parents want them to, Eric. You and Jason were no exception."

JOURNAL ENTRY: July 20

Even with muted and darkened skies, the weather has turned pleasantly warm, and the town has settled into a productive routine. Everyone works their share in Bradley's Backyard, sometimes even if they have their own garden to tend, which most of them do. In part, I think, it's something to do, and partly to socialize.

With the lack of instant communication, no one is supposed to venture anywhere alone. Small groups go out fishing, mostly on Lake Meade. When there is a reasonable catch, the excess is turned over to Marsha to dole out during meals.

Tom spends fewer and fewer hours at the office, and since that one altercation, Jim's security team has little to do except patrol. Occasionally all they do is help someone move or lift something heavy. The security team has a good reputation in town. Often I see people riding the streets with their bicycles, and for a while it was difficult to spot the security guards, until someone came up with the idea of putting a rod with a red, white, and blue mini-flag attached to the back. Now they are easy to find.

With Ken and Karen in the house down the lake, they are now back leisurely patrolling the town too.

Life has taken on a blissfully boring air.

~~~

July 21

It was mostly a peaceful afternoon, with high, dark clouds and a soft breeze. The dim daylight was now a constant companion. The colonel, Tom, Eric, Perky, and myself were in the office discussing the duty schedule, while Emi sat on the ham chatting.

"DAD!" Emi screamed from the other room.

We all ran into the small office that was once the township treasurer's space and now was home to our communication to the world. Eric reached her first.

"What's wrong, Emi?" he asked, panic lacing his voice.

She turned to face him, setting down the radio earmuffs. "It's Mom."

Eric took the mike reluctantly. "Beth?" Emi reached over and pulled the plug on the muffs so we could all hear.

"Oh, Eric it is so good to hear your voice. I've been trying to get in touch with you through military channels but my messages have never gotten through," Emilee's mother said. The relief in her voice was obvious.

"How did you find us on the ham?" he asked.

"Dad, I've been trying to reach Mom for weeks," Emi confessed, looking chagrinned. "I finally found a ham operator in northeast Florida that agreed to get a message to her at the District Emergency Operation Center."

"When the operator told me of Emilee's regular radio time schedule, I kept trying to get on during that time, but I'm on the move so much it was difficult and I kept missing the window," Beth said. "I'm thrilled to finally talk to her. I've missed her so much, Eric, but I know she is much better off up there with you than down here. Just knowing she's safe means everything to me."

"We've been doing as well as could be expected. Life gets hard at times, though we always make it, and it's relatively safe here," Eric assured her.

"It would have to be better than here! It's very dangerous now since we lost the southern half of the state." There was a long pause on the other end. "Eric, I want to set up a regular time to talk with her, maybe every couple of weeks."

"Of course, Beth," Eric answered. After catching up, he turned the seat back over to Emilee and she plugged the muffs back in. As we went back to the other office, I could hear Emi talking to her mother.

"I've been doing good in school, Mom, don't worry. All A's," she said with pride. "We only go to school three or four days a week, but we're in class all year." There was a pause while she listened. "Sometimes during the winter we can't get out because of the snow, and dad or Uncle Jason homeschools me and Jacob." There was another longer pause, and then Emi said, her voice quivering, "I miss you too."

CHAPTER 35

July 22

I brought egg salad sandwiches for lunch, and Jim joined me.

"Have you seen Ken or Karen around town?"

"No, why?"

"Today is their regular patrol day and no one has seen them. They usually check in first and then cruise on their bikes," Jim said. "Want to take a ride with me over to their house? I can't imagine them sleeping in *this* late."

*

We pulled into the long gravel driveway, and I could see the Passat sitting in the parking spot.

"Their bikes are still here, too," I said to Jim as we approached the door where the bicycles were leaning.

Jim suddenly thrust his arm out to stop me. "The door is open." He pulled his Beretta and pushed the door open with the barrel. "Ken?

Karen?" he shouted into the silent house. We stepped across the threshold into chaos. Blood was splattered and smeared everywhere.

Ken was lying on the floor in the living room; a large pool of crimson had formed under him. Only one small chair had been turned over. That was the only sign of a struggle in the room other than the trail of blood left by Ken crawling to where he was now, face down on the cream and gray tile. Jim knelt beside the body and felt for a pulse.

"He's dead," he said angrily.

I turned toward an open door and caught a glimpse of the bed. I pushed the door further open and caught the coppery scent of more blood. Karen had been stabbed multiple times in the chest and neck. I didn't bother checking for a pulse – no one could live after that vicious of an assault. I let out a sob.

Jim came rushing into the room when he heard me. As I turned toward him my attention was grabbed by the wall behind the door. I stood, shocked, and pointed. "**JUSTICE**" was written on the wall in dripping red - likely Karen's blood.

*

Outside on the deck overlooking Lake Meade, I took a couple of deep breaths, trying to get the stench of death out of my nose.

"Are you doing better now, Allex?"

"Yeah, I guess." I leaned my forehead against Jim's broad chest. "Who would do something like this? And why?"

"I think the why is easier than the who," he said. "I would venture that someone felt Karen needed to be punished for that shooting six weeks ago, which may also take us to the who." He stared out at the lake. "While we were going through all those pricey houses in Marquette, you had a real knack for figuring out the death sequence when we found bodies. I know Ken and Karen were close friends of yours. Do you think you can put that aside for now and do a forensic walk with me?"

I straightened my shoulders. "Let's do it."

We went back to the entrance. We both looked at the door, the floor, and the walls.

"I don't think it started here," Jim said.

"No, I don't think so either. Let's try the bedroom." I stood by Karen's body and detached my feelings. "There are no defensive wounds. She was killed or disabled in her sleep, with the first blow."

"There's no blood on this side of the bed," Jim observed. "The perp probably woke Ken and he got up before *he* was attacked. Maybe he chased the assailant out into the living room where he was stabbed." We walked the crime scene as we described what we saw, what we felt.

"The assailant, younger, stronger, turned when Ken came after him and… can we turn Ken over to see the stab wounds?" I asked. Jim carefully nudged the body over. I almost lost my lunch. "One wound. Either the knife was double edged or it was turned upward and it was very, very sharp." The slash started low in the abdomen and traveled several inches up to the sternum, effectively eviscerating Ken.

"My guess is the fatal wound was inflicted by the back door, and Ken crawled to where he is now. He tried to get up, toppling the chair in the attempt," Jim said, mirroring my thoughts exactly.

"Once the assailant saw Ken down, he went back to finish off Karen." We stepped back into the bedroom. There were so many stab wounds it was impossible to say which was first or last – they all could have been the fatal one. "He was in a rage by this time." I pulled the bloody sheet over Karen's face with shaky hands. Jim pulled an afghan off the couch and covered Ken.

It was now three o'clock in the afternoon.

"Your thoughts, Allex?" Jim's voice was calm and washed over me like a healing salve.

"I'd rather hear yours first."

"The writing on the wall points to an act of vengeance. Who would want revenge? Jeremy Smith or Loraine Misko may feel that justice wasn't served," Jim said.

"Jeremy was the only other one there that heard me call out to Karen to not shoot. He knows she didn't *have* to shoot his father, that it was an act of passion." Jim started to say something, and I held up my hand to stop him so I could finish. "I couldn't see what Karen was seeing, and it's quite likely she felt they were still in danger. All I know is what I saw from my angle." I turned in a circle, looking up at the ever-gray sky. "And Jeremy didn't have to kill either of them," I said, gesturing toward the house.

"Let's go question the boy," Jim said.

*

The Misko house was several houses away from the Giffords', placing it between the crime scene and our house. It was a small bungalow, clad in white siding with deep green shutters. Loraine was in the yard hoeing in the spacious and lush garden.

"Mrs. Misko, is Jeremy here?" I asked her, as pleasantly as I could force myself to be. She looked up when I called her name.

"I think he's still sleeping. He's been staying up all night and sleeping all day," she shrugged, and reached down to pull a weed. "It's very strange for me to suddenly have an adult child. I don't know what to do with him and—"

"We need to talk to him, *now*," Jim interrupted.

She had an air of defeated resignation as she led us into the house. She walked over to a closed door and knocked. "Jeremy, you have company." There was no answer. She turned the doorknob. "It's locked. He does that."

Jim moved her aside and kicked the door open. There was Jeremy, hanging from an open ceiling beam, a note pinned to his bloody clothes. "**VENGEANCE IS MINE**," was all it said. Loraine sank to her knees and wailed.

JOURNAL ENTRY: July 23

We laid Ken and Karen to rest beside Bob and Kathy in the baseball field, with Father Constantine officiating in the rain. Everyone in town joined us. Most wept openly for our loss and the loss to the town. Jeremy was buried over in Camp Tamarack. Only Loraine knelt beside his grave.

~~~

August 1

Jim's hand had completely healed and Dr. James gave me permission to start therapy on it.

"That feels good," Jim sighed, as I massaged his palm. I worked my way down his wrist and up the forearm to the elbow. Many don't realize that most of the control in the fingers start in the arm and elbow.

"The rest might not," I warned him, as I worked the tips of my fingers into the muscles of his ring finger. The muscles were stiff from lack of use and he had a hard time bending that digit. He winced as I dug in but I didn't stop.

Jim sucked air in through his teeth when I forced the knuckle to move. I worked his hand and finger for several more minutes, and then had him soak it in hot water to further relax the tiny muscles.

Later I caught him flexing the hand and forcing movement on his own. He's a stubborn man and I could see him regaining full use in record time.

August 10

"Allex!" Jim called out, opening the door to my bedroom. With dawn still hours away, the night was coal black.

"I'm awake now," I answered, my breathing ragged.

"I could hear you in the other room. Another nightmare?" he asked gently, sitting down on the edge of the bed.

"Yeah," I said, rubbing my feet.

"Tat?"

"Yeah."

I shifted over to the center of the bed so Jim could slide under the covers. He held me close.

CHAPTER 36

August 20

The nights were getting cooler already and that was worrisome. An early frost would damage the crops that were doing so well now.

Emilee pedaled her bike down the long driveway where I was working at stacking wood inside the garden area, getting ready for needing the smudge pot.

"Nahna! Rayn's in labor! Dad said I should get you in case you wanted to be there." I was surprised she wasn't riding the new four-wheeler, and then realized she likely came in the truck with her father and Rayn.

"Of course I do. I was there when you were born down in Florida, and I was present when Jacob was born too." I rushed to put my tools away, then dipped my dirty hands into the bucket of water I kept nearby to rinse off the mud. "You go on back to the hospital while I get my keys and I'll see you there." I darted into the house, pausing to wash my hands with soap. The baby coming in mid-August concerned me, as I thought he wasn't due until September.

*

"How is she doing?" I asked Eric, who was pacing the narrow entranceway of the small hospital.

"Contractions are four minutes apart," Eric told me. "Dr. James is examining her now. He said for you to scrub as soon as you got here."

"Would you send Emi over to the offices and tell Jim and Tom where I am and what's going on? I don't want either of them to worry when they can't find me."

I waved to James as I passed the partially closed curtains that surrounded Rayn's bed to let him know I was there. I scrubbed and donned gloves and mask, then joined Eric by his wife's side just as another contraction hit.

"You're doing fine, Rayn. You need to dilate just a bit more before you can start pushing," Dr. James said. I could tell his confidence level had grown tremendously since his first delivery.

"Have you selected names yet?" I asked to fill in moments between contractions.

"We've decided on Alan for a boy and Harmony if it's a girl," Eric said, wiping the sweat off Rayn's forehead.

"Both beautiful names…"

A half hour later the baby was crowning. "Okay, Rayn," Dr. James said, "on the next contraction you can push." And she did. We welcomed little Alan into the world at six-ten in the evening.

I wrapped the baby in a soft blanket and laid him on his mother's chest. I caught Eric wiping tears from his eyes as his son latched on to his finger with a tiny fist. Dr. James worked the afterbirth out, and then tied off the umbilical where I had clamped it.

"I'm going to wash him and wrap him in a clean blanket," I said and took my grandson. I had a small basin of warm water waiting and quickly sponged the birth blood from him. Once he was covered in a fresh, warm blanket, I set him on the baby scale I once used for measuring shredded cabbage. Alan weighed in at six pounds eleven ounces, exactly what his father weighed at birth. This baby was not premature. Then I remembered an old saying my mother repeated to me a very long time ago: "The first baby can come anytime, the rest take nine months."

*

"I feel like a grandfather," Jim grinned when I stepped out into the small lobby where he and Emi waited.

"You have a new brother, Emilee. Would you like to see him?" I asked. Knowing she would, I had brought an extra mask with me. I fixed the loops around her ears, then tiredly smiled at Jim and told him I'd be right back.

*

Jim greeted me with a hug when I came back out. "You look exhausted, Allex. Did everything go okay?"

"It went perfectly. Labor was relatively short for a first baby, only seven hours," I said after glancing at the clock. "Why is the power is still on?" I asked in confusion. It was now seven o'clock and the generator should have shut off an hour ago.

"We made a quick executive decision to keep the gennie going until the baby was born," he answered. "This baby is too important to us to interrupt the birth. Jason is getting ready to switch the hospital over to the standby generator now and shut down the main one." Jim brushed a lock of hair out of my eyes. "Are you ready to go home?"

"Yes. Let me go tell them I'm leaving," I said and then added with a grin, "Grandpa."

*

I accepted a drink from Tom, took a swallow, and let it warm me as the alcohol slid down my parched throat.

"I want to thank both of you for keeping the generator on."

"It was the least we could do," Tom said.

"By the way, did you notice how chilly it's gotten?" Jim asked.

"Yes, I noticed it earlier. I've started stocking some firewood inside the shelter, just in case we have to use the smudge pot. I think tomorrow we should also alert the other gardeners to the possibility of an early frost so they can cover their plants. It would be a shame to lose the harvest after so much work."

August 25

I slipped out of Jim's bed, intent on an early shower. The view through the enclosed deck stopped me cold. It was white outside, and it was snowing! I was stunned for a moment, and then I rushed back into Jim's room.

"Jim, wake up!" I shook him until he opened his eyes. He looked at me dreamily until he realized I was distraught.

"What's the matter, Allex?" he sat up, now fully awake. The down comforter slipped off his bare chest to expose a mat of curly gray hair.

"It's snowing! We need to cover the gardens!" I rushed back to my room for appropriate clothing.

Pulling on a jacket I hurried to our small garden of raised beds, thankful I had dropped the sides a few days ago, though it was still very cold under the shelter. Inside the enclosure I wadded up some newspaper and stuffed it into the smudge pot. Then kindling and a few larger sticks went in. I struck the lighter that was always in my pocket. On the third try I got a weak flame and lit the newspaper. The wood was well seasoned and soon the fire was sending up billows of smoke that hung at the top like a heavy fog. I used a long pole and opened the plastic flap Jason had installed. The gray smoke drifted out and the air cleared. I put a couple more pieces of wood into the half barrel and went back into the house.

The battery clock on the wall said it was only six-thirty. How were we going to alert everyone so early?

Tom stepped out of his room, concerned over the activity. Apparently I hadn't been very quiet in my rush to get outside.

"What's going on, Allex?" he scowled.

"It's snowing, Tom, and if we don't let everyone know so they can cover the gardens, all the vegetables will freeze!" Instinctively I reached for the coffee pot to make our morning brew. Within ten minutes, the three of us were out the door, dressed, with coffee mugs in hand.

Jim ran next door to wake Harold. That house wouldn't need any further protection, and we needed his help up at the community garden.

Tom and I grabbed some sheets and tarps from the barn and took off for Bradley's Backyard with Harold close behind. Jim piloted the Humvee around the town, blasting the loud horn to wake people.

*

By noon, the gardens were mostly covered, but the snow was coming down even heavier. Inside the church, people were gathering to get warm and for guidance.

"It may be premature or too late to worry about the plants, so I would highly suggest everyone pick the mature produce and quickly," Harold said from the podium. "The root crops should be okay for now. However, beans, tomatoes, peppers, tender greens, and anything above ground will get frost burned if left out."

"There are a lot of beans out there, Mr. Wolfe, we can't possibly eat that many," a young woman called out from the back.

"Keep some fresh for eating over the next two or three days, and the rest we will start with mass canning," he looked over at me and I silently nodded. We had days of processing ahead of us.

"What about those of us who have our own gardens?" another voice asked. "I planted all corn in my backyard. What am I supposed to do with all of that?"

"Yeah, we were encouraged to do a single crop. Now what?" That voice was tinged with anger.

"Harvest your own gardens first," I replied. "The idea is to get the food out of the damaging snow. It's going to be a great deal of work, I won't deny that. Just keep in mind this is *your food* for the winter! There is no waiting until a better day. It has to be done *now!*" I looked over this sea of unfamiliar faces and wondered what I was doing here. "We've set up a house as a food processing station and storage. Most of you are already aware of that. After you have separated what you want fresh, take the rest to that house and we will set a schedule to help you process it. I know we thought we had another month of growing and could tackle the harvest in stages. Well, we were wrong. Now let's get busy!"

*

"Are you going to start harvesting, Allex?" Tom asked.

"No, we don't need to. That shelter has bought us some time. Not much, but some," I answered, knowing it should be done soon or the weight of the snow would collapse the plastic sheeting. "What I need to do right now is get to Eric's garden and help them."

"I think the community is expecting you to work with them first," Tom continued.

"There are a hundred people out there working to save their produce," I said in exasperation. "My sons have each other, Amanda, and Emilee. That's it! I'm going to save my family first." I turned to leave and bumped into Jim standing behind me.

"I'll come with you," he said. "Tom, would you make sure the fire in the smudge pot keeps going? Remember, that's *our* food, too."

*

We spent three hours at Eric's picking vegetables and digging root crops with the snow falling around us. In the end, there were bushels of small and medium sized potatoes, onions, beets, and rutabaga, and more bushels of ripening and green tomatoes, peppers, and eggplant, all of which were stacked in the greenhouse to stay out of the continuing snow.

"I think your pumpkins and acorn squash will continue to ripen in the cold pantry," I said to Eric when Jim and I were getting ready to leave. "I left you one of the quart canners and dozens of jars with enough seals."

"Thanks, Mom. We wouldn't have gotten this done in time without you," Eric said, giving me a hug.

*

People struggling with small wagons and wheelbarrows continued to beat a path through the snow, taking the harvest next door for storage or processing.

The three of us worked nonstop to harvest the small garden that would keep us fed.

"Don't pull the plants yet. It's a long shot, but we might still have some growing time.

Jim, Tom, and I harvested two bushels of green and yellow beans and I intentionally left six plants of each unpicked that might be our seed for next year.

"I'm surprised there are this many tomatoes," Tom said, looking at the basket of nearly ripe tomatoes and two more boxes of green ones.

We used the plastic milk totes for the potatoes and onions, leaving some still in the ground. Many years in the past I've dug spuds only to have missed a few and they came up the next year. Leaving some may be our only way of propagating. I instantly thought of Jacob's French fries and Emilee's chips and my heart heaved.

"We can dig half of the carrots now and they will keep well. I think if we mulch the rest down with the compost we just might be able to dig more in a couple of months."

We did the same for the beets and rutabaga. I had no idea what we would do with two dozen green peppers, except share them with Marsha.

"Where are we going to put all of this?" Jim asked.

"Right now, we just need to get it into the house so it doesn't freeze. We'll work on storage later."

*

The blanket of snow was now a foot deep and snowflakes drifted down in a lazy spiral. The temperature hovered at thirty-five degrees. Tom stared out the glass door to a curtain of all white and shivered. He looked worried.

"What are we going to do?" he said.

The lights blinked and went out. It was six o'clock.

"Tom, I think it's time for you to move downstairs with us," Jim said, clamping his large hand on Tom's shoulder. He looked forlornly at Jim, and then at me, and grimly nodded.

"Tom," I said, "we *are* going to make it. It won't be easy. It's going to be a bad winter and there will be more losses, but we *will* survive."

The End

*

History is written by those who can, not necessarily just by those who survived it. I survived it and I hope I've written the facts as best as I can remember them, so those who come after know where they came from.

*

Emilee closed her grandmother's journal. She got up from the old rocker, wiped her tears with a cloth hanky, and put the journal back on the shelf.

ABOUT THE AUTHOR

Deborah Moore is single and lives a quiet life in the Upper Peninsula of Michigan with her cat, Tufts. She was born and raised in Detroit, the kid of a cop, and moved to a small town to raise her two young sons, then moved to an even smaller town to pursue her dreams of being self-sufficient and to explore her love of writing.

Being a life-long Prepper, Deborah has done numerous articles for magazines, and speaking engagements at conventions regarding the subject.

Her first published novel, *The Journal: Cracked Earth*, made the Best Seller's list in just six weeks. Book Two of the series, *Ash Fall*, went to the printer eight months early because of the unprecedented popularity and Book Three, *Crimson Skies*, is proving to be even more popular. *Raging Tide*, the fourth book in the series was to be the final chapter, but Deborah is delighted to announce that book #5 is right around the corner.

CPSIA information can be obtained
at www.ICGtesting.com
Printed in the USA
FSOW01n1158040217
30293FS

31901061140580